CLEAN KILL

John Rourke was flat against the roof now, climbing toward the peak. Once there, it would have to be quick—a series of perfect shots. He would have to stand up, kill them and hope there weren't any more of the trained assassins to kill him back.

When he reached the peak, he could see the three men clearly. There were three rounds in one of his twin stainless Detonics .45s, six in the other. Straddling the pitched roof, Rourke raised himself to his knees, then drew his feet under him, so he could stand quickly.

Taking the safety off both guns, Rourke breathed deep and rose. "Up here!" he shouted.

The three men wheeled their weapons toward him and Rourke opened fire. The first man caught a single bullet in the head and crumbled. Rourke cut the other two down with four shots in rapid succession.

"Five shots to kill three men," Rourke mumbled to himself as he began to climb down. "Two shots too many."

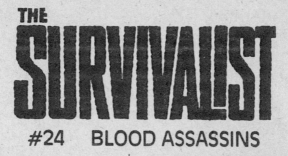

THE SURVIVALIST

#24   BLOOD ASSASSINS

BY JERRY AHERN

ZEBRA BOOKS
KENSINGTON PUBLISHING CORP.

For Steve Fishman, a friend to the Rourkes and the Aherns, all the best to someone John Rourke would be proud to fight beside . . .

Any resemblance, etc . . .

ZEBRA BOOKS

are published by

Kensington Publishing Corp.
475 Park Avenue South
New York, NY 10016

First printing: September, 1992

Printed in the United States of America

One

The knife in his hand—it was designed and executed after the style of a British implement of war, but no matter—was double-edged, forming a triangle with long equilateral sides and an extremely narrow base. The sides made the double edges, and they were sharpened past any usefulness as a working blade, good only for shaving and one thing else.

That one other thing was taking life.

Helmut Spitz, hands double-gloved in leather over synthetic rubber (this to protect his hands from injury and guard against blood-transmitted infection), drove the blade of his dagger into the sentry's carotid artery. Spitz's left hand was closed over the about-to-be-dead man's mouth in order to stifle any sort of sound. Spitz was not worried (concerning his eyes) over the blood spray that the torn artery would produce, because he wore a gas mask fitted with goggles.

From historical records, Spitz knew that in the days prior to what had come to be known as "the Night of the War," commandoes were taught to attack the femoral artery on the inside of the thigh whenever possible and to be cautious should a hand blow be delivered to an opponent's mouth lest the skin of the knuckles be broken, all as a precaution against communicable disease. Many of mankind's physical ills had been conquered since those days, but Spitz was careful; there was no reason compelling him to be otherwise.

The sentry's body sagged into Spitz's arms and only then did Spitz withdraw the weapon, the knife a copy of the Fairbairn-Sykes commando blades of World War II. Two wars and six and one-half centuries away, in the hands of a descendant of the Nazis for whose killing this knife was originally designed, it was still marvelously effective. Spitz was a student of edged weapons, and for that reason he carried more than one: a general-purpose pocket knife of the type still called "Swiss Army Knives"; a heavy, short, stout, fixed-blade utility knife; and, this commando dagger.

Helmut Spitz dragged the dead body back into the shadows, holding his breath in order to enable him to hear any sounds which might trigger a mental alarm; his left hand was still over the mouth of the now-dead man, on the off chance that there might yet be a death rattle. There was a sound indicating that the dead man's bowels were loosening, but there was no way to prevent that.

It was so still here that, had Spitz used the knife against a kidney or along the inside of the sentry's thigh or merely plunged the knife through the chest and into the heart, the sound of steel cutting fabric might conceivably have been heard.

That was why he went for bare flesh.

None of the sentries in this vast hall was helmeted and that was a positive advantage to Spitz and his unit, aiding in unhampered access to the neck and voiding any possibility for potentially noise-producing headgear to tumble to the marbleized synthetic stone of the floor. The cryogenic storage facility at New Germany in Argentina, perhaps because of the two bodies still entombed here, seemed cathedral-like—ceiling of great height, vaulted and buttressed, but the walls windowless. The floor of this, the main room, was enormous, nearly adequately sized for a soccer field, barren of ornamentation.

And the guards were sworn to secrecy concerning this location. Although chosen (it was supposedly a great honor to stand watch here) from among the most trusted men in the crack units of the Trans-Global Alliance, they filled a need that was essentially ceremonial. After all, the cryogenic facility was fully self-contained and self-sustaining, located in such a remote spot that most conventional forms of access were impossible. The entryways were guarded, equipped with computerized sentry systems and armored against anything short of a nuclear strike.

The slings of the guards' energy rifles were white synthetic leather, as were the pistol belts and holsters for their energy pistols. And they wore dress uniforms.

The man whom Helmut Spitz had just killed was a German, but the guards at the entryway, killed only moments earlier, were Chinese and American, the latter a Marine in "dress blues," as they were called.

It was a Chinese, a descendant of one of the survivors of the Second City, who had betrayed the installation, allowed Spitz and his commandoes entry. The man harbored hate for the Rourke Family, the Rourkes causing the defeat of the Second City and responsible for its fall from power. The Chinese was among the few surviving believers who worshipped in the Second City's death cult. Spitz had the man killed for his troubles, because he disliked traitors.

The two bodies which slept in this supposedly impregnable repository were, at this point in human history, of enormous value. One of the sleepers—Spitz heard closer to dead than alive—was Sarah Rourke, the wife of the hated Doctor John Rourke, nemesis of the Führer, Deitrich Zimmer, and the Führer's son who was leader of Eden and heir apparent to the Reich, Martin Zimmer. Sarah Rourke was also Martin Zimmer's mother.

The second sleeper, by all reports fully healthy, was another historic enemy of National Socialism. He was Generaloberst Wolfgang Mann, key to the overthrow of The Leader one hundred and twenty-five years ago and the establishment of the hated democratic republic of New Germany under the betraying leadership of Herr Doctor Deiter Bern. Next to the Rourke Family, with whom Generaloberst Mann chose voluntarily to sleep one hundred twenty-five years ago, Mann was the Reich's greatest enemy.

The Bern government still survived through the generations, still harbored racial inferiors within it, still pandered to the democracies of the Trans-Global Alliance led by the United States, still condemned National Socialism, without which it would not have existed in the first place.

All of that would soon change, and the work done here would facilitate that circumstance, Helmut Spitz

8

believed, because he was told so in a private briefing by Deitrich Zimmer.

Destiny.

In the days prior to the Night of the War, the descendants and some few survivors of the Third Reich—men who had actually touched Hitler's hand, heard his voice, seen his glorious face, marched in his heroic armies—planned for the destruction of the lesser races in the aftermath of inevitable warfare between the Union of Soviet Socialist Republics and the United States of America. These magnificent few planned for their progeny to survive, return, rule. For this purpose, in what was then Argentina, a mountain redoubt was built at enormous expense and populated with the cream of Nazi youth from around the world.

For five centuries, while the Earth's surface was uninhabitable, the civilization which would rule the new Earth prospered. Science, technology, all disciplines thrived under the enlightened leadership of National Socialism. But, gradually, because persons of inferior race had been able secretly to insinuate themselves into what was known as "New Germany," a small group of heavily armed traitors arose. They were led by Generaloberst Wolfgang Mann and, with the help of the infamous Herr Doctor Rourke, overthrew by violence and deception the rightful government.

Evidence subsequently came to light, Spitz recalled, that Generaloberst Wolfgang Mann's great-great grandmother was suspected to be a Jewess.

Spitz inspected the knife wound in the dead sentry's throat. The men under Spitz in his Abteilung each knew the historic purpose of what would be done here this day, and to a man the brave young ones were ready

9

to die for the SS, for the Party, for the mission, and for their Hauptsturmführer, Spitz himself.

One of the humblest of the Abteilung's number, a mere Rottenführer, but as brave and as dedicated as any man in the SS, brought with him a disc player. As the Abteilung travelled here by aircraft before the High Altitude, Low Opening parachute insertion some miles from the facility, the young Rottenführer played on his machine Richard Wagner's immortal "Siegfried's Funeral Music" from *Der Ring des Nibelungen* tetralogy— played it in order to remind them all of the gravity of what lay before them. Before the green jump light was lit, however, the fellow changed his music to something which inspired them with purpose and courage. Its heroic strains still rang within the corridors of SS Hauptsturmführer Helmut Spitz's mind, filling him with determination and pride. The music was, of course, that unparalleled theme, telling the tales of Wotan's daughters, the "Ride of the Valkyries."

The body of the sentry was now fully withdrawn behind the support pillar at the entrance to the main gallery, and Helmut Spitz wiped clean his blade on the dead man's clothes, silently sheathing the steel.

Soon, the assault.

The hall was longer than it was wide. Pillars of shimmering synthetic marble were set every four meters apart, ranking from the low, arched entryway where Spitz crouched to what had become a shrine to the forces aligned against National Socialism. At the hall's furthest end, before the ranked flags of the nations of the Trans-Global Alliance, lay seven coffin-shaped transparent chambers, five of these open, two only—one just to the right of the centermost chamber, which had been that of Doctor Rourke, and the other on the far left side—operational. These latter two cryogenic chambers were illuminated from within, swirling clouds of gas, a translucent blue in color, surrounding the bodies cocooned there.

In the chamber just to the right of that in which the vile Herr Doctor Rourke had slept, Frau Rourke lay in uneasy repose. In the other chamber was Generaloberst Wolfgang Mann.

But all of that would change.

Very soon.

Spitz looked at his wristwatch, counting down the seconds. Had any one of the men of his Abteilung not been in position, the radio receiver built into the gas mask which Spitz wore would have been used, alerting him. Had one of his men failed, an alarm would have been sounded, at the least an energy weapon discharged.

The digital readout on the face of his wristwatch arrived at the zero hour and, in that very second, pneumatic weapons were fired from both sides of the great hall toward the two guards patrolling just before the seven cryogenic sleeping chambers, both men crumpling to the floor, before any alarm could be sounded, Spitz hoped. Each of the sentries, as did sentries of all the world's major armies, carried an alarm signal strapped to his palm. If danger seemed imminent, the sentry could pre-activate the alarm so that any release of pressure would give the signal. These men would not have detected that which had been about to claim their lives, therefore their alarm signals would not have been preset, would have required that extra split second for manual activation. Swiftness robbed them of their chance.

11

Now all potential for resistance within the hall was quelled.

And Helmut Spitz stood up, hissing into his radio, running across the vast emptiness toward the cryogenic chambers, "Quickly! Quickly!"

The vidcams monitoring the hall were computer linked and would, by now, register that there was something terribly wrong, but as long as silence was maintained there might still be some precious moments before there was a full alert and the rest of the small but well-trained garrison turned out. Already, the two men of Spitz's Abteilung who had dispatched the last two guards (the young Rottenführer who liked Wagner was one of these) had reached the two remaining cryogenic chambers.

Without being told, Spitz's men set about laying out the explosive charges on the two still-occupied cryogenic chambers. Soon, history would be changed forever.

TWO

Paul Rubenstein stared at John Rourke, watching the lines in his friend's face etch more deeply, it seemed, by the second. And, John's hands were alternately twisted together as if two violently opposed living entities were struggling with one another and covering John's face.

John paced, sat, stood, paced again across the private conference room adjoining Admiral Hayes's office at Pearl Harbor.

Michael sat slumped in the far corner, Natalia standing beside him, nearly as motionless as a statue. Periodically, Natalia's hands would move as John would walk past her, as if to touch him. But she never did.

Annie merely sat and stared at the wall, tears periodically overflowing her eyes and spilling down across her cheeks. Annie, Paul Rubenstein knew without being told, was undergoing an empathic experience with her father, adding his grief to her own.

Thorn Rolvaag, the vulcanologist, was already

airborne in a high-altitude observation craft for the purpose of studying the eruption of Kilauea, which had nearly claimed all their lives. Both Rolvaag's graduate student and the pilot of the helicopter—which had brought Rolvaag in but could not get him out—were hospitalized and in good condition.

One thing was in doubt, another a certainty.

That which was in doubt was the fate of Commander Emma Shaw, who had violated orders, endangering her life and her aircraft in what turned out to be a successful attempt to rescue the persons stranded on Kilauea. She had saved all their lives—except for those of Annie, Michael and Natalia who were still en route to the site of the eruption when Emma Shaw arrived there—and Paul did not delude himself as to why Emma Shaw had done so.

She was in love with John Rourke.

It was her fate that was in question. Would Admiral Hayes, who had been the first female commander of an attack submarine in the history of the United States Navy, act with compassion and forgiveness toward a disobedient officer? Or would she have Emma Shaw arrested, held for charges?

The thing which was a certainty was that John Rourke had sealed his own fate while successfully attempting to save the lives of everyone aboard Emma Shaw's V-stol fighter bomber. John fought his third child, Martin, the adopted son of the Nazi leader Deitrich Zimmer, trying to prevent Martin's energy pistol from discharging again and bringing down the aircraft. In the process—Paul had witnessed it with his own eyes—John was forced to strike his son across the jaw. And Martin fell back, out the open fuselage door, falling to his death in the volcanic eruption below.

When—if?—someday John's wife, Sarah, was successfully returned to consciousness, she would learn that the son whom she had brought into this world—almost at the very moment she was shot in the head by Deitrich Zimmer—was killed by the hand of her husband, her child's father.

Of all the Rourke Family, Paul Rubenstein knew Sarah the least well. He was married to the Rourkes' only daughter, Annie. The Rourkes' only surviving son, Michael, was, along with John, one of two men Paul Rubenstein counted as both brothers and best friends to him, albeit Michael was his brother-in-law and John was his father-in-law. And, of course, in the same way that he, Paul Rubenstein, was a member of the Rourke Family, so also was Natalia Anastasia Tiemerovna. Natalia, once in love with John, perhaps still in love with him, was Michael's mistress, would one day be Michael's wife.

Sarah lost Michael and Annie to adulthood when John manipulated the cryogenic chambers in order to age his children into adulthood for the purpose of their survival, indeed perhaps the survival of the human race. As Paul understood it, John and Sarah's marriage had been shaky Before the Night of the War. After she was awakened from cryogenic sleep and discovered that her two small children were adults, the Rourke marriage did not improve.

Then the baby. The child seemed like a blessing, Paul had always thought, as if somehow divine intervention had decreed that—in what was the first time John Rourke had made love to a woman since his last time with his wife Before the Night of the War—Sarah

15

should become pregnant.

Sarah was actually happy, enjoying her life after the War, assisting John with his hospital at Eden, readying herself to be an absurdly young grandmother someday (Paul and Annie had been seriously talking about having a baby then), waiting for her child to come so she could raise their child.

Then, all of that fell apart.

The hospital was attacked. Sarah delivered her son by herself in a hospital corridor. One of the Nazi commandoes, Deitrich Zimmer himself, shot her in the head. The bullet lodged inoperably deep within her brain. John was injured, comatose. The baby was kidnapped, for a time thought to be dead.

And so, John's life was now destroyed. The one bargaining chip John Rourke had held which would have enabled him to coerce Deitrich Zimmer, perhaps the most brilliant surgeon who ever lived, to perform a life-saving operation on Sarah was destroyed. That bargaining chip was Martin, whom Zimmer had raised as his own son, trained to be his successor as Nazi leader. Sarah was doomed to cryogenic sleep, perhaps eternally. If, by some miracle Sarah could be revived, restored, the bullet removed from her brain without killing her or destroying her faculties, when she learned that John had caused Martin's death (even though Martin had precipitated the circumstances leading to it), she would never forgive John.

John would be alone.

And, whatever happened, John Rourke lost.

That was unfair, wrong. John Rourke's entire life was spent fighting for the survival of humankind. As his reward, happiness would forever be denied him.

Paul Rubenstein watched as Natalia lit a cigarette, wishing for the billionth time that he had not given up smoking Before the Night of the War, then pushing the image of smoking from his mind.

John began pacing again.

The door leading between Admiral Hayes's office and the private conference room opened.

Emma Shaw stepped through, still wearing her flight suit, her helmet under her left arm. She ran the fingers of her right hand back through shoulder-length auburn hair that was losing its curl.

John stopped pacing. "Well?"

"The Admiral will enter a reprimand on my personnel file. If, within six months, there's no similar incident, the reprimand will be removed," Emma Shaw said, her voice low, without inflection.

A slap on the wrist, Paul thought. That was good.

"She pulled me off rescue duty for two days. Told me I needed the rest. I tried talking myself back up, but she wouldn't go along with it."

A massive rescue effort was going on now to evacuate the population of the island of Hawaii, because of the ongoing eruption.

"The admiral said there'd be plenty to do in two days. Even if the evacuation was completed, medical stuff and supplies and everything would have to be ferried out to the camps that are being set up. And Eden's forces are still massing for what looks like an attack. Admiral Hayes said I'd get plenty of flying in then."

"Rest," John told her. "You need it. And thank you, from all of us, Emma." John extended his right hand to her. She took it. They shook. She released his hand.

17

She glanced at all of them briefly. She left the room. John spoke again. "I think all of us need a rest. There's a lot to be done. And I have to do some thinking, alone. All of you, I—" And John's voice cracked as he rasped the words, "love you," then stormed out of the room.

Emma Shaw heard the footsteps in the corridor behind her and turned around. She started to speak. John Rourke's eyes streamed tears as he walked past her, not looking at her, saying nothing. "Ohh, God help him," she whispered, closing her eyes.

Three

John Thomas Rourke stood on the summit of the mountain. When he looked to his left, he could see the ocean, limitless, the sun rising far off the windward coast. When he looked to his right, the darkness was not fading, the smoke and ash of Kilauea dominating the sky.

But the sunrise was beautiful, beyond his descriptive powers. He had never been a man of many words. Beauty and darkness would soon meet above him.

He felt almost evil, wasting ammunition, but he truly had plenty and weapons in the calibers he used were not in the strategic inventory of the Trans-Global Alliance. And, he had come here to do this at any event.

He drew one of the little Detonics CombatMaster .45's from beneath his left armpit. He examined the gun closely. It was the one with his name on it, otherwise essentially identical to the gun beneath his right arm.

How often had he used this and its mate? How many lives had he taken in what he perceived as a good cause? And, for what?

His life was now nothing but ashes, like those at the tip of the thin, dark tobacco cigar he smoked, like the ashes spewing forth out of the volcano so far away, yet close. To have tried to sleep would have been an exercise in futility. He had killed his son, Martin, as surely as if he had shot him. And he had sealed his wife's doom, because without Martin there was no way in which he could coerce Deitrich Zimmer to utilize his almost magical surgical procedures to save Sarah's life. So, in one fateful instant, he had killed his son and effectively killed his wife.

And John Rourke had never felt loneliness more intensely in his entire life. Even Natalia was totally gone from him; she would be happier with Michael anyway.

This was a good place. A shot would never be heard, would disturb no one's predawn sleep. John Rourke hefted the pistol in his right hand, then cocked the hammer as he took one last drag on his cigar . . .

It was Admiral Hayes's voice on the telephone. "Yes, Admiral."

"Mr. Rubenstein, I felt it best to speak with you concerning a very recent development. I'm afraid it's too tragic to discuss over the telephone, and I'll confess I don't think I have the courage to tell either your wife or your brother-in-law, or, for that matter, Major Tiemerovna."

"What is it?"

"I'll be waiting in my office." The line clicked dead.

Paul Rubenstein looked across the room. Annie lay on the couch, an afghan she had crocheted herself covering her. She was sleeping, but mumbling incoherently, tossing her head every few seconds. Was she seeing something?

A shiver passed along Paul Rubenstein's spine. He was tempted to wake her.

Instead, he scribbled a note on the pad beside the telephone and told her he was going out to speak with Admiral Hayes about something, would be back shortly. Where to place the note if she awakened? He set it on the coffee table, beside the couch, bent over his wife, touched his lips lightly to her forehead as he drew the afghan up closer around her.

She was seeing something, because her eyelids were fluttering and, once one returned from the Sleep, one did not dream. But Annie did, if she were in the empathic state. And that only came upon her, he knew from past experience, when someone she cared for deeply was in danger.

He went back to the telephone, took it off the table, walked about the room with it in his hand for a few seconds. Even if Michael and Natalia slept, he would wake them. He dialed their apartment at the BOQ. Natalia answered. "Yes?"

"Me, Natalia. You and Michael okay?"

"Tired. We cannot sleep. And you and Annie?"

"Fine. Same way. Where's John?"

"Michael checked. John took a car from the base and drove up into the mountains. I think he wanted to be alone."

"You guys get some rest," Paul said, then hung up.

He stuffed his battered old Browning High Power into his trouser band and left the apartment, electing to walk the two blocks to Admiral Hayes's office. It was just past dawn, cool, damp, the air fresh and clear, his lungs still relishing that, after the hell of the volcano.

What was it that Admiral Hayes could not relate over the telephone? Could not tell Annie or Michael? Paul Rubenstein quickened his pace. Something about John? His walk became a jogging run, one block down, another only to go. There were extra guards on duty near the Admiral's headquarters complex, and as he narrowed the distance to the building to under a half-block, the guards nearest him already came to alert. "Relax. Paul Rubenstein to see Admiral Hayes."

"Yes, sir!"

Paul jogged past the Marine who'd spoken and the other man standing guard with him. He reached the front door in another few seconds.

Paul slowed his pace as he entered the building, catching his breath. The combination of Admiral Hayes's cryptic yet frightening telephone call and Annie's obvious dream state ate at his nerves. What had happened that was so terrible that only he could be told, that was too terrible for a veteran line officer like Thelma Hayes to relate?

Paul Rubenstein could see Admiral Hayes now. She stood at the end of the corridor, waiting for him, her uniform jacket off, her sleeves rolled up, her hands lost in the pockets of her skirt. Behind her glasses, the muscles around her eyes seemed bunched, tight, her smallish mouth's corners turned down.

Paul Rubenstein stopped walking. He stood a few feet from her. "What is it you couldn't tell me over the telephone, Admiral?"

Her hands came out of her pockets, a lighter in one, a solitary cigarette in the other. She lit the cigarette, exhaling smoke through her nostrils as she said, "Some things cannot be said very easily, even less easily when you can't see the face of the person you're talking to, Mr. Rubenstein."

"What happened?" There was a sick feeling in Paul Rubenstein's stomach, a cold sweat in his palms.

"There has been a death," she said, simply, quietly.

Paul Rubenstein felt the tendons in his neck go tight.

Four

She could not sleep. She didn't try. Maybe she would run over to the other side of the island after a while. A friend of hers owned one of the larger cattle ranches there and would lend her a horse. A ride really wouldn't help, but it was something to do.

Emma Shaw stood on the front porch of her little house, changed out of her flight suit into a loosely woven long-sleeved grey pullover sweater and a midcalf-length full skirt, rose colored—cotton, like the sweater—with deep side seam pockets, her hands buried in them. She wore no stockings and only wore flat sandals on her feet. And, she was a little cold. Wrapped about her shoulders was her one handicraft, the shawl she'd crocheted and practically hung under John Rourke's nose in order to impress him with how domestic she could be.

It was just past dawn.

She'd washed her hair twice as many times as usual in order to get the volcanic ash and dust out, turned up the hot water between showers and soaked under it for more than fifteen minutes, trying to get the stuff from the pores of her skin.

"Almost blew it this time, Emma," she told herself. As she took her cigarettes and lighter from the porch railing, lit a cigarette, exhaled, she remembered what her portside engine air filter had looked like by the time she landed at Pearl. It was very much like a sandbox.

She'd flown back to Pearl Harbor on forty-percent engine power.

By the book, that wasn't enough with her weight load. But she made it anyway, by the seat of her pants. And that was the best way to fly, even in this era of computers and autopilots and everything else.

If Admiral Hayes had brought her up on charges, if she'd been tossed out of the Navy, it would have been worth it. She started to cry now, just thinking about it. "I am stupid!" Emma Shaw said to the morning, to any wild creatures which might be listening, but most of all to herself. Women were stupid, she thought. Risk everything for a man she was nuts about who saw her as a war buddy. But, as she sniffed back her tears, she knew she would have done it again.

Emma Shaw was in love for the first and maybe the only time in her life. Two days from now, she'd be back in the air, and at any minute the forces of Eden and their Nazi allies would launch an attack against the United States and the rest of the Trans-Global Alliance. And, she'd be in aerial combat. And, maybe she would die. Takeoffs and landings from a carrier in rough seas were dangerous in and of themselves, not to mention other aircraft and ground batteries and everything.

Cigarettes weren't like they used to be in the days

26

when John Rourke was growing up. Tobacco was now totally noncarcinogenic. So, unless one smoked to excess and contracted emphesyma or injured the heart, smoking was okay. Under the circumstances, as she lit a fresh cigarette from the butt of the one burned down between her fingertips, she would have smoked anyway, even if there hadn't been noncarcinogenic cigarettes and even if cancer weren't curable.

Life like this was nothing to lose.

Annie Rourke Rubenstein sat up, screaming.

The afghan fell from her body to the floor."

"Dead?" What had she seen? She could not bring it back from the dream. There was a note on the coffee table. She picked it up and read it. Paul had gone off to see Admiral Hayes about something.

She stood up.

She looked down at her clothes. The wrinkles would fall out of her skirt. She straightened her blouse. She walked to the window and looked out. It was raining, huge drops streaming down over the panes of window glass like tears, like tears down a cheek.

And, without warning, the memory of her dream flooded over her and Annie screamed as she fell against the window frame.

Five

Paul Rubenstein sent Natalia over to keep his wife Annie company, not telling Natalia what Admiral Hayes had told him. He could not tell her, but knew that soon he would have to, tell Annie, tell Michael, too.

He borrowed an F.O.U.O. car, its Tracer unit tuned to the frequency of the F.O.U.O. car which John had taken when he drove off the base. The Tracer unit allowed one F.O.U.O. vehicle to home in on another, a very simple thing since each of the vehicles emitted its own signal code from the moment it left the base until it was returned (unless the solar cells ran out of energy first).

This signal was strong.

Paul followed it out of the city and into the mountains, along a highway that a few hours from now would be well travelled during the rush hour, but now was all-but-deserted. He passed through small suburban Honolulu communities, climbing with the road, his eyes occasionally drifting down to the automatic

29

controls which drove the car instead of him. He didn't trust them, kept his hands very lightly on the steering wheel even though he didn't have to.

What Admiral Hayes told him, in the aftermath of Martin's death, was almost beyond absorption. Tears still came to his eyes when he thought of it, and he would then focus his attention all the harder on the automobile's automatic controls, as a means of forcing reality away from him.

They—he and the car's computer—were out of any trace of real civilization now, and Paul Rubenstein, a New Yorker centuries ago, breathed more easily. Now, cities compressed his spirit, were slightly maddening to him.

It—the computer—kept driving, turning the car off onto an unpaved side road now.

The car drove at a "safe" speed, neither so fast as to enable him to get this over with soon, nor so slow as to postpone the horrible inevitable.

Instead, at what was the perfect speed, the computer drove him calmly toward what would be the worst moment of his life.

His left arm was a little sore, still.

But exercise was the best thing. He flexed his fist and put his hand into the borrowed glove. Michael Rourke took the ball from inside the glove and hefted it. His baseball experience was limited to distant memory and the occasional game of catch with his sister in the years when they were growing up alone at the Retreat.

He took the ball and threw it against the concrete wall, and the ball rocketed back toward him. Michael

30

dashed left, barely getting his glove on it. But he caught it. He threw the ball again, caught it more easily this time. He could get a baseball and glove of his own. If he stayed here at Pearl Harbor long enough, he might get involved with one of the teams. Every unit had its own, and there were several teams from among the ranks of the civilian employees, too.

Michael Rourke had discussed this with Paul. "You mean you really played on a team?"

"Well, it wasn't as if I played for the New York Yankees, Michael. I just played with some teams on the Air Force Bases my dad was assigned to. It was kind of fun."

"Can you teach me to hit?"

"You serious?"

Michael told his brother-in-law that he was serious.

Paul agreed to teach him to hit.

Michael nearly missed the ball—but only nearly. As a boy, his father had played catch with him, swatted flies with him, done all the father-son stuff. But his true boyhood ended the morning after the Night of the War when he saw his mother about to be molested and, rather than stand there, or cry, he took the boning knife out of their hastily put-together cache of supplies and killed the man who was about to hurt his mother. He put the knife in the man's kidney. He hadn't known anything about where to place a knife for killing, and he doubted that instinct was working upon him—more like dumb luck.

But, childhood ended.

If this was his second childhood, it would really be his first.

He kept playing with the ball, getting generally

better at getting his borrowed glove on it each time. He was worried for his sister. Paul had said she was upset, restless, dreaming. That did not bode well. But, Michael supposed, Natalia was the best to keep Annie company, take care of her, comfort her if Paul himself could not be there.

Paul had not said where he was going.

And, that was odd, very unlike Paul.

Michael stopped throwing the ball, took off his glove, just stood there. He decided to go see Natalia and his sister after a quick shower.

Six

It took a moment before Paul Rubenstein was able to see John Rourke. John lay against a rock, as if asleep.

Tears filled Paul Rubenstein's eyes as he forced his legs to move along the narrow, rocky trail.

It was full daylight now. Admiral Hayes had offered to detail some men to accompany him, but he had told her simply that some things had to be done alone. First Martin, now this, one life that was evil and vile by any judgement, another that was noble and good, yet both lives shared the same genes. And, how would he tell Annie? He'd have to tell her; it was only right that he did. He was as used to being orphaned as anyone ever got to it, Paul Rubenstein supposed. But how did one tell someone that a parent, a loved one, someone who had become quite literally larger than life because of circumstance, was dead?

Paul reached the top of the rise, the end of the path. He stooped over to pick up a spent brass cartridge case. It was from a .45 ACP, one of the German production rounds, of course, but headstamped as if it were made by Federal Cartridge, John's perennial brand of preference.

Paul stared at John Rourke.

Paul sniffed back a tear.

He started to walk closer to him and the rock against which his friend lay. Why had this had to happen? It wasn't right.

"It's not like you to come up so quietly, Paul. What's up?"

Paul Rubenstein breathed. There were more yellow brass cartridge cases on the ground near Paul's feet. He crouched, began picking them up.

"Came up here to think. I haven't shot for anything but self-defense in longer than I can remember. I can police up that brass. I just hadn't gotten around to it."

"Gives me something to do," Paul told his friend. "Uhh—"

"What?"

This was needless cruelty to John, prolonging it to save himself. "The cryogenic facility in New Germany was hit by Nazi commandoes. Blew it up. Sarah and Colonel Mann are both dead."

He'd said it.

He stayed there, crouched over the pieces of empty brass.

John said nothing.

"I didn't know how to tell you. Annie and Michael and Natalia don't know yet. But, I'll tell them. I'm sorry, John. She was a magnificent woman. I don't know what else to say."

John lit a cigar, but his hands shook and, as he exhaled smoke, John coughed, sounded for an instant

34

as if he were choking. He just dropped the cigar and lowered his face into his hands. And Paul could hear the sobbing, see his friend's face as John's fists hammered down into the dirt on either side of him.

"Jesus!" John exclaimed. John stood up, walked to the edge of the drop, stood there, beating his right thigh with his right fist. "After all—all she—she went—went through, God!" And John Rourke raised his voice into a cry across the valley beyond "Sarah!"

Paul Rubenstein opened his hands and let the empty brass fall through his fingers. His throat felt tight. He stood up, walked toward his friend, put his arms around him and John Rourke rested his arm across Paul's shoulders and wept.

Seven

Annie already knew that something terrible had happened, but not quite what. While Natalia kept talking with her, she dressed, telling Natalia nothing at all about her dream-initiated fears.

"Michael's been thinking about trying to pass himself off as Martin with Deitrich Zimmer. I don't seem to be able to talk him out of it," Natalia said despairingly.

Annie was pulling her slip over her head, stopped with it still bunched up over her breasts. "He shouldn't do that. There's been enough tragedy, Natalia." She finished putting on her slip, smoothing it along her thighs, then walked over to the dresser, picked up her brush and started doing her hair. She'd showered, washed her hair, dried it. She would have to look her best, today. Her mother always liked her to look her best. "Besides, Michael could never convince Deitrich Zimmer. It would be like Martin having tried to convince daddy that he was Michael, instead. It'd never work."

"I know that. But Michael feels he has to do something. Men are crazy."

"We let them be, even admire it in them, don't we?"

"Paul is so sensible."

Annie smiled. "He's exciting. Trust me."

"Ohh, I didn't mean that!" Natalia told her hastily.

"I know you didn't mean anything," Annie replied.

"It is only that Paul doesn't seem to have to be spectacular, that he does what needs to be done without any—what's the word?"

"I'm amazed!" Annie said. "Fanfare?"

"Yes, like that. 'Fanfare' isn't the sort of word one uses every day, you know."

Annie shrugged her shoulders, straightened her straps. The sides of her hair were caught up in a barrette just near the crown of her head, the rest of her hair hanging down, almost to her waist. Natalia had helped her a few days before, trimming off about two inches of split ends.

It was a cool day. She took down a long-sleeved medium blue blouse, began putting it on. "Michael is just like Daddy; he's naturally heroic. And it's unnatural for him to be otherwise. Paul is just naturally competent; when it's competent to be heroic, he's heroic, but he doesn't go out of his way to constantly do that. Do you know what I mean? It doesn't define him."

"Yes. I want Michael's baby." And Natalia laughed. "Can you imagine that? Me? A mother!"

"You'll make a wonderful mother. What's Michael think about it?" Her blouse was buttoned except for the button at the neck. She closed the cloth-covered buttons at her cuffs.

"I haven't mentioned it to him, not yet, anyway."

38

Natalia lit a cigarette, stood up from where she'd been sitting on the edge of the bed, walked to the window. Natalia wore black slacks and a loose-fitting, black, long-sleeved cotton sweater with a round neck. Except for very small pierced earrings—diamonds—and her Rolex wristwatch, she wore no jewelry. As usual, she looked stunning.

Natalia was frequently in black. Annie felt a chill along her spine, that the color might be especially appropriate today. Natalia's hair was up, making her look very sophisticated. But she was always that, at least in appearance.

"Why did Paul go off like that, Annie?"

"I'm not sure. I think there's something going on and he didn't want to worry me." Annie closed the button at her collar and tied the collar into a long, drooping bow at her throat, then stepped into her skirt. It was straight and navy blue. She pulled it up, closed the zipper, then the double waist buttons at the small of her back. She picked up the skirt at its hem, smoothed her slip beneath it, then let the skirt fall back, its hem only a little bit above her ankles.

In China's First City, Annie had become much taken with high heels, for the way they looked and made her feel. She stepped up and into a pair of blue pumps, then saw to her jewelry. This consisted of only a thin gold chain at her neck, a gold bracelet on her right wrist, her wristwatch on her left wrist and a pair of gold pierced earrings.

She liked dressing well, and the mere process was usually a way to clear her mind, get her thinking of something else. "Could you do my eyes, Natalia? I've never been good at it."

39

"All right. Sit down. How about a very pale blue?"

"It wouldn't be too much blue?"

"You're right. Here we go. Close your eyes."

Getting her mind on something else had worked a little. But when she closed her eyes in order for Natalia to apply the eye liner and eye shadow—she didn't use mascara and hated the stuff anyway—Annie could still see the dream. It was as if she had been inside one of the cryogenic chambers in New Germany, and then there was fire and there were explosions.

Perhaps she should have contacted the German authorities right away, alerted them. Tell them she'd had a bad dream? That she never dreamed unless someone she loved was in danger? If Colonel Mann had not himself been in cryogenic sleep, he would have believed her.

She was tempted to tell Natalia, but somehow felt she should not. Not yet, at least.

"There, kid! You look great."

Annie smiled, kissed Natalia's cheek. "You look great. I look okay," Annie corrected, going over to the mirror to inspect Natalia's handiwork. "You have to show me again, sometime. I always get too much on so it looks like I got my eyelids dirty or something." She did her lips. All men got to do was shave. That couldn't be much fun. Maybe she should tell Natalia. "I had a dream."

"Ohh, God," Natalia almost whispered.

As Annie started to explain, she heard the door to the apartment opening. In the mirror, when she moved her head just right, she could see beyond the bedroom doorway and into the small living room. Paul. Michael. Her father.

"Annie?"

"In here. We're decent. Come on in, Paul."

She turned away from the mirror, looked at her husband as he filled the doorframe. He wasn't as tall as her father or her brother, but he was tall enough, and even though he was lean, he had good muscles and solid shoulders. There was a look of terrible sadness in his eyes. "It's Momma, isn't it?"

"Your mother's dead, Annie." Her father wasn't even in the room as he spoke.

Natalia ran back to the window, clutched at the curtains, leaned her head against the glass.

"We're gonna get the damn—" Michael began.

Paul crossed the room, folded Annie into his arms. Annie realized only then that tears were already flowing down her cheeks, thought absently that her eye makeup was waterproof. She closed her eyes as she sagged into her husband's arms, saw the dream again. "The cryogenic chambers were burned. And there were explosions," she related, her own voice sounding muffled to her, her head so close against Paul's chest.

"You should have said something." It was Michael's voice "But it was already done, wasn't it?"

"I, uhh—"

"She doesn't know," Paul said for her. "She had a headache, was feeling sick to her stomach earlier. I suggested that she should lie down. She probably experienced it without knowing it, then only saw it after she was alseep."

"Yes," Annie said, trying to nod, but Paul was holding her so tightly she couldn't. Her voice was gone and that was the last word she could say for a time.

Michael's voice sounded strained, as if he were

41

holding back tears. "They'll pay, but never enough."
On the last word, his voice broke.

She pulled away a little from Paul's embrace, looked
past him. She saw Michael, his head against the
doorjamb, his right forearm over his eyes, his body
shaking. Natalia went to him. She saw her father, John
Rourke, dark circles under his eyes, his face expressionless, his cheeks drawn down, the tendons of his
neck—visible under the open collar of the black knit
shirt he wore—pulsing.

She could hear Natalia crying. Paul wept.

Annie put her arms around her husband's waist,
touched her lips briefly to his cheek, let him hold her
while the tears came and her body shook.

She said the word, "Momma."

Eight

It was nearly four in the afternoon when Emma Shaw heard the crunch, the muted hum of synth-rubber leaving pavement and coming onto gravel. The news broadcasts had been full of the events which had unfolded at New Germany in Argentina. The death of Sarah Rourke and of the heroic German General Wolfgang Mann at the hands of Nazi terrorist commandoes almost overshadowed the continuing eruption of Mt. Kilauea and its resultant devastation.

There was definitely a car outside.

Emma Shaw picked up the .45 automatic from under the couch and walked across the great room toward the windows.

She almost dropped the gun when she looked out, realized that the man in the car was John Rourke.

She had wanted to call him, not known what to say to him. "I'm sorry your wife is dead?" It would have sounded as hollow to him as it did to her. But, she really was sorry. She'd never known Sarah Rourke except from history books in school and that silly movie that was made in Eden. But she'd resented the woman, a woman who was more dead than alive holding a man who was so wonderfully alive but who refused to live, a man she wanted for herself and knew she could never have.

The driver's side door of the F.O.U.O. car was open, but John did not get out, just sat there. Emma Shaw watched him, her hands shaking. She set down her gun, ran the palms of her hands over her skirt, dug her hands into her pockets in order to stop her hands from shaking. Now her shoulders trembled instead.

Why had John Rourke come here?

"Ohh, God," she whispered aloud, her own conjecture terrifying her.

He just sat there, still. What was he doing? Should she go out onto the porch? And what would she say then. "Want a drink? Coffee? Tea?"

Or herself.

She couldn't say anything that wouldn't sound trite and, at the same time, cheap, about them both.

She saw a long-fingered, strong, graceful hand reach out to the door and pull it shut, heard the soft purr as the electric motor restarted.

"No!" She shouted the word, but he couldn't hear her, of course. She pulled open the door, ran out onto the porch, shouted louder, "John, wait!"

The car stopped.

What had she done? Emma Shaw almost verbalized.

The door opened.

Should she run to him, should she—

John Rourke stepped out of the car and she took a step back closer to her open door.

John wore the same brown leather bomber jacket

he'd worn when she picked him up off the slope of the volcano, the leather just as scarred and ash-smudged now as then. Black knit shirt, black BDU pants, black combat boots.

A black mood?

And, why not, his wife and a son dead within less than the span of half a day. And, he would blame himself. Men did that. "John?"

"I, uhh—" The words came out of him like a sigh. He took off his dark-lensed aviator-style sunglasses and she could tell from his eyes that he'd been crying. And, before she was conscious even that she was moving, she was running down from the porch, running to him. She stopped, less than a foot away from him, balanced on the balls of her feet, the hem of her skirt swaying back and forth against her bare legs, her hands away from her sides, fingers splayed. "I had nowhere else that I could go, no one else that I could talk to. Paul and Annie needed to be alone. And Michael and Natalia, too. It's my wife, you see. The Nazis killed her and I have to talk to somebody."

John Rourke's voice was tight sounding, his breath coming in short gasps as, she realized, he fought back tears.

That was why men died younger now as they always had, always would. Because they had to be men all the time.

Emma Shaw's hands moved, jerky and awkward-feeling to her—moved slowly toward John Rourke's face, touched him gently, caressed his face. "Talk to me."

John Rourke nodded.

"And let me hold you," Emma Shaw whispered,

drawing John Rourke's head down toward her, his arms folding gently around her, his head bowing. She heard his tears, felt them against her own cheek, brushed her lips against his face, whispered, "I'm here for you, John."

For such a long time that her arms and legs began to go numb, she held him like that, afraid to let go of him, or that he would let go of her.

Nine

Alternately, but not often, he would sip at one of the drinks on the table. One was a cup of decaffeinated coffee which had to be cold by now despite the self-warming cup in which she had served it. The other was a glass of red wine.

Neither the coffee nor the wine was very much gone. She had finished her coffee, sipped at her wine, watched John Rourke from across the table, listened.

"We were really going to make it," he told her. "The baby, the hospital, her work and mine. We were going to make it this time. No going off ever again, no leaving her. And after one hundred and twenty-five years, Zimmer finished what he started."

"My dad always told me that the one comfort he had as a cop was that the ones he didn't catch up with on this side, God'd catch up with on the other side."

For the first time since he had arrived more than an hour ago, John Rourke smiled. Then the smile left him. "God won't have the chance, at least not before me, unless Zimmer drops dead before I find him."

"There's a whole world war about to happen between you and him, John." She lit a cigarette, almost absently offering one to John. He just shook his head. She told him, "Go ahead and light a cigar. I've got air freshener."

He nodded again, took a cigar from the coat beside him (his coat was getting her couch filthy from dried mud and volcanic ash, but that didn't matter). He lit the cigar with his battered old lighter, the lighter perhaps only a few years younger than he was.

He set it down on the coffee table. She'd read once that psychologists believed that a man setting down some personal object—like a lighter, a key ring, something like that—was symbolic of feeling at ease, in control.

"May I see your lighter?" Emma Shaw asked him.

"Of course," John answered almost absently, picking up his lighter and reaching it across to her.

She leaned forward, took it, leaned back in her chair and turned it over in her hands. The lighter was bare brass, and she was uncertain whether it had started that way or had once been possessed of a finish. Engraved across the bottom beneath the word *Zippo,* partially obscuring the words *Bradford, Pa.,* were the intitials *JTR.* "How long have you had this, John?"

"Since I was a kid," he told her.

"And you were always very careful with it; I don't mean the finish, but careful to keep it functional, never lose it?"

He looked up from the glass of wine he seemed to be studying with microscopic intensity and asked, "What's your point, Emma?"

48

"That sometimes we lose things—or people—even though we tried our best not to. And, it's not our fault. When my mom died, for a long time I wondered if maybe something I'd done or hadn't done could have changed things. After a while, I guess I learned that nothing I could have done could have changed things. If you had a hole in your pocket, and your lighter fell out, you might never find it."

He smiled. "I know it sounds obsessive, but I always check my pocket seams before I put on a pair of pants. The same with jackets." He shrugged his shoulders. "And anyway, this is different."

"Why? Because when the Nazis hit your hospital a hundred and twenty-five years ago, you survived and she didn't survive as well? So, you should be feeling guilty for living? I don't buy that, John. Want some dinner?"

"Maybe I should go."

"Where?"

"I don't know."

"You're the sensible one. Eating regular meals is good for your health. If you want to be healthy enough to go after the men you want to kill, then you'll need your strength."

"Mother?" John asked, smiling. But the smile faded again.

"Maybe that's what you need, and maybe not. But, that's not what I am. But I like cooking for you. Want some fresh coffee or are you planning on poisoning your digestive system?"

John Rourke said, "Well, since you put it that way."

She got up to start dinner.

49

He ate little, having no taste for it, despite the fact that she was right and the food was good. He'd eaten nothing all day.

She sat across from him, looking at him now and again. Finally, John Rourke said to her, "You're a good friend."

Emma Shaw stirred her coffee with a spoon, didn't look up from it as she said, "What's on your mind?"

"I don't know." He got up from the table, walked across the room and went out onto the porch.

After a few seconds, she followed him. He was lighting one of his thin, dark tobacco cigars as she came up beside him.

"Those things taste any good?" Emma asked him.

John Rourke just looked at her. "What?"

"I asked if they taste any good, the cigars."

"I like them," Rourke told her, exhaling smoke through his nostrils. What a peculiar woman Emma Shaw was, Rourke thought.

"Let me try," she said, her hand touching his, taking the cigar from between his fingers. She inhaled; to her credit, Emma Shaw did not cough. "Strong. Sure these things aren't carcinogenic?"

"The ones I smoked in the Twentieth Century were, even the ones Annie made for me out of tobacco she raised herself. These are German. Won't cause cancer."

"And when there's the war, will the Germans fly them into Hawaii just for you?"

"If I asked them to," Rourke nodded, "they'd get me a few."

She inhaled again, this time exhaling smoke through her nostrils. "But you'd go without before you'd do that, smoke cigarettes. Strategic material would take preference, right?"

"Uh-huh," Rourke nodded.

"But I suppose you've planned ahead, have a long-term supply laid up."

"Uh-huh," Rourke nodded.

Emma Shaw puffed on the cigar again. "Figured out what's on your mind yet?"

"Not yet."

"Want to hear what's on my mind?" Emma asked him.

"Sure."

"You feel like you could burst inside? Because of what's happened?"

Rourke didn't answer her.

"Do you feel so sad you almost want to die?"

John Rourke took back his cigar, inhaled the smoke deeply into his lungs. He looked out into the night. There was a beautiful, albeit not majestic, view. "Nice just standing out here in the fresh air," Rourke said.

"Sarah is dead. Natalia is Michael's woman. You're lonely. Everybody has somebody, except you. Do you want me?"

John Rourke turned around and looked at her. "What?"

"Do you want me, John? Like I want you, John? I love you. I don't expect you to love me back, but maybe it wouldn't hurt to be held, to let whatever happens happen. I mean, maybe I'm awfully brazen or callous, with your wife just dead. And I'm sorry. But with the war coming, maybe I'll be dead, too. Or you. I admit you've given it a good try, but even you're not immortal. I'd like to have you, however you'd like to have me, John." And she looked away from him, shook her head, seemed to force a little laugh. "There! I've said it." She exhaled loudly, then barely whispered, "And you think I'm a slut or an opportunist or—"

John Rourke snapped the cigar into the gravel beyond the porch, his hands going to her shoulders, turning her around. "I think you're a marvelous woman. I respect you—"

"Ohh," she whispered, looking down.

John Rourke still held her shoulders. "That's not what I meant," he told her.

Her face turned up toward his and her grey green eyes met his eyes squarely. "Then maybe you should tell me what it is you do mean, John."

John Rourke almost whispered, "I don't know what I feel, what I mean, but you were right. Being with you, I mean, uhh—"

"Are you going to kiss me, John?"

"I was thinking about it."

"Well, then whenever you're ready." Emma Shaw whispered.

John Rourke, his hands moving down across her arms, to her waist, settling there, drew Emma Shaw up and toward him, lowering his face to hers.

He looked at her.

He folded her into his arms.

John Rourke touched his lips lightly to Emma Shaw's lips, then crushed her against him, his mouth hard against hers, her mouth opening beneath him, her body going limp in his arms, molding against his thighs, his abdomen, his chest.

The fingers of John Rourke's left hand knotted into her hair, cocking her head back. Her mouth drew out into a thin, beautiful smile. He kissed her throat. Her hands, bound within his arms, touched at his face.

His fingers wove more deeply into her hair, the nape of her neck in the crook of his left elbow, the fingers of his right hand splayed over her, rising from her waist and across her back. Rourke bent over her, kissed her mouth, her cheek, then her mouth again.

He let her go, but only a little.

She lay in his arm, her breathing reduced to short rapid panting.

John Rourke swept Emma Shaw up into his arms, cradling her there against his body.

Wilhelm Doring watched as the old man from the little diner—Luther Haas, the ranking Nazi intelligence controller in the Hawaiian Islands—conversed with these racially objectionable persons he had hired as assassins. Doring watched and he listened. "You all know what to do, as we have discussed. Nikita, why don't you go over it once more, hmm?"

"Right, Mr. Haas." Nikita was a tall, broad-shouldered expatriate Soviet, involved in the drug trade here in the islands and credited, as Luther Haas recounted it, with several contract murders on behalf of the party, and many more which he privately arranged. "We close in from both sides of the house and get the woman and anybody else inside. Just shoot 'em down dead. Don't blow the damn place up or nothin', cause we want that son-of-a-bitch cop Tim Shaw to know he fucked with the wrong people this time."

"Exactly, Nikita. One thing more. You will carve a swastika on the dead body of Shaw's daughter. Then get out of there. Now, you and your men be on your way. And remember that the man with her is John Rourke. He did not survive all these years by being inept, hmm? Heil Zimmer!"

"Yeah, sure thing, Mr. Haas," the very American-sounding Russian said, nodding his head and shaking his shoulder-length blonde hair as he walked off.

Doring looked after Nikita, watching as he walked down the hillside toward the ten men waiting for him. All of them were armed with caseless projectile firearms, not a plasma energy weapon among them. The house that Commander Shaw had lay across a narrow valley which looked like it might once have been a river course. Through binoculars, Doring had watched the disgusting scene between Rourke and the woman. And, how appropriate it would be to have this despicable Rourke fellow turn up dead in this love nest with his little Naval officer whore!

When Herr Haas had insisted on contracting a revenge plot against the American policeman, Inspector Shaw, for the deaths of half of Doring's commando team, Wilhelm Doring had been against it. He and his four men were more than adequate to the task (He discounted Marie Dreisling completely). But Herr Haas had insisted that Doring not risk the remainder of his unit in an unplanned operation, and that speed of retribution was required. Hence, Nikita and his drug friends.

But now, having seen Doctor Rourke, Wilhelm Doring felt even worse about at last agreeing to Herr Haas's plan. These eleven scurvy fellows were easily too many to deal with Fräulein Commander Emma Shaw. Were they enough, however, these street ruffians, thugs, to deal with the almost legendary Herr Doctor John Rourke?

To have gone with these men would have been madness, however. If they were good, they could succeed on their own. If they were not and he accompanied them, they would succeed only in getting him killed, perhaps.

So, he waited, Luther Haas lighting a cigarette. They stood together, each watching through night-vision binoculars. Rourke and the woman would be inside the bedroom by now.

John Rourke's hands moved over her body, his touch easy, gentle as he slowly removed her clothing.

At last, she was naked. She thought she should be trembling or something like that. But, instead, she felt safer, happier than she had ever felt before.

John was stripped to the waist. And he was magnificent. Shoulders almost terrifyingly broad. His arms and his chest veritably rippled with muscles at his slightest movement. Her hands caressed his bare back, powerful, hard. The hair on his chest was more than partially grey. But it was the only bodily sign that he could have been much more than thirty years old, even though she knew that biologically he was closer—one side or the other—to forty. His stomach was flat, muscled and hard, too.

There were no scars on his body and for a moment she was amazed that with all his near-death encounters—just those talked about in the history books—he remained unscathed. But she remembered a property of cryogenic sleep (biology was never one of her strongpoints in school). It was discovered that cryogenic sleep had a restorative effect on the human body, curing minor illnesses, even healing the skin as if the body, given time to rest, could repair itself.

"What are you thinking, Emma?" John almost whispered, bending over the bed, his hands on her again, his lips brushing hers.

"How good you look and how much I love you," she whispered back.

John smiled, kissed her lightly again, then stood up. "Are you sure?"

"Uh-huh. Never surer of anything in my life. You?"

"Yes," he whispered, starting to open his trouser belt.

"Wait a minute," she told him. And she knelt up on the bed, her hands going to his waist. "You undressed me. Let me undress you."

"If you want," John said, smiling easily. But there was a far-off look in his eyes, sadness mingled with loneliness. And more than ever, she wanted this to be the best moment in John Rourke's life, just as she knew that it would be the best moment in hers. She started to undo his belt, her lips touching at his abdomen, at his chest, at his throat, her bare body against his chest, her breasts hot, her nipples feeling so hard she could barely stand it.

Emma Shaw had told herself in that first moment that she was able to think after he kissed her for the first time that she would be more than foolish to suppose he would be hers for ever, stay with her always.

But John Rourke was at least a little bit hers now. And she would be his for as long as he wanted her, and after that, too. There was never a man like this in all her life, probably not in all the world.

She opened the button at the waistband of his trousers.

There was a very soft sound from beyond the room as John's lips touched hers, her face in his hands.

His body went rigid.

Over the sound, not over her.

His lips moved to her cheek, to her ear. "We're not alone."

She didn't have a cat. Pests like mice and rats had gone from most places on the Earth over six centuries ago when the sky caught fire in the Great Conflagration. John had closed the door behind them as he'd carried her into the house, so no bird or squirrel (such animals were returned to the wild more than a century ago and thrived) had followed them in.

She looked over into his eyes, then looked away and glanced to her right, but without moving her head. He was right. They were not alone. Her .45 was in the great room by the front door. Her Lancer pistol was on the kitchen table; she'd disassembled it for cleaning then gotten caught up in the television broadcasts about Sarah Rourke and not reassembled it yet.

If she'd believed in spirits roaming the Earth she

could have convinced herself it was Sarah Rourke out there, come to prevent them from becoming lovers.

John Rourke's little pistols—every school kid grew up knowing they were Detonics .45s—were still in their shoulder holsters, on the chair in front of her dressing table, the chair halfway between the foot of the bed and the door. His little knife, the black double-edged one he usually carried inside the waistband of his trousers, was with the guns.

The noise had been from beyond the doorway, in the great room.

"When I tell you to, you drop to the floor, Emma. And grab my shirt as you do. I'm going to my guns. If there's trouble, run for it. Get to the car and get out of here." His right hand left her body for a split second, then returned, something cold in it as he pressed his hand against her left breast.

She realized it was a coded entry car key, the one to the electric car in which he'd driven here.

John slid his hand down along her body to the left cheek of her rear end and she felt the coded entry key slipped under her between the flesh of her bottom and her calf.

She looked into his eyes as his hands started to tense on her. "I really love you."

He touched his lips to her forehead. Then he rasped a single word, "Now!"

His hands were gone from her in the same instant as he spoke, his body a blur of movement racing away from the bed and toward the chair where his guns lay. For a split second, Emma Shaw was powerless to move.

The bedroom door was already open.

Two men came through, submachineguns in their hands. John wasn't going to make it to his guns. Emma Shaw screamed, turning her naked body fully toward the two armed men, her hands cupping under her breasts. Not because she was frightened. She was that. But if she could divert their attention for a split second, get their eyes on her instead of him.

John's right hand clasped to his belt buckle, ripping his belt from the trousers loops, snapping it outward, toward the face of the man nearest to him. John's left hand reached out to the double shoulder holster for his guns. Grabbing it near the center of the harness, he swung both pistols outward.

The military belt's brass tip struck the first man across his eyes knocking him back, his submachinegun firing into the bedroom ceiling, huge chunks of plaster falling down around him as he stumbled to the floor.

The two pistols John swung in the shoulder holster hit the second man on the side of the head. John kicked the first man in the face.

Emma Shaw rolled off the bed grabbing for John's black knit shirt with one hand, the coded entry card for the electric car with the other. But she had no intention of using it.

She pulled the shirt on over her head stuffing her arms into the sleeves, the garment impossibly large for her. Under the circumstances, since she had nothing else even close—her clothes lay on the floor on the other side of the bed—the shirt's size—and more importantly its length—was an asset. As her head emerged from inside the shirt and she looked over the top of the bed, she saw John Rourke use a classic judo throw on a third man just through the door, John's right hand catching the man's gunhand wrist, pinwheeling the arm, rolling the man over and down.

John had his double shoulder holster in his left hand, was reaching with his other hand for a submachinegun which lay on the floor next to one of the men, unconscious or dead. But as John Rourke reached for the gun a line of bullets tore into the floor from the submachinegun of a fourth man.

From behind her, Emma Shaw heard one of the bedroom windows shattering.

She wheeled round one hundred and eighty degrees, grabbing the lamp from the nightstand and hurling it toward the man coming through the window. The lamp struck him in the head and he stumbled toward her. To her feet, Emma Shaw rotated ninety degrees right, snapping her left elbow out from shoulder level, impacting the man at the right temple.

She tried grabbing for his gun but another man was already at the window stabbing his submachinegun through it and toward her. Emma Shaw launched herself over the bed as the submachinegun opened up, bullets tearing across the bed, into the carpet as she hit the floor and rolled.

John at last had one of his pistols free, stabbing it toward a man levelling a submachinegun at John's chest. Emma Shaw almost screamed for real this time, her heart in her mouth. John fired first.

Ears ringing, the smell of gunpowder hanging on the air like an invisible foul-smelling cloud filling her nose, Emma Shaw reached out and rolled, grabbing for the submachinegun John had reached for instants earlier. As her hand closed over it—she recognized the submachinegun as a Lancer copy of the HK MP 5, considered the best of the best among brass cartridge submachineguns—the man beside it reached out and grabbed at her.

John Rourke's booted right foot kicked out and connected with the man's face.

Then John was hauling her to her feet and toward the shattered window. The man beside it threw the muzzle of his submachinegun toward them and John fired twice, the man's face instantly smearing with blood and his head snapping back.

John Rourke let go of her arm, shoving her toward the window, telling her, "Be ready to use that!"

As she brought the submachinegun up into a firing position, at the far right edge of her peripheral vision she saw John shifting his little .45 from his right hand to his left, catching up the submachinegun belonging to the man he'd just shot with his right. The submachineguns were the SD variant with integral suppressors. The other guns she'd seen were Lancer versions of the Uzi, these not suppressor fitted.

John stabbed the HK submachinegun toward the window, shouting to her, "Head down!" She dropped to her knees, careful as she could be to avoid the glass shards. John's weapon fired and Emma Shaw looked up. A man at the window was dead, his body falling back.

"Run for it!" John sprayed out the submachinegun toward the bedroom door. Emma Shaw ran for the window, starting to clamber up. But John swept her up into his left arm, half throwing her through the shot-out window.

She dropped to the ground, stumbling, getting to her feet.

John vaulted through, reaching down to the dead man just beside the house wall, grabbing up the dead man's submachinegun.

The little .45 was in his waistband. The two submachineguns in his hands sprayed back through the open window.

"Now watch your bare feet!"

She ran beside him as he ran, seeing him hurl away one of the submachineguns—empty she assumed—and redraw the little Detonics .45 from his trouser band.

They ran along the wall of the house, toward the front, where John's car was parked—her own car was garaged and impossible to get to, she realized.

As John turned the front corner of the house, Emma Shaw beside him, three men rose up from behind the F.O.U.O. vehicle in which he had driven here, toward which they had been running. Submachineguns in the hands of the three men opened fire. Chunks of the outside wall shredded under the impact of the bullets and John knocked her breathless, slamming her back against the wall behind the corner.

He stabbed his submachinegun around the corner, firing a short burst. Then he flattened himself against the wall beside her. "You all right?"

"Sure. I'm more than half naked. Some damn assholes shot up my house and I'll just bet I won't get you to get me back to bed."

"You're a wonderfully candid person," he told her, smiling.

"What are we gonna do, John?"

He smiled, said nothing for a moment, then, his eyes following the downspout near them, said, "I'm going to give you both submachineguns. You watch out behind you. Don't know how many there are. I'm going up on the roof. Fire a couple of shots, not more than three if you can manage that short a burst. You don't have more than a dozen rounds left in this." He handed her the submachinegun.

"What are you gonna do on the roof?"

"Kill those men." Then, as if to himself, more like thinking out loud rather than talking, he added, "Wish I had some pliers."

"Pliers?!"

But John Rourke was already moving . . .

His old OSS friend years ago had related to him once how two pairs of pliers were often used in conjunction with a gutter downspout to climb to the roof of a building. John Rourke didn't even have one set of pliers, but he climbed the downspout anyway.

The double Alessi rig across his bare shoulders, only three rounds in one gun, six in the other, his spare magazines on the bedroom floor, fallen there when he ripped out his belt, his knife still on the chair by the dresser, he had one option and one only. Get on the roof and as quickly as possible, kill the three men by the car. It was that or die, and more than his own life—he realized he feared for Emma Shaw's life. Did that mean that he loved her?

It was a thought at once comforting and terrifying.

His hands worked along the downspout, his feet

63

locked around it, helping to shove him upward along its length. He was halfway to the roof. Below him, Emma Shaw fired a really nice, clean-sounding short burst.

From his position, he could not see the three men, or for that matter the car.

His right hand reached the gutter—it was integral to the structure, not an add-on as gutters had been six centuries ago. Rourke hoped it was not only integral but sturdy, because the gutter was the only handhold for him on the roof line. He hauled his body weight up against it, rolled over it onto his back, the shingle material rough against his bare skin.

Almost literally, he'd been caught with his pants down.

Including the men both inside the bedroom and outside, not discounting these three, there were eleven. That was an odd number for an assault, but none of the men seemed wonderfully professional, just violent. There was a decided difference between the two qualities.

John Rourke, flat against the roof surface now, started climbing toward the peak. Once there, it would have to be quick, not a sniping situation. That would be too slow. Just stand up, kill them and hope there weren't any more of them to kill him back.

Another admirably controlled burst from Emma Shaw below.

She loved him, she said. John Rourke was not prepared to tell any woman he loved her. There had been only two women he'd loved that way, Sarah and Natalia.

Sarah was dead. "Jesus," Rourke hissed through gritted teeth. The thought alone tightened his throat, his chest, made him want to stop all this, regardless of the men there on the ground by his borrowed car, just stop it all and sit down where he was and let the tears come. His temples throbbed. His mind and body ached.

And there had been Natalia. He had loved Natalia, perhaps still did. Sensibly, she had let herself fall in love with Michael and now she was Michael's, as much as a woman of Natalia's strength and courage and independence could be any man's woman.

And Emma Shaw?

He'd come here to her, lonely and full of greater sadness than he had ever known, knowing what would happen, afraid to let it happen, wanting it to happen, still deep inside himself feeling he was somehow cheating on Sarah, albeit she was dead. He almost felt as if to these armed men who had come here to kill, he owed a thank you rather than death. They had kept him from doing something that he would have regretted, something that someday might have stood between him and Emma Shaw.

To have come here now was wrong.

One didn't mourn a lost wife by having intercourse.

Throughout his life, he had never believed in the inevitable, yet he had come here wanting the inevitable to cancel out his thinking, to take away his pain.

Marriage, he had always believed, despite the arguments he and Sarah had, despite the difficulties that their marriage at most times seemed unable to endure, was for life.

Did that mean that since, for the moment at least, his life went on, that their marriage still was, still continued to endure?

He was at the peak of the roof.

He could see the three men clearly, and as yet they clearly did not see him.

There were three rounds remaining in one of his twin stainless Detonics .45s, six in the other. Although functionally perfectly ambidexterous all his life, the right was his master hand. He shifted the pistol with three rounds to his left hand, the one with six in his right.

Straddling the peak of the roof, Rourke rose up to his knees, both pistols cocked and locked. He drew his feet under him, so he could stand quickly, testing his balance, too, lest he lose it and fall.

His left thumb swept behind the tang, wiped down the safety, then swept back. More easily, he thumbed down the safety of the pistol in his right hand.

John Rourke stood.

"Up here!"

The three men wheeled their weapons toward him and John Rourke opened fire. A single bullet from the gun in his left hand to the head of the man in the center of the three behind the car. A double tap from the gun in his right hand to the chest and thorax of the man to the already dead man's left. A double tap from the gun in his left hand, emptying it, chest and thorax again.

The slide of the pistol in John Rourke's left hand was locked open, empty.

Four rounds remained in the pistol he held in his right hand.

The three men were down without firing a shot in return.

"Stay where you're at, Emma, in case there are any more of them!" Rourke ordered. He was already moving along the roof line and lowering his body profile, just in case.

Ten

Tim Shaw's eyes were on his daughter's clothing. He would have expected grass stains or something on her skirt, but there were none.

And he looked at John Rourke, and wondered.

In all, there were eleven dead men here, and like Nikita Kamasov who was one of them, they were all in the drug trade, most of them documented killers, all of them armed with submachineguns. And John Rourke had killed them all, the majority of them inside Tim Shaw's daughter's bedroom.

Doctor Rourke was reloading magazines for his .45s when Tim Shaw walked over to him. Rourke looked up from his guns. "Doctor Rourke, these guys just—"

"Yes?"

"One father to another, huh?"

"Yes?"

But Tim Shaw didn't know what to say. After all, Emma was a grown woman, and even though John Rourke had a daughter close to her age, it wasn't as if John Rourke was anywhere near old enough to be her father. Rourke had to be about forty. Rourke's children were as old as they were because Rourke had played games with the cryogenic sleep process, intentionally aging them into adulthood. Everybody grew up reading the story in history books. "Just wanted to say I'm sorry about the death of your wife, real sorry. Lost mine when Emma was just a tyke."

John Rourke nodded. "Thank you." Rourke's every gesture, right down to his breathing, seemed to suggest exhaustion.

"These guys just popped in on you."

John Rourke looked Tim Shaw square in the eye. "Your daughter and I were in the bedroom, as you've obviously deduced. And judging from the condition of her clothing—no blood stains, no grass stains, no mud—you've probably guessed at a few other things. Gentlemen don't discuss personal relationships with women, as we both know. Under the circumstances, however, suffice it to say that I was feeling terrible. I still do. Your daughter, a friend, was very kind to me; she's as fine a woman as I've ever had the good fortune to know."

"Know?"

John Rourke loaded one pistol after the other in turn. "Whatever might have happened was never allowed to happen, by the circumstances attendant to what you see here." And Rourke gestured toward two of the morgue men who were carrying a body in a black rubber bag on a stretcher between them.

"Okay, John," Tim Shaw said. "Who you think these guys were after?"

"I wasn't followed up here, and the F.O.U.O. car was randomly selected, so I doubt there was any electronic

70

trace. I'd say the Nazis hired these men to go after your daughter as part of a revenge plot against you. Get her out of here. Back on base would be safest."

"In one of her damn airplanes," Shaw nodded. "The bastards. Can't come after me, gotta go after my daughter."

"For the operation you pulled off at that condo, when you nailed six of the ones who did the massacre at Sebastian's Reef Country Day School. You got six of their people and you got a lot of their equipment. If there were twelve, as we suspect, you cut their commando group by fifty per cent. Easy to see why they want back at you."

Tim Shaw, looked toward the house's little front porch. Emma sat on the railing, her skirt sagging down between her knees, her hands kind of buried inside it. And she looked sadder than he'd ever seen her look since her mother died.

He looked at John Rourke again. "None of my business, but do you love her?"

John Rourke stared at him blankly for a split second, then, his eyes hardening, said, "I don't know." Rourke lit a little cigar, holding his lighter while Tim Shaw took out a cigarette. Then Rourke lit it for him. "I get the impression with all the things they've put in history books about me—and that's stupid, because I didn't do anything special—but that people think I'm supposed to be some guy out of a novel or a movie."

John Rourke hadn't done anything special? If that were true, then George Washington was just a soldier with bad teeth. "You mean people expect you to be more than human, and that means less than human,"

71

Shaw opined.

"I lost my wife. I just killed a son. My head isn't on straight. I don't really know what I know, except Emma's a marvelous person. That make any sense, Tim?" Rourke exhaled smoke through his nostrils.

"Yeah, probably, John, if anything does these days," Shaw answered, nodding, his eyes focusing on the glowing tip of his cigarette.

Emma Shaw watched the two men she loved. She loved her brother, of course, but that was different. And it was a different sort of love, too, of course, that she had for her dad, Tim Shaw the cop—different from the way she loved John Rourke.

And now it was over before it was begun.

She just sat there on the porch railing, hands clasped in each other between her knees. When she swung her feet forward, she could see them beneath the hem of her skirt. When she swung them back, it was as if they weren't there. She was perched, waiting, waiting for her father to say something, maybe even for John to say something.

But she'd said it all to herself already. This was too soon for John, too soon after the death of Sarah Rourke. And maybe she'd messed up any chance they might have had in the future. And her father was too good a detective not to have figured out why all the carnage within the house was confined to the bedroom.

"Shit," Emma Shaw murmured under her breath.

As she watched her father and John still talking, one of the Shore Patrol investigators began walking hurriedly from his car, toward them.

Emma Shaw swung her legs around and slipped off the railing, started walking across the porch, then started running, down the low steps, across the yard where evidence technicians still worked and only a little while ago there had been three dead men.

She quickened her pace now, seeing the Shore Patrol investigator—Lieutenant Ned Barringer—approaching her father and John.

He gave the usual salute military people give to important civilians. And, after all, John was technically a general.

John nodded to him.

She slowed her pace, stopped a few feet away from John and her father and Lieutenant Barringer. She could hear what he was saying. ". . . received word from Deitrich Zimmer, sir. The communiqué states that despite the damage done to the cryogenic repository in New Germany, both Mrs. Rourke and Generaloberst Mann are alive, in cryogenic sleep, and will be traded for Martin Zimmer. But if there is no trade, they will be killed. We're working on getting independent confirmation now, but the message source appears to be genuine, sir. Not one body has yet been found in the wreckage of the cryogenic repository. The fires caused by the explosions are still burning, but the German government says it will send in a team in fire-resistant gear to check. That may take several hours."

Men didn't faint, and certainly not men like John Rourke. But he leaned back against the hood of the F.O.U.O. car, his face suddenly white as a sheet, his eyes closing.

And, when he opened his eyes, he looked at her.

73

She felt tears and there were a million contradictory reasons why she should, but she couldn't let them show.

Her father said, "You mean to say they never fuckin' checked!"

"I, uhh—"

John didn't say anything.

Eleven

The pale blue gas swirled away for just an instant. She had a lovely face, just as he remembered it from that brief moment one hundred and twenty-five years ago when there had been the shared communion of death between them, he the giver, she the receiver. Her hair, almost too meticulously brushed it seemed, almost funereally perfect, was a rich, dark auburn, the arrangement softening with time. The hair grew, of course.

Generaloberst Wolfgang Mann's hair was well past military length, and a healthy growth of beard adorned Mann's traitorous countenance.

Deitrich Zimmer's thoughts returned to Sarah Rourke. With her eyelids down, of course, it was impossible to see her eyes. But he remembered them as they had been in that instant more than a century ago when they had flashed up at him, defiantly, proudly. She was, of course, a remarkable woman, full of courage and strength and determination and not at all unattractive. She was the mother of his son.

Several courses of action lay open to him now, possessed of her body as he was. With her, he would assuredly be able to trade for the return of Martin. With her, he could control John Rourke, and hence at least to some degree control the Trans-Global Alliance's attempts to interdict his actions.

Zimmer looked past the cryogenic chamber in which she lay, toward the wall which was covered by a mural-sized video screen, a map displayed on it, showing the constantly updated positions of forces of the Reich and of Eden, all but one in the same. The attack on Pearl Harbor would be critical, of course. And, with the good Herr Doctor Rourke out of the way, there would be a decided advantage.

He—Zimmer—would arrange the trade for young Martin in such a manner that John Rourke would have to accomplish the trade himself. And he—Zimmer—would not only have Martin back, but have John Rourke as his prisoner, or dead. But he hoped for the former, the latter—an eventuality—coming to pass all in due time.

And if the good Herr Doctor Rourke had any compunction about personally involving himself in the trade, that would fade away instantly.

In the event that he was unable to carry out his plan of preference, he had made arrangements to accomplish his intended scheme by other means. A video crew and specialists in laser holography would be his "ace in the hole," as the Americanism went.

This promised not only to be challenging, but amusing as well.

The one problem with his ice-bound redoubt was that there were no windows, and he felt just slightly claustrophobic. The feelings passed with activity, of course, and there would be an adequate supply of that.

There was a secret, and he must know it, possess that secret himself. And the secret was the greatest prize, even greater than the death, final and complete and ultimate, of Doctor John Thomas Rourke. And only John Rourke could unlock that secret, retrieve this knowledge.

This ultimate knowledge posed the ultimate risk of course, but what knowledge was, after all, without risk to the knower?

Deitrich Zimmer licked his lips.

He could taste it.

Twelve

"It's very simple to give you artificial fingerprints, Mr. Rourke, but that's the least of your worries." Natalia watched Michael's eyes as they squinted slightly, the doctor from the police department forensics unit lighting a cigarette as he continued. "You can get anyone to alter your fingerprints, either temporarily or permanently. Corneal imprint is what's most reliable. But, you have to remember that Deitrich Zimmer, when he isn't being a Nazi dictator, is one of the finest medical minds ever. What's known of Zimmer's techniques—and that's precious little—is studied in medical schools from New Germany to Lydveldid Island to the Chinese First City to Mid-Wake—hell, you name it. He's going to be able to spot fingerprint changes unless they're done perfectly, and he might even spot them then. And what will you do about cranial measurements? Dental records? No, you could pull off a deception that would last until he examined you. That's it, Mr. Rourke."

"I have to try," Michael said in reply.

Natalia sat on a stool at the far end of the morgue, her legs crossed, a cigarette in her hand. She flicked ashes from it to the floor—Dr. Robinson had said she could, that the floors were swept every night—and a few specks of ash settled on her stocking. She brushed them away, rearranging herself on the stool, straightening her dress. Michael, the moment he heard about Deitrich Zimmer's communiqué, was determined to go through with the charade he had planned before the—thank God—totally erroneous information concerning his mother's death.

When Natalia Anastasia Tiemerovna thought of Sarah Rourke, she thought of Mark Twain's famous line, about reports of his death being premature.

All the toughness and courage and ability which Michael and Annie had in abundance weren't solely inherited from their father. For the first time since the night one hundred and twenty-five years ago when Sarah was shot in the brain by Deitrich Zimmer, Natalia saw real hope of Sarah's return to the living.

Dr. Robinson was saying, "Think of it this way. Dr. Zimmer may be evil incarnate—I don't know—but I do know he's not a fool. He knows you exist, and he knows you've impersonated Martin—successfully—once before. He will anticipate it, Mr. Rourke. I read somewhere that you once entertained plans for following in your father's footsteps in medicine."

"I still do, maybe."

Dr. Robinson's teeth looked like ivory against his chocolate brown skin as his face beamed with a broad grin. "Well, then put yourself in Zimmer's place, for goodness' sake! He'll be expecting to be deceived. If Martin Zimmer were still alive and your father actually brought Martin Zimmer in trade for your mother's life, Deitrich Zimmer would check Martin Zimmer just as carefully! From what you've told me this evening and from the scuttlebutt I've picked up, it seems clear that Deitrich Zimmer essentially built Martin Zimmer! He started with the raw clay of your brother, added surgically the genetic material from a descendant of Adolf Hitler, made Martin. Don't you think he'd know every measurement it was possible to know, every minute scar, every blemish! You don't even know if Martin Zimmer was circumcised. Were you?"

Natalia felt her cheeks warming slightly. Michael was most definitely circumcised.

Dr. Robinson smiled again as he looked at her, apparently recognizing the answer to his somewhat rhetorical question. "How are you going to check now with Martin's body buried under a couple of tons of still molten lava on Kilauea? I don't mean to be too blunt, Mr. Rourke, but you'd never get away with it. What would you do—pursuing the thing with the circumcision, for example—if before he did the trade he asked 'Martin' to drop—" And he looked at Natalia, didn't finish what he was about to say.

She finished it, "Pants?"

"Yes."

Michael smiled. "I'd piss in his face, all right?"

Natalia looked at the tip of her cigarette, stood up, ground it under the sole of her high heel. "Stop being macho and be smart. As long as he can examine you Michael, you cannot hope to succeed."

In the next instant, Natalia wished she'd never said what she had said. Because Michael started to laugh. And he kept laughing. Dr. Robinson looked at her, then back at Michael. Michael said, "That's it!"

"What is 'it,' Michael?"

"What the hell are you laughing at Mr. Rourke?"

Michael stopped laughing, only chuckling a bit, smiling as he said, "They put me into cryogenic sleep, but with two gases. My father has a remote. He lets off the finger pressure—like what they used to call a dead man's switch—and the other gas flows into the chamber."

"What other gas?" Natalia almost whispered.

"Cyanide?" Michael suggested, shrugging his shoulders, then laughing again.

Thirteen

Annie's nails dug into the flesh of his abdomen.

They had gone to bed early, exhausted from the emotional low, then the emotional high. She slept behind him, her right hand and forearm resting across his body. When his wife's nails pierced his skin, Paul Rubenstein awoke instantly. Gently, he pulled her hand away, holding her hand as he turned over onto his right side, looked at her in the darkness. He could not see her face, but he knew she was dreaming.

Her mother?

Was something happening to Sarah Rourke?

Should he awaken Annie and find out?

Paul Rubenstein lay on his back, still holding her hand. Annie mumbled something incoherent. Paul Rubenstein stared up into the darkness. Michael's brave but stupid scheme for substituting himself for Martin Zimmer. Annie's dreams.

Paul shook his head.

And, John's despair.

What had happened at Emma Shaw's house in the

mountains was obvious. And Paul Rubenstein applauded John for it. Sarah, wonderful woman that she had always been, even if she wasn't dead, was the next best thing. Because of his love for Sarah and the entire Rourke family, his wife chief among them, Paul Rubenstein prayed that Sarah would return from her living death. On a rational basis, however, he knew that any chance of that was so remote as to be effectively impossible.

And John had a right to live, too.

The Rourkes were his family.

He loved them all, but most of all his wife.

And when Michael brought his lunacy to fruition, John helping him, Paul Rubenstein knew he would be there, too. His wife's father and brother were like brothers to him.

Annie snuggled more closely against him. Paul Rubenstein smiled. "Most fortunate of sidekicks," he whispered to the darkness.

That was him.

Fourteen

John Rourke poured a glass of his German-made Seagram's Seven into the small tumbler, sipped at it. Never a regular drinker Before the Night of the War or since, he had always had his preferences. Seagram's was his favorite hard liquor. When the Germans had offered to duplicate for him whatever he might require from the Retreat supplies, he had suggested the whiskey. One hundred and twenty-five years ago, it was made in small quantities only for him. Nowdays, as he understood it, the whiskey had become one of the favorite alcoholic beverages of New Germany, and Mid-Wake and Hawaii as well.

He was watching the white-foamed surf breaking over the slick blackness of the rocks. This was his second small glass of whiskey in two hours. He had no intention of getting drunk, nor had he ever been so by design or otherwise.

But, John Rourke could not sleep.

Too much had happened for him to be able properly to deal with it. Less than twenty-four hours ago, he had precipitated the death of his third child, Martin Zimmer. Then he was informed that his wife was dead, and along with her his old friend and comrade Wolfgang Mann. Then, out of despair and loneliness, in seeking the comfort of a woman, he had betrayed his wife, cheated on her, albeit unknowingly and incompletely—but not for lack of trying on his part. Fate intervened in the form of the eleven men sent to kill Emma Shaw in her home. In the aftermath of this episode, he was informed that, in fact, his wife was not dead (nor was Wolfgang Mann).

The news that Sarah lived filled his heart with happiness, but even in that very moment his joy was muted by the fact that her life still hung in the balance in two ways. He was not certain of just how yet, but in some way he had to force Deitrich Zimmer to perform a life-saving operation to remove from Sarah's brain the bullet which Deitrich Zimmer himself had put there. And, he had to get Sarah away from Zimmer. Even in this modern age of highly advanced medical technology and speeded-up healing, there would be a reasonable limit to how far and how fast someone recovering from brain surgery of the most delicate nature could be moved.

And there was the matter of the trade itself, in order to be in a position to accomplish all or any of this. Martin, the person for whom Deitrich Zimmer wished to trade, was dead. Michael clung stubbornly to the idea of impersonating Martin, indeed their only viable option, but one which would not get them very far at all and, in the end, might result in Michael's death as well.

And if, through some miraculous combination of luck on their part and ineptitude on the part of their adversaries, Sarah was saved, once she was well enough, John Rourke would have to tell her that Martin was dead, killed by his father's hand.

Regardless of the circumstances—Martin had been attempting to destroy the aircraft which Emma piloted, endeavoring to force it down into the volcanic lava flows below, killing them all—Martin's death was a fact. Sarah would never forgive him—John Rourke—for that. And their marriage would end.

And, there was the matter of Wolfgang Mann, whose life John Rourke wished to save as well. And Mann, it was clear, had taken the cryogenic sleep for one reason only—Sarah.

John Rourke lit a cigar, inhaled, held the smoke in his lungs, exhaled, watched the smoke as the wind caught it, danced with it, dissipated it into nothingness, like a dream in the light of morning. He sipped at his whiskey.

This had all started very simply six hundred and twenty-five years ago in the declining years of the twentieth century. Now it was the dawn of the twenty-seventh century A.D. His only intention was that if the unthinkable became reality, his wife and son and daughter would be able to survive that with him. He had built the Retreat, stocked and provisioned it. Now, his children were, in terms of physical age, merely a few years his junior. His daughter was married, his son had been married, then widowed, losing an unborn child in the process. John Rourke's wife, their mother, bore a third child and, effectively, had been murdered in the moments following giving birth.

And, without the hands, procedures and appliances of the man who nearly killed her, she was doomed to cryogenic sleep for God only knew how long, perhaps forever.

Simplicity into complexity.

He took another sip of his drink.

And he thought of two women, neither one of them his wife. He had been in love with Natalia, and she with him, but because of his marriage they had never consummated that love. And now Natalia belonged to Michael, and he to her, what John Rourke had planned on what, for all he knew, might be humanity's last morning.

And then there was Emma Shaw.

It seemed to John Rourke that he could not have feelings for a woman without bringing her pain.

He finished his drink, then sat there for a time longer, smoking his cigar.

In the morning, he would embark upon the most desperate gamble of his life.

Tonight, he would be alone with his thoughts . . .

The ceiling of her BOQ was stippled, meaning that it had an almost infinite number of tiny bumps in it. The drapes open—she was on the second floor—there was enough ambient light from outside that when she strained her eyes, she could make out subtle patterns in them—the bumps.

Her nightgown, of soft, natural cotton, felt rough against her nipples each time she inhaled, moved. And there was a slightly sick feeling in her abdomen, like an ache.

Emma Shaw could not sleep.

For a while, she'd thought that perhaps even John's

friendship would be lost to her, that he would somehow blame her for the terrors of the day, terrors which would have destroyed a lesser man. Although she admired many things about John Rourke, Emma Shaw realized that the man's resiliency was perhaps his finest and most unique quality. After the talk with her father, after being informed that the earlier reports that Sarah Rourke was dead were erroneous, that she was, instead, held prisoner by the leader of the Nazis, he had come over to her where she'd sat on the porch railing, sat down beside her. "Emma, I'm very sorry."

"I'm so happy for you, John, at least there's a chance for you and your wife, now. I, uhh, got carried away." She'd tried to smile.

"No. I was carried away by you," he told her. Then he said the oddest thing. "And, I guess I still am." And he kissed her cheek and walked away.

She could still feel that kiss.

It burned against her cheek.

Alone in her bed, staring at the ceiling, Emma Shaw realized that she was starting to cry.

Fifteen

The communications center at Pearl Harbor was a series of interconnecting rooms built about a central hub, allowing for expansion or contraction of the facility depending on the demands of the situation. The main portion of the complex—the hub itself—was surprisingly attractive by comparison to most military decor, John Rourke felt. The walls—what could be seen of them where there was not equipment—were so deep a grey as to be almost black, and the floor was of synthetic black and grey marble.

The first communiqué arrived precisely at four in the morning, saying nothing but that a second communiqué would arrive in two hours. The second communiqué arrived precisely when it was supposed to, John Rourke returning to his quarters, shaving and showering in the interim.

The eruption on Mt. Kilauea had slowed, and plans were already well along to put into action the plan of vulcanologist Thorn Rolvaag for diverting the lava flow. John Rourke had wanted to be with Bjorn

Rolvaag's descendant, but that was impossible now. It was hard to equate the survival of two people, one his wife and one his friend, with the lives of so many that would be ended or altered if the volcanic eruption continued unabated, and perhaps he was selfish to look to his own concerns first. But, out of selfishness grew the value for all other things. And, he had to do what he had to do.

Intelligence data to which John Rourke was privy had arrived, indicating that the suspect poison gas facility in Eden City was confirmed by James Darkwood and other Allied Intelligence personnel. Rourke scanned the abstract of Darkwood's report; reading between the lines allowed him to appreciate the danger to which Darkwood had subjected himself in order to get the information. Like Thorn Rolvaag, James Darkwood was also cut from the same heroic cloth as his ancestor.

A volunteer group of Trans-Global Alliance fighter-bomber pilots was already being assembled for a preemptive strike against the facility.

War was at hand.

Dressed in the color which best fit his mood and his outlook—black—John Rourke read the communiqué to the Family. It was from Dr. Deitrich Zimmer: "You will fly to sixty-two degrees, forty-one minutes, fourteen seconds North Latitude, one hundred eighteen degrees, seventeen minutes, forty seconds West Longitude."

The rendezvous time was in exactly twenty-four hours. "You will bring with you my son, Martin. Since you will need assistance in moving the sarcophagi, you may bring with you three other persons beyond the crew of the aircraft. It would be absurd to demand that you arrive unarmed, but any use of weapons or any other action which I might deem threatening will be dealt with accordingly, i.e., the occupants of the cryogenic chambers killed immediately. Should you fail to bring Martin, or attempt to intervene with troops, the result will be the same. The lives of Frau Rourke and Generaloberst Mann are in your hands."

"Sixty-two, one-eighteen. That's near Great Slave Lake, in the lower portion of the Northwest Territories in what used to be Canada," Michael said, turning away from the map which dominated a substantial section of the far wall.

"People of your generation were often accused of having a poor knowledge of geography, Michael. But you were always good at it." And John Rourke smiled approvingly at his son. Michael, despite his tender years when the Night of the War occurred, had always shown academic promise, a natural intellect coupled with a keen desire to know.

"There are five of us," Natalia said, "and he'll only allow four." She was slowly, inconspicuously opening and closing her Bali-Song. In the days prior to the Night of War, when butterfly knives had first become popular, they were occasionally referred to as the macho pacifier, like worry beads, the opening and closing of the two-handled knife something to occupy the hands and free the mind. "But, if Michael goes through with his idea of impersonating Martin," Natalia went on, "all five of us will be there anyway."

Admiral Hayes stood overlooking a tabletop display showing communications satellite positions. Commander Washington waited beside her. A third person, in charge of communications security for Pearl, was with them. Rourke walked toward the lighted table as this third person, Lieutenant Commander Wilma Jones, said, "We naturally took shots off the first communiqué, then set up for the second. His transmitter is bouncing off satellite, of course, but we feel it's actually in the neighborhood of sixty-two North, one hundred eighteen West. You and your family will be walking into his domain, General Rourke, if I may say so, Nazi Headquarters."

"Opinion noted, Commander," Rourke told her, standing beside her, looking down at the display. "He's evidently quite confident of pulling off more than a trade or he would have picked a more neutral spot in order to safeguard the location of his facility.

"Agreed," Commander Washington nodded. "It'll be a tough insertion, but we can put a specially equipped SEAL Team in there to back you up. Arctic gear, the works."

"Have them standing by, but don't insert," Rourke advised Commander Washington.

Admiral Hayes cleared her throat. "Dr. Rourke?"

"Yes, ma'am?"

"We can't afford to lose you to him. If Zimmer had you he could dictate terms. Even if military thinking were to the contrary, public opinion would be such that we would have no choice. Have you watched the television lately, or read the compunews?"

"I'm afraid I haven't," Rourke admitted. Television news, with its ability to editorialize through selective revelation, had never engaged his interest. Compunews was fine, but in the last few days there had been no time to boot up the computer terminal in his quarters and read.

"There's a cult of personality growing up around you, Dr. Rourke, as a symbol of what the United States once was. If there were a Presidential election being held tomorrow, you'd win in a landslide."

John Rourke smiled, feeling slightly embarrassed. "Political aspirations are something I've never possessed, Admiral, let me assure you. And if Zimmer were to get the upper hand on us, I'm sure I speak for my entire family when I say I would expect you to do whatever you had to do as regards safeguarding national security. If we make our bed, we'll lie in it."

"It's fine for you, Doctor, to encourage us to do what is logical rather than what is expedient. Nonetheless, you're risking a great deal, Dr. Rourke, a very great deal. This is an obvious trap, we're all agreed. Five of you will be no match for Zimmer's elite SS units."

Commander Washington interjected, "That SEAL Team can be positioned to close in within under two minutes, barring terrain in the immediate vicinity being too flat for cover. And even then, we can pull it off. Unless the Admiral says I can't have my men there, they'll be there, Doctor."

John Rourke looked at Washington as he said, "You can't be close enough for Zimmer to spot you. Not just visually but electronically. We're talking about the lives of not only my wife and Generaloberst Mann, but also Michael's life."

"Then you'll do it!" Michael almost shouted.

John Rourke turned to his son. "What choice do I have but for you to pass yourself off as Martin?"

There was no choice. Putting Michael into cryogenic

sleep just might work, if they could outguess how Deitrich Zimmer would have planned to outguess them, assuming they might substitute Michael for Martin as part of a countermeasure. But correspondingly, Michael would be highly vulnerable and unable to be of any direct assistance to them.

However he figured it, for once John Rourke was unable to plan ahead.

Sixteen

His methods were considered almost mystical by some, he knew, and the thought amused him, especially that they had remained so for more than one hundred twenty-five years. The key to his success at the operating table in procedures of the most extraordinarily delicate nature was the use of virtual reality techniques coupled with computer simulation, an area in which he had pioneered.

Computer simulations were employed in all manner of disciplines ever since the latter portion of the twentieth century, when virtual reality methodology was also developed. But the combination of the two was in its infancy then. Computer simulations were high-tech and complex, while virtual reality was still relegated to being little better than interactive video.

The concept of virtual reality was quite simple, but its perfect execution required equipment which, in the twentieth century, was not yet perfected. Virtual reality was a means by which a living human being could, via physical stimulation, mentally enter another universe, which could be so believable that, when used properly and assisted by drug therapy, the subject could be convinced that he had actually been there physically. In its more conventional application, indeed what it was designed for in the first place, it allowed the subject to vicariously experience physical action inside a computer program.

In the beginning, there was cumbersome headgear, and one or two motion-sensor-equipped gloves, the headgear giving visual stimulation to the wearer's eyes and ears and the gloves, linked as well to the computer program, allowing the program to read hand movements and simulate their results within the computer image which was also transmitted through the headgear.

It was possible, in the earliest days, for a person outfitted properly to reach to a "wall inside a room" on the computer screen and strike a "light switch," none of which of course existed at all. The possibilities for the system, in the days Before the Night of the War, were seen as limitless.

In that respect, Deitrich Zimmer saluted those pioneering researchers; they had been quite right.

Through the use of virtual reality Deitrich Zimmer was able to perform simulated operations, actually perform them, not just rehearse. He had added his own special twist, and in it lay the reason why no one had yet attained his degree of perfection. Utilizing a high-speed digitized video-editing apparatus and wearing a complete body suit designed to read and translate his motor responses, he could even experience the sore feet and locked knees of standing for hours at the operating table. The video material was of actual patient operations, in all stages, both the successes and the failures. The programs which controlled the digitized video edits were keyed to his responses, constantly shifting to meet the demands of the situation.

It was bloodless surgery which could be done and redone until it was not only gotten right, but done perfectly. Appliances of his own design enabled him to expand his skills still further.

In some ways, however, the operation which he was about to perform—he had rehearsed it for more than a year—was his most delicate yet. Not only the life of the patient depended on it, but so did the life of his son.

His one last review—an edited video from his final and most successful virtual reality practice session—was complete. Deitrich Zimmer stood up from the console, activated the foot controls and signalled for his surgical assistants to begin.

Looking through the glass of the control booth, he could see the pace quicken as the personnel surrounded the table.

Zimmer activated the door control switch—again, foot controlled—and went through the doorway into the operating theater. Like the other personnel, he wore a state-of-the-art surgical environment suit, the design his own, physically matching the feel of his virtual reality suit, completely self-contained, even for breathing.

There was no possibility of contamination either way, from surgical staff to patient or patient to surgical staff.

Entry to the area containing the operating theaters was through a series of clean rooms employing air locks.

Dietrich Zimmer approached the table.

Below the neck, yet allowing for access to the heart, should that be required, the body was tented. Only a very small portion of the skull—six centimeters square—was shaved.

Zimmer made a last survey of his instruments.

He looked to each of his assistants in turn, getting eye contact and moving on. That each person was in top form was mandatory, because the operation would, perforce, have to move with total efficiency.

Lastly, he looked at the face of the patient. A mask would be placed over the face, allowing for instantaneous application of additional oxygen when required.

Sarah Rourke was rather pretty.

Seventeen

She had just done the stupidest thing anyone in the military could ever do, volunteer.

"Oddly enough, Commander Shaw, if you had not volunteered I would have requested that you do so. I couldn't think of a better pilot or wing commander."

She didn't know what to say. Finally, "Thank you, Admiral."

"Just remember something, Commander. In one respect, I'm letting you go against my better judgement."

Emma Shaw looked at Admiral Thelma Hayes and realized that she blinked.

Admiral Hayes's eyes softened and she smiled. "Nothing to do with your abilities, Commander. I realize there was something between you and Dr. Rourke. And, well, with his wife perhaps back in the picture, I didn't want your mind on anything besides your mission. I'm not trying to interfere in your personal life, but I've known you on and off for years, and followed your career in naval aviation. You're a hot shot, and sometimes that can be great, but most of the time it isn't."

Emma Shaw didn't know what to say.

Admiral Hayes continued. "I'm not implying that your performance in training or in combat has ever been less than exemplary. Otherwise, you wouldn't have made it past Lieutenant Commander a year ago. No, it's just that you are one of those rare pilots who is naturally gifted at his or her work. That's a handy thing, but it's also a dandy way to overreach yourself. I don't want you doing that here. The mission against the poison gas plant in Eden City will be dangerous enough. I checked your records. You're fully trained on the new SR-901. It's a lot of aircraft."

Emma Shaw almost slumped in her seat. The SR-901, she had thought, was still experimental. She'd helped in some of the high speed maneuverability testing over the Phillipines, done two of the high-altitude check flights. It was the true descendant of the old Twentieth Century SR-71, but capable of Mach Nine and equipped with plasma cannons and every state-of-the-art weapons system they could pack aboard her. From a distance, this new Blackbird even looked like the old ones. "The SR-901, Admiral?"

"Do you have a problem with that, Commander Shaw?"

"No, ma'am. The 901's the best there is."

"You'll be ferrying over your own aircraft. The route is to Australia, then the southern tip of Africa, then to Venezuela. That means flying through the Eden antiaircraft net around Cuba. Once you're past that, it's a straight shot to Eden City. You'll have several tactical options for the return flight, depending on latest Intell. Are you in?"

"Yes, ma'am."

Admiral Hayes smiled. Emma Shaw just sat there, knowing she should be getting up out of her chair, leaving the Admiral's office, but she was uncertain for a second whether or not her legs would work.

The old Thad Rybka holster carrying the Metalifed Colt Lawman MKIII .357 Magnum was positioned at the small of his back. The Smith & Wesson Centennial was inside the waistband of his black BDU trousers, suspended there on its Barami Hip Grip. The old Metalifed and Mag-Na-Ported six-inch Colt Python, rebuilt for him while he slept by gunsmiths at New Germany, could have been back on his right hip, but in the full flap holster there instead was the Metalife Custom Model 629 with its six-inch Mag-Na-Ported barrel. The 180-grain Jacketed Hollowpoint .44 Magnum round was the better choice for his needs these days. Someday, Annie or the children that she and Paul would someday have could inherit the Python. Michael was into the .44 Magnum as well, having little use for .357.

Rourke slipped the double Alessi rig onto his shoulders, the twin stainless Detonics CombatMaster .45s already holstered chamber loaded, hammer down, his usual preference. He normally used the old gunman's trick of sacrificing the extra round over basic magazine capacity for the surety of feed derived when the top round was stripped out of the magazine into the chamber and the round beneath it edged slightly forward.

Two Milt Sparks Six Packs were on his belt, one

holding six standard length seven-round Detonics magazines, the other holding six six-round Detonics magazines. The Six Pack for the mini-gun magazines was given to him in the days prior to the Great Conflagration by Commander Robert Gundersen, skipper of the USS *John Paul Jones,* the submarine which had carried Rourke and Natalia to the Pacific Northwest, involving them in a bloodbath there which had nearly turned into a nuclear incident.

Either the full-sized or abbreviated magazines would work in the miniguns under his arms. The shorter magazines only worked in the CombatMasters, but not in the full-sized Scoremasters that he would carry holsterless in his waistband once they were on the ground in Canada.

He had been asked once why he carried so many handguns in preference to all other arms. Indeed, he had a rifle, the HK-91 in 7.62mm/.308 (a better bet for him these days than his old CAR-15), and three knives, the twelve-inch blade Crain Life Support System X that he wore at his left side, the AG Russell Sting IA Black Chrome that he wore inside his trouser band near his right kidney, and a little Executive Edge Grande pen-shaped folding knife concealed in his jacket pocket. This was one of the items he recovered when he and Paul raided the museum exhibits at the Retreat.

But he liked handguns.

Before the Night of the War, one of John Rourke's closest friends and a frequent shooting buddy was Steve Fishman of Augusta, Georgia. Steve, ex-Special Forces, was a fine martial artist, both practitioner and teacher, and more than proficient with any gun or knife one cared to put in his hand. On one of many pleasant shooting sessions with Steve—this time when Rourke was driving back to Northeast Georgia from a conference in Charleston, South Carolina—a mutual friend of Rourke's and Fishman's had been in the area as well. The friend, Hank, was a professional soldier and occasionally over a drink or a cup of coffee would tell a wild story or two about his adventures, invariably involving some insane joke supposedly accounting for the loss of his left eye, the socket covered with a black patch or by sunglasses when appropriate.

Whether Hank's stories were true or not, John Rourke and Steve Fishman enjoyed them. And one thing Hank could do as marvelously well as his eyepatch jokes and the recounting of his adventures was shoot.

This one day, then, Rourke had been shooting his twin stainless Detonics .45s, Steve Fishman his much-engraved, ivory-gripped Beretta 92SB Compact 9mm and Hank a Metalifed Browning High Power with worn-smooth black rubber Pachmayr grips. Rourke was returning from teaching a security course when he made the stop-off in Charleston, then the subsequent trip to Augusta and consequently had all his working handguns with him. Hank remarked, "Now Steve there has his Beretta and I've got my Browning and my TEC-9, but you've got enough handguns to fill Steve's store."

Steve owned an Augusta gunshop which was literally a Mecca for police, federal agents and security professionals from all over the Southeast. Rourke smiled at Hank's remark, saying, "I doubt I've got enough handguns to fill even one shelf in one of

Steve's display cases."

Steve laughed, adding, "But I wouldn't mind if he tried."

Hank persisted. "You know my background. I get along on this Browning and the TEC-9 and an M-16 I get in country, if that."

John Rourke lit one of his thin, dark tobacco cigars. "I've always realized the importance of long guns, and made myself satisfactory with them."

"Satisfactory?" Steve Fishman exclaimed, laughing again. "I've seen you with that Steyr-Mannlicher SSG, remember? You could shoot the whiskers off a gnat with that 7.62."

"Gnats have whiskers? What do they shave with?" Hank asked, lighting a Camel with a Zippo windlighter nearly as battered as John Rourke's own. Hank removed his eyepatch so quickly and deftly, substituting a pair of dark lensed sunglasses that, even had Rourke been trying, he could not have seen the one-eyed man's disfigurement.

Rourke laughed, forcing it a little. "I'm being serious, guys. Both you guys were Special Forces, all that. Me, well—"

"Spook stuff," Hank said, nodding, alluding to Rourke's background as a case officer in the Central Intelligence Agency.

"Yeah, but not that," Rourke told them "I just trained myself for the long gun being a luxury. Most people these days don't expect close-range firearms combat, right? Because at close range you can get killed too easily. But most gunfights take place at a distance of a few feet to a few yards. So, you walk in close and you've got firepower. Rifles don't get you in close. And, like they say, the fastest reload is a second gun, or a third or a fourth or fifth." Rourke smiled.

"You're a gunfighter," Steve Fishman said with an air of definitiveness.

They went back to their shooting, Steve eventually turning in the best twenty-five yard group of the day.

Rourke wasn't certain at the time whether or not Fishman had intended the remark as a compliment or not. Over the intervening years, however, Rourke had come to accept Steve Fishman's remark as a statement of fact.

John Rourke was a gunfighter.

This would be a gunfight when they got on the ground in Canada, pitted against Deitrich Zimmer's people. That was the only option, because there was no other choice.

As he caught a glimpse of himself in the closet door mirror of his BOQ apartment, John Rourke reflected that if he was a gunfighter, he was dressed for the part.

Eighteen

The old days were back.

Dressed in one of her black jumpsuits and a pair of high black boots, Natalia Anastasia Tiemerovna buckled on the double-flap holsters carrying the matching stainless steel Smith & Wesson Model 686s, the twin L-Frame .357 Magnum revolvers given her by the President of the United States more than six centuries ago. Round-butted, action-tuned and with the barrels flatted by revolversmith Ron Mahovsky, each bore a proud American Eagle on the right flat.

She put on the Null shoulder holster with the suppressor-fitted stainless Walther PPK/S .380. John's philosophy of handgun combat was contagious, she suspected. He used multiple guns, minimizing his necessity to reload. He was better at it than she, but his technique was perfected over a longer span of years. She had not gotten into multiple gun use until the L-Frame Smiths were given to her.

Stowed away in her gear for their mission to Great Slave Lake was the Lancer copy of the SIG-Sauer

P-226 which she had recently acquired and thoroughly shot-in. The P-226 was her favorite of full-sized 9mm Parabellums Before the Night of the War, and would ride in her belt or in the pouch she'd had built into her arctic parka when they were on the ground.

She picked up the Bali-Song, flipped open the clasp and did a fast opening and closing, locked the clasp and secured the knife in the pocket along the seam by her right thigh.

Natalia took one last look in the mirror. Her hair, just past her shoulders, was down. When she got into combat, she would probably bind it back if there were time. For the moment, it was fine as it was.

Her duffle bag was already aboard the aircraft, so all she had to carry was her big black purse which could be converted into a day pack, and her rifle, this an M-16. Carrying two cartridge revolvers and an M-16 these days, of course, was like carrying a brace of Colt 1851 Navy .36 caliber percussion revolvers and a Henry rifle in the days Before the Night of the War. But, she didn't care.

She slung her purse to her left shoulder and the rifle crossbody on its sling, left shoulder to right hip, pushing it rearward and carrying it muzzle down along her back. The sword she'd had made up just prior to taking this last Sleep was strapped to her duffle bag, just in case.

Natalia let herself out of the BOQ apartment she shared with Michael, but Michael was, of course, not there. He was being readied for the Sleep. His appearance had been subtly altered by means of state-of-the-art makeup techniques to make him appear even more physically identical to the now-dead Martin Zimmer—Michael's brother—than Michael had been before.

As Natalia walked alone along the corridor, she remembered the first time Michael had taken the Sleep, how she had given Michael and his sister, children then, the injections of cryogenic serum, to allay potential guilt for their parents should the formula, computed to their body weights, be incorrect and the results disastrous. Now, Michael was chronologically older than she was, her lover, the most accomplished and at once gentle lover she had ever known.

As she rounded the bend of the corridor, she saw Paul and Annie waiting there for her. Paul was all in black, after the fashion of the Mid-Wake battle dress utilities of more than a century ago, the style of dress John had recently adopted as well. Along with his other weapons, Paul carried his inevitable German MP-40 submachinegun, the Schmiesser as it had been erroneously called throughout its history. His subgun was even more of an antique than her M-16. Annie, ever disliking trousers of any sort, wore a midcalf-length full skirt of heavy Oxford grey wool, combat boots, and a long-sleeved, round neck sweater, the white cuffs and little white collar of the blouse she wore beneath it visible. Annie's double holsters were at her hips, one carrying a Beretta 92F 9mm, the other a Detonics Scoremaster .45. As with Natalia herself, there was an M-16 swung to Annie's back.

Paul and Annie nodded and abreast, Paul at the center, Annie on his right, the three of them walked down the corridor.

John would be waiting for them out front.

As they reached the base of the staircase, the open expanse before the double glass doors of the BOQ visible, they stopped. John stood just on the other side, and with him stood Emma Shaw.

Natalia felt herself smile. John and Emma were apparently deep in earnest conversation. Natalia silently wished Emma Shaw better luck with John than her own had been.

For the briefest instant, John took Emma Shaw into his arms kissing her quickly, her body molding against his. They broke, holding hands for a second longer; then Emma Shaw ran down the steps and away.

She was already in her flight gear, and Natalia surmised that Commander Emma Shaw would be a part of the assault on Eden City's poison gas production facilities; it was her type of mission, demanding a pilot with consummate skills and nerves of steel.

After a respectful moment, Natalia said to Paul and Annie, "Let's go, shall we?" And she started ahead.

Michael Rourke sat on the edge of the cryogenic chamber. His feet this time touched the ground. His father stood near him saying, "When you wake up, all of this will be over."

"One way or the other," Michael added, nodding his head. "The timer works. I checked it myself."

John nodded to him.

Natalia had checked the timer, too. Normally cryogenic sleeping chambers were designed—clock-like—to awaken the sleeper. This timing would be critical. Were something to happen to the rest of them or even if they were merely separated, the timer might well be Michael's only chance at survival.

Built into the base of the coffin-shaped chamber was a secret compartment, only accessible from within the chamber itself. Within this compartment was an arctic parka and snowpants, emergency survival gear and weapons also included.

Michael's sister went up to him, kissed him lightly on the mouth, said, "You're my real brother, and I don't want to lose you, okay?"

"Okay, Sis," and Michael took her into his arms, embraced her.

Paul went up to him, shook his hand, and the two men embraced.

John shook his son's hand. "You're a brave man, son, and a good friend. I love you." And John leaned over, kissing Michael on the forehead.

Natalia realized that it was her turn. They had made love this day, said their farewells. But she held him, touched his hair with her fingertips, kissed his cheek. His hands felt strong on her body as he kissed her mouth hard. "I love you, Natalia. Don't worry. This isn't goodbye."

She nodded, temporarily unable to speak, kissed him lightly on the lips, then again, then stepped back, only watching now.

John—damn his always having to be the responsible one, hence the guilty one should something go wrong—administered the injection personally. As the drug which would allow the brain to be reawakened,

113

without which the sleeper would be in perpetual, irredeemable coma, entered Michael's system, Michael looked at them all in turn, then at last said, "When I awaken, my mother will be restored to us. That's what I believe. God bless you all; I love you all." And Michael—he wore only a loose-fitting pair of black slacks and a loose black shirt—raised his bare feet, swinging his legs over into the coffinlike cryogenic chamber.

Buttons were pressed by the cryogenic specialist, the chamber's transparent lid started closing, lights flashing from within the interior panel, the bluish-white gas immediately beginning to circulate.

It was so much like death that Natalia could feel tears rim her eyes. Whether Michael Rourke lived or died, she knew, she would always be his. And John had been right, aging him for her by use of the cryogenic process so many years ago. His two best friends—herself and Paul Rubenstein—were now the mates of his children.

Only John Rourke's own life was in disrepair.

If Sarah survived, possessed her faculties, she would almost certainly leave John after the death of Martin, irrational as that was. She would not leave John out of hatred, but out of a need for her own survival, the reason Natalia had at last given up any hope of becoming John's lover.

Wolfgang Mann, should he survive this ordeal as well, stood waiting in the wings, as it were, had taken the Sleep with them one hundred twenty-five years ago for no other reason than his love for Sarah Rourke.

Natalia let the tears roll down her cheeks for a

moment, and not just for Michael, but for John.

A man who had lived for six and one-half centuries all but alone. Would he continue on alone, someday even losing them? She shuddered at the thought, grateful that, unlike Annie, she—Natalia—possessed no mental gift/curse. Annie, of course, could not foretell the future. Natalia doubted that anyone could, hoped no one could.

She was glad that she could not.

Nineteen

The aircraft's shadow over the white of the glacier below was suddenly there, almost as if the plane had broken through from one dimension to another in some science fiction story rather than inserted from the upper atmosphere so as to come streaking downward in what amounted to a controlled power dive.

As much as John Rourke was familiar with all the conceptual data concerning transatmospheric insertion—it had been discussed as a means of faster intercontinental air travel as far back as the 1970s—the actuality of it still amazed him.

And it made John Rourke think about Emma Shaw. Her mission to Eden City could not utilize the rapidity of this technology because of the air defense systems involved. In the old-fashioned way, even though the new SR-901s could do Mach Nine in a pinch, she still had to stay atmospheric, following terrain as much as the speed of her aircraft would allow.

The new insertion system was quite simple, really. The aircraft was equipped with sufficient thrust in order to allow it to break free into the upper reaches of the atmosphere. Then it vectored downward toward its target destination. The old transpolar flights were close to the theory, yet utilized the standard Euclidean geometric truism that a straight line was the shortest distance between two points; but distance was sacrificed in favor of speed with transatmospheric insertion.

Long range trans-Pacific flights, which could consume the equivalent of a day's travel in the Twentieth Century, were now accomplished in hours, as this flight had been.

In less than fifteen minutes, they would be on the ground.

John Rourke looked away from the window and into the cabin, his eyes taking a moment to adjust to the contrasting light. Around him sat Natalia, Annie and Paul. Michael slept in the cryogenic chamber positioned well aft. John Rourke lit a cigarette, mindful of the smell of his cigars within the confines of the cabin. "Michael's chamber, as was his idea, is equipped with a cylinder of cyanide gas. The ploy that we'll release the cyanide gas if Deitrich Zimmer's personnel attempt to overpower us has two major faults, however. First, I won't release it, of course. Secondly, if Zimmer believes the body in the cryogenic chamber is Martin's or Michael's, Zimmer might well be willing to gamble I wouldn't use the gas and cause the death of my son. Again, correctly. We had to utilize genuine cyanide gas in the event, of course, that it came down to testing the gas, in order to prove our sincere intention of using it.

"Our chances," Rourke continued, "overall are not very good. We'll be heavily outnumbered and deep inside territory controlled by the enemy. Unless someone sees a flaw I don't, I'm planning on us playing this tough, as if somehow we have the upper hand and they don't. And, even assuming we can pull off a trade, we won't be out of the woods. And, just getting back to the aircraft won't insure our escape, because as we all know, the area will be blanketed with air defenses.

"Commander Washington's SEAL personnel," he went on, "will be close at hand and well equipped, but not close enough, nor equipped to fight off a truly sizeable force. Similarly, the low level approach pattern they utilized, coming in over Hudson's Bay out of Lydveldid Island, cannot easily be utilized as a return method. Commander Washington's people will know that and so will Deitrich Zimmer's people, should the SEALS engage. So, you might ask what we'll do."

Paul grinned. "What'll we do?"

John Rourke smiled. "Funny you should ask. I don't have a real plan, because I can't second guess Deitrich Zimmer. Our only ploy is to let the trade start to progress and do what the situation seems to suggest, and hope for the best. That's beyond 'loose' I know, and I'd welcome any suggestions at all."

There were none.

Too many variables with which to contend.

Paul began a last-minute weapons check.

Twenty

John Thomas Rourke's eyes squinted against the sun on the glacier and he took the dark-lensed aviator-style sunglasses from his pocket, putting them on. From his youth, John Rourke's eyes had always been light sensitive. Yet, disadvantage turned to an asset, because his night vision had always been particularly acute.

Rourke stood in the open rear bay of the vertical takeoff and landing cargo lifter, staring out toward the crescent of vehicles and men approaching the aircraft from the west.

Arctic Cat-style tracked vehicles, painted white with the occasional splotch of dark grey, camouflaged from casual aerial visual observation to one degree or another, rolled over a ridge of ice and down onto the plateau where the V-stol aircraft had touched down only moments before.

The men were nearer than the vehicles and moving more rapidly, too. Clad in snow smocks, with the hoods up and their eyes goggled, all other exposed skin toqued, they looked faceless. They moved astonishingly swiftly on their skis, but most of them without the use of poles, balancing themselves expertly instead and (it seemed) easily with their energy rifles rather the way a tightrope walker would use a balance bar.

The air over the glacier was cold and clear. The ozone layer here was severely depleted. Rourke wore sunscreen, as did the rest of his family, even Michael in the cryogenic chamber, ready for the moment when it would be opened. Although Rourke could hear the sounds of the tracked vehicles, louder still because they were closer, were the swooshing noises made by the skis of the Alpine troops. As Rourke exhaled, his breath turned to steam. The cold—ambient temperature was about six below zero Fahrenheit—was not as bad as Rourke had anticipated it would be, the wind almost calm, at least for the moment.

Even as a child, John Rourke had always preferred cold weather to warm, the tingle of skin touched by icy wind to the greasy feel of sweat derived from merely standing still. He'd grown up in the days before private home air-conditioning was the accepted norm, and despite his fondness for the out of doors, unlike other children, he always waited for the balmy weather of summer to end and the cool breezes of autumn to begin.

Warm weather was not a problem here.

At all.

There had been permanent glaciation here for the last several hundred years, partially he suspected as the natural cycle of the global climatic conditions, but in large part due also to the effects of the nuclear detonations on the Night of the War. Yet the sun was more a problem now than in the summertime of his youth. Nearer the equator, the ozone layer was sufficient under normal conditions to ensure that the effect of sunlight on human skin was not potentially lethal. With prolonged exposure, however, or in higher latitudes or at higher altitude, the threat from sunlight was severe. Cancer had effectively been conquered, but that was no reason to flirt with it.

The lead elements of the Alpine troops stopped some fifty yards distant, gradually encircling the aircraft. Natalia moved into the bay beside Rourke. "Well, at least we won't be lonely here, John."

"No," Rourke almost whispered, smiling at her but not looking at her. "Cover us, you and Annie. Paul!" And Rourke started down the ramp, Paul Rubenstein falling in beside him. "If you have any brilliant ideas," Rourke said to his friend, "now would be a wonderful time to share them."

Paul laughed. "We're crazy, but I've known that for six centuries."

Rourke smiled again.

They stepped down from the ramp and onto the surface of the glacier.

The tracked vehicles were forming an outer ring—about sixty yards away—around the Alpine troops.

All except one of the vehicles joined the ring.

The circle of armed ski troops opened, admitting this solitary vehicle, little Nazi flags on each fender, stiff even though there was no noticeable wind. "Reinforced," Paul remarked.

"That ugly thing needs all the help it can get,"

Rourke told his friend. He had thought of finding some means by which to leave Paul behind, Paul of course being in the greatest danger of any of them because Paul was a Jew. But Paul would never have stayed behind out of fear for his safety while the rest of them ventured here, so Rourke never even brought it up.

The solitary tracked vehicle was through the circle, the circle closing behind it, the vehicle approaching to about twenty-five yards from the tail section of the aircraft. Rourke's ears were a little cold, so slowly he reached back and pulled up the hood of his parka. Then he settled his hands near his belt, his gun-belt over his coat and the two Detonics Scoremaster .45s, chambers loaded, ready to his lightly gloved hands.

In this sort of temperature extreme, one normally wore a glove liner and an outer shell. The glove liners Rourke wore were of silk, thin, tailored to his hands. They would protect his flesh from contact with metal and retain a modicum of warmth, but more importantly they would allow him full dexterity with his weapons.

The tracked vehicle's gullwing door opened on the right side, drawing back into the body and disappearing.

Four snow-smock-clad SS Alpine Corps troopers raced out, their assault weapons coming to the ready. "Easy," Rourke hissed through his teeth to his friend.

"I'd love to shoot those bastards, but good guys don't do that sort of thing," Paul said under his breath.

"Not until the bastards give us a reason," Rourke added.

A fifth man stepped out of the vehicle.

Unlike the others, he wore no snow smock, but rather a class A uniform of SS Field Grey, covered by a nearly ankle-length greatcoat of the same color, brilliantly polished high black boots disappearing beneath its hem. Gleaming like the leather of his boots was the brim of his cap. The runic symbols of the SS adorned both the hat and the lapels of the coat.

On his hands were gloves of soft grey leather. A pistol belt was at his waist, a smallish flap holster all that it supported. In the man's left hand was a riding crop.

"This guy's been watching too many World War II movies," Paul suggested.

"Hardly; he'd know that the Nazis are the bad guys and they always lose."

"We can teach him that ourselves, John."

Rourke smiled, taking his eyes from the SS officer and glancing at Paul for an instant. "Or certainly try."

The SS officer advanced across the snow, his men remaining on station at the vehicle. He stopped three yards from them, his heels coming together with a barely audible click, his right hand rising in the classic salute of his ilk, but with the riding crop for added flare. "Herr Doctor General Rourke! It is a great honor." He dropped the salute, continuing to say, "Allow me to introduce myself. I am Hauptsturmführer Gunther Spitz, at your service."

"I'd say it's nice to meet you Captain, but why begin

125

a relationship based on a lie," Rourke told him. "Very impressive show of force by the way. I take it you're expendable to your Führer?"

"How so, Herr Doctor General?"

"I could kill you now, and I might if your men make the slightest move closer to the aircraft."

Hauptsturmführer Spitz laughed. "You Americans! What a flare for colorful language, and such thinly veiled threats. The cowboy philosophy of course. Those guns, for example, which you wear. They are classic!"

"Rather like your uniform, a bit anachronistic, but in the case of my guns, they're serviceable and they are not repugnant to anyone save the hoplophobic. And most of those people are already dead. On the other hand, any civilized person is offended at the sight of your SS insignia."

"You attempt to provoke me, Herr Doctor General," Hauptsturmführer Spitz said softly, smiling. "But you shall not. I am a German officer and—"

"You're a Nazi. Your German heritage is coincidental only."

"You shall not provoke me, Herr Doctor General," Spitz reiterated, smiling again. He reached to his greatcoat pocket, Rourke edging his hands toward the butts of the Scoremasters in response. "A cigarette case only, I assure you." Indeed, it was that, slim and silver, deeply engraved with the swastika symbol surrounded by clusters of oak leaves. Spitz opened the case, offering from its contents to Rourke. Rourke shook his head. The case was not offered to Rubenstein.

Spitz took a cigarette himself, fired it with a lighter

built into the top of the case. Rourke had never had anything against cigarette cases, but had always secretly considered the kind with a lighter built into the top as somewhat foppish. Rourke reached into his own pocket, took a cigarette, lit it in the blue yellow flame of his battered old Zippo windlighter.

"You attempt to insult me, Herr Doctor General."

"No, not really. Your very existence is insult enough. Where's my wife and Generaloberst Mann?"

"Your wife awaits you. But, as a symbol of good faith, Herr Doctor General, we have brought the traitor Mann here to you."

John Rourke felt the muscles around his eyes harden, the tendons in his neck go taut. "Where is Generaloberst Mann?"

Hauptsturmführer Spitz smiled wolfishly. "In my vehicle. Shall I send him to you?"

John Rourke, his voice almost a whisper, spoke slowly, evenly. "Let me explain something to you first. You obviously realize that at the merest inkling of trouble, Mr. Rubenstein or I will shoot you down dead. If there's body armor under your greatcoat, or even if the garment itself is armored, that will be of no avail. Your face isn't armored and that's where you'll get it, right between the eyes.

"You also probably think that it will be easy work for your vastly superior force to overrun us and take over the aircraft, then seize Martin Zimmer. So, I should make clear to you a few points here. Even if you are sufficiently commited to your cause to die for it here and now—and regardless of the cause, that is a type of bravery which I will not disparage—your sacrifice

127

will achieve nothing.

"In order to protect our interests," John Rourke went on slowly, "we have placed our half of the trade in cryogenic sleep." Hauptsturmführer Spitz's eyes hardened, brightened with some inner passion, perhaps hatred. His face was otherwise expressionless. "In addition to the usual cryogenic gas, there's a second gas, in a canister inside the cryogenic chamber. That second gas is cyanide gas. You're familiar with its properties?"

SS Hauptsturmführer Spitz nodded curtly, said nothing.

"Then you realize, Captain," John Rourke continued, refusing to use the SS rank, "that even with the vastly decelerated metabolic rate of a cryogenic sleeper, one whiff would still kill the occupant of the chamber before any remedial action could be taken. I have a control, so does Mr. Rubenstein, so do the other two members of our party. As a backup system, if the cryogenic chamber is not opened in a specific, rather unnatural fashion, the cyanide gas will be released into the chamber's atmosphere, regardless of the condition of the control units. If you enjoy chess, then you're in luck because it's your move," John Rourke concluded.

Hauptsturmführer Spitz said nothing, did nothing for a very long moment, then rocked back on his heels once. "You will forgive me, Herr Doctor General, but I must consult my superiors."

"Virtually everybody in the human race is your superior, pal," Paul Rubenstein said through clenched teeth.

Spitz glared at Rubenstein for an instant, saluted John Rourke with the riding crop, then turned on his heel and walked back the way he had come, toward his tracked vehicle—and, presumably, a private radio communication.

Deitrich Zimmer's king was in check.

Twenty-One

Deitrich Zimmer read the message as it was handed to him.

He'd been perusing Sarah Rourke's chart, and, after returning the message blank to the man who had brought it, he continued reading Sarah Rourke's chart. All vital signs, all signs of electrical activity within the brain, everything was promising. He looked at the physician he had stationed by her side in the recovery room. "She is doing satisfactorily. Be vigilant."

"Yes, Herr Doctor!"

The physician saluted, of course, but Deitrich Zimmer merely raised his right hand palm outward, then turned away.

The messenger was still waiting for him, by the door leading into the recovery room of the clinic. "Herr Doctor! There is a reply?"

Deitrich Zimmer smiled. "I will deliver my reply personally, not to the Hauptsturmführer, but to the good Herr Doctor instead."

Zimmer said nothing more, turned on his heel and

began walking along the grey corridor. The clinic here was the best he had ever had, ideally suited to all his purposes. Required subjects were brought to him, as many as needed for the perfection of a new surgical technique. The process by which he had, he was quite certain, saved the life of Sarah Rourke had required the use of sixteen persons, the last nine of them women. The last four remained alive, the final two in excellent condition, as well as they were when brought to him for surgical experimentation. The others who lived experienced various degrees of disability, but all in the quest for perfection, their sacrifices, however personally great, insignificant in the grander scheme of things.

With his new procedures, he could not only successfully enter into the deepest recesses of the human brain to remove some object, he could also place something there. That idea intrigued him.

As a young man, Deitrich Zimmer had read many banned books, and the great majority of those were from among the works of science fiction written throughout the Twentieth Century. The theme of many works dealt with man creating man. The engineering requirements for the construction of a manlike robotic entity had not yet been met. Doubtless, had five centuries of warfare not intervened, either civilization would have collapsed of its own weight or entered into a new era of technology Before the Night of the War and now undreamed of.

Yet, if a man could be made to perform independently of his own free will, perhaps that would be the greatest robotic creation of all.

A man. Or a woman.

Natalia Anastasia Tiemerovna sat a little distance away from John Rourke, her eyes on the Alpine troops. The men—at least from her Twentieth Century perspective she assumed that they were all men—seemed impervious to the cold. She was not. A silk scarf was tied over her hair and ears, bound closed at the nape of the neck, covering part of her forehead as well. A similar scarf covered her from the bridge of the nose to where the heavy turtleneck she wore over her jumpsuit rose to beneath it at her throat. The snow goggles which protected her eyes covered what little exposed skin there was between the two bandannas.

Her M-16 rifle lay beside her on the open cargo platform. She sat there on a warmed air cushion, wiggling her toes inside her boots, drawing up her fingers inside her gloves, folding them into the palms.

She looked at John Rourke. The man she had wanted as her lover for five centuries would, if they survived, be her father-in-law.

Life and insanity were synonymous.

She had always heard about women who tried to remold the men with whom they fell in love. She had always thought that this was disgraceful. Now she felt slightly differently. She hoped that she could just ever so slightly remold Michael Rourke. She loved his brashness, feared his contemplative self-sacrifice. Natalia could not let the son become the father, for his sake more than her own.

Had John Rourke been the character in a Shakespearean tragedy, his fatal flaw would have been his perfection. Unlike the creations of Shakespeare, however, this fatal flaw would not be his undoing—she hoped.

John's face was masked in a toque, his dark-lensed aviator-style sunglasses replaced with goggles similar to her own. Although she could not see him clearly she knew what lay in those eyes and that face: the reckless uncertainty of improvisational genius.

And, if he had been wearing mittens rather than gloves, she might have guessed that he was keeping his fingers crossed.

Twenty-Two

John Rourke's eye muscles tensed.

The man exiting from one of the seven newly arrived tracked vehicles was Deitrich Zimmer—the man who had kidnapped his son, turning the boy into something vile, evil—the man who had also nearly murdered Sarah. Reflexively, John Rourke reached toward his guns, but did not touch them.

Natalia whispered, "Easy."

Annie came up to stand beside John Rourke, between him and her husband. "If I'd never understood the concept of revenge, I'd understand it now, I think."

"And we can't touch him," Paul said, an edge to his voice.

"Not yet," John Rourke almost whispered. "Not yet."

The years had, evidently, been kind to Deitrich Zimmer. Although logic indicated that Zimmer was, chronologically, in his sixties—these days essentially middle-aged—Zimmer looked more like a vigorous man in his late forties. What was visible of Zimmer's hair from beneath the foraging cap he wore was yellowish white. There were lines in his face, but somehow they denoted strength.

Deitrich Zimmer stopped just a few yards from them, and through the goggles Zimmer wore his eyes looked bright blue and clear. As he spoke, his teeth almost sparkled. "You know who I am."

"Of course," Rourke nodded.

"And I know you would wish to kill me, but do not because I hold the power of life and death over your wife."

"As do I over the man in the cryogenic chamber," Rourke responded. "Your flunkey mentioned Wolfgang Mann. But we haven't seen him yet."

"Yes," Zimmer said, smiling almost conspiratorially, as if he were about to share a secret with them. "Well, you see, we had not anticipated your charming little ploy with the cyanide gas. I assume you were not misleading my officer?"

"You assume correctly. The gas cylinder has been designed so that you can test its contents, should you feel that is actually necessary," Rourke told him.

"No," Zimmer shrugged. "I would never doubt you, a colleague. No, but there is a bit of a problem with the little surprise I had arranged for you with Generaloberst Mann. But back to that in a moment. A question, first, if you will."

Rourke's eyes were on Zimmer's eyes. And those eyes were madness incarnate. "Of course."

"Do you expect to escape with your lives?"

John Rourke smiled. He took one of the thin, dark tobacco cigars from a pocket within his parka and lit it in the blue yellow flame of his battered Zippo. Rourke answered through an exhalation of blue grey smoke. "Of course."

"Very good!" Zimmer seemed genuinely pleased. "I have learned that one should never accept defeat, even when it seems that all else but defeat is impossibly elusive. I applaud you."

"Generaloberst Mann. You were going to tell us about him," Paul said.

John Rourke exhaled smoke through his nostrils. "Yes."

"I will have him come to you now, as a symbol of good faith. Because, you see, I have a little added request before I release to you Sarah Rourke."

"Request," Natalia said, just repeating the word.

"What kind of request?" Annie asked, her voice almost a whisper.

Doctor Zimmer smiled at her, his eyes like death. "I believe that you have brought—" and he looked at John Rourke when he said this—"our son back to me with the added touch of the cynanide gas in order to force me to perform an operation on your lovely wife, our son's mother. Anticipating that, I performed such an operation."

John Rourke's hands balled into fists and he did not know whether to shoot the man or—"She's—"

"Your wife will be fully restored," Zimmer said, smiling, Rourke breathing, Annie grabbing at his arm, Paul clearing his throat. "In a few days, she should be up and around and active. She's already been walked a bit, to promote proper circulation."

"And Sarah's faculties?" Natalia asked, her voice barely audible.

"As best I can ascertain, she is as she was before she

was shot. Whenever one enters the brain, there is always the possibility of some very minor damage, the loss of a small memory byte here or there. But that can be restored. There was little cosmetic damage from the entry wound, but that has been taken care of as well. I believe the old Americanism was, 'good as new'?"

"I don't know whether to thank you or kill you," John Rourke said, his voice a low rasping whisper.

"Thanking me would be out of character to the situation would it not? And, certainly, prematurely killing me would only precipitate your own deaths in the same instant as my own. I will have Generaloberst Mann brought to you. He can even assist you in the little task I have in mind."

"What is that task?" Paul asked.

Zimmer laughed. "One that you in particular, as a Jew, should find most morally challenging. You see, you will have the choice, Herr Rubenstein, of failing your friends, your family, or being the greatest traitor to your rather disgusting kind who has ever lived."

Paul started forward.

Annie, already holding his arm, grabbed at him harder.

John Rourke said nothing.

Deitrich Zimmer said, "In effect, it is poetic irony. A Jew helping to restore to the world of the living—Adolf Hitler."

Twenty-Three

Wolfgang Mann walked with the same almost casual, natural straightness John Rourke remembered from their first encounter more than a century and a quarter ago outside the Eden Project encampment.

He wore a black parka over black fatigue pants, his trouser bottoms bloused into black jackboots.

The hood of Generaloberst Mann's parka was down. Mann's sandy colored hair, with just a hint of grey, looked very short, shorter than Mann's usual modified military cut, almost as if the hair were just growing back from being shaved away.

But that was impossible, of course, because Mann had only been in Zimmer's hands for days, not weeks.

John Rourke very suddenly had an icy cold feeling in the very pit of his stomach.

Mann walked toward them without blinking, without acknowledging them, the high-cheekboned face expressionless.

Mann stopped a few feet from them.

"What is wrong with him?" Natalia whispered, taking a step toward him, the M-16 in her hands shaking slightly.

"I had originally programmed your Generaloberst to kill Herr Rubenstein as a—"

"What?" Rourke rasped, walking between Zimmer and the others, going up to Mann.

"As the Jew, I naturally felt Herr Rubenstein was the least important among you. But, since your introduction of the cyanide gas, I decided to alter that program. Generaloberst Mann is quite harmless to you now. See?" And Rourke's eyes flickered toward Zimmer as Zimmer looked at Mann and commanded, "Kneel in the snow, Herr Generaloberst!"

Wolfgang Mann dropped to his knees.

"Kiss the boot of Herr Doctor Rourke, Generaloberst!"

Wolfgang Mann lowered his face toward John Rourke's feet, but John Rourke dropped to his own knees, grabbing Mann's head, drawing Mann's head against his chest, his eyes scanning over Mann's scalp beneath the close cropped hair. There was a spot closer cropped still, but there was no scar. Mann tried pulling away from him, tried carrying out Zimmer's order. Rourke held him tighter, but his eyes shifted upward toward Zimmer.

Zimmer was laughing. "He is quite perfected." Then Zimmer called toward the vehicle which had brought him over the snow, "Send out the captured American pilot."

For a moment John Rourke held his breath. There was an answering reply, and as Rourke looked toward the vehicle, a youngish woman—Emma's age—stepped from the vehicle. Wearing only a dark blue knee-length shift, barefoot and seemingly oblivious to the cold, she walked toward them. "Stop, Lieutenant Klein," Zimmer called.

It was then that John Rourke noticed the pistol in the woman's bare right hand.

"Put the pistol to your head and pull the trigger, Lieutenant Klein."

John Rourke was up, moving, running toward her, a blur of motion beside him as Paul and Annie started toward the girl.

The pistol was an ordinary cartridge arm, and in the same instant as the shot echoed across the frigid air the left side of the girl's temple blew out and away from her head, and her body began to crumple lifelessly into the snow.

John Rourke stopped running.

Annie and Paul passed him.

John Rourke looked at Natalia. The muzzle of her weapon had shifted, now halfway between Wolfgang Mann—his face was in the snow, his lips trying to kiss the boot that was no longer there—and Zimmer, who was laughing.

John Rourke said nothing.

Zimmer very abruptly stopped laughing. "You see, Lieutenant Klein was an earlier experiment. She was really very automationlike. On the other hand, Generaloberst Mann, Herr Doctor General Rourke, is perfectly natural in everything he does, unless I order otherwise. If you fail me, Herr Doctor General, I will reenter the brain of your wife and she will be like this, ready to obey my slightest whim, even at the cost of her own life."

Rourke started walking very slowly, across the glacier, toward Zimmer.

Zimmer kept talking. "On the other hand, if you cooperate, assuming Martin is well, I will not only restore to you Sarah Rourke but I will disable the device within the brain of Generaloberst Mann."

John Rourke's face was so close to Zimmer's face when Rourke stopped walking that the glowing tip of Rourke's cigar was inches from Zimmer's skin.

Zimmer kept smiling. "I should inquire concerning your other son. He is well?"

John Rourke said, "Yes."

"I take it he was otherwise occupied? I do not see him with you."

"Michael suffered an arm wound in an assault against a group of Nazi saboteurs a little while ago. It was a knife. There was risk of infection." Rourke did not lie, because all of what he said was true enough. Zimmer would draw whatever conclusions he might.

"I almost asked myself if you would attempt, Dr. Rourke, to substitute your boy for mine."

"And what did you almost answer yourself?" John Rourke said, exhaling, breathing, actually feeling lighter in spirit than he had for some time. The truth did that.

"You would not allow the boy to be so foolish, because then you might indeed have your wife restored to you, but your son would be in my hands."

"A man would have to be a fool to risk losing so much of his family," John Rourke almost whispered.

"You will bring me the frozen remains of Adolf

142

Hitler. From those remains, I will gain the genetic material with which to recreate him."

"What sort of horror or science fiction have you been into recently, Zimmer? Robbing graves? Building a Frankenstein's monster?"

"No, a savior."

Twenty-Four

Lifeless-looking, Wolfgang Mann stood on the glacier, almost at attention.

Deitrich Zimmer, hood up now against the growing cold, a cigarette lit between his gloved fingers, said, "At the close of World War II, when the Führer knew full well that he would be hideously tortured at the hands of the Allied invaders, and that all sorts of confessions of lies would be attributed to him, he did the courageous thing."

"He shot himself in the head with a Walther PP series pistol," Natalia whispered.

Zimmer smiled. "You know your history, Fräulein Major. The Allies knew, however, that even in death the power of the Führer would only continue to grow. So that his body might not become the object of the veneration it so deserved in future generations, it was spirited out of Germany aboard a B-17 bomber, flown to a secret airfield in the eastern portion of the United States, then taken by truck in dead of night to a location in the northern portion of the state of New York, near what was then the St. Lawrence River. It was a mountainous area. Deep within the mountain there was a storage facility.

"The Führer's remains were packed in ice and frozen, then the block of ice surrounding him was cut away from the rest. It was desired that this block of ice should never melt. A frozen storage locker was specially constructed, built to accomodate the block of ice. The storage locker was closed, then set inside a room. The locker and the room were refrigerated electrically, utilizing a closed system. The storage locker and the room were separately powered, so that in the event that one unit somehow failed, the other would continue on. The room itself was fitted with a backup system which would be actuated should the primary system fail. The facility was part of a larger complex.

"In the years following, in the early days of the so-called Cold War between your country, Herr Doctor Rourke, and yours, Fräulein Major Tiemerovna, the mountain facility was expanded, becoming the first of the Presidential war retreats. In many ways, it was the best, although in the years following, the location was changed several times.

"Too close to too many A targets," John Rourke supplied, his cigar out, but still clamped tight in his teeth.

"Indeed," Zimmer nodded. "The facility was utilized for the storage of strategic materials."

"How do you know all this?" Annie asked him.

Zimmer started to answer, but John Rourke

answered for him. "After the war, the United States brought over a considerable number of German scientists, some of them former Nazis, but seen as potentially useful despite their previous affiliation. Evidently, at least one of those affiliations was not a previous one."

"Bravo," Zimmer enthused. "Martin's superior intelligence, indeed, is in no small part thanks to yours, Herr Doctor."

Rourke said nothing.

Paul asked, "Then why did you guys wait until now?"

Zimmer did not ignore the question. "Following what has come to be known as the Night of the War, there was of course no opportunity for centuries. The Leader, the man whom the revolution led by the despised Deiter Bern overthrew, was planning that his spiritual antecedent's body should be recovered, and accorded the veneration which it so richly deserved."

"Pardon me while I puke," Paul observed.

Zimmer went on. "When Bern and his stooges seized control of New Germany, several of our leader's most trusted men, myself among them, were able to escape or go into hiding. The records concerning the repository of the Führer's remains went with us."

"Why now?" Paul asked again.

"Yeah!" Annie echoed.

"In large part thanks to your mother, young woman."

Annie started to speak, didn't.

Rourke looked away from her, back into Zimmer's

eyes. "You see," Zimmer continued, his voice like that of a patient schoolteacher explaining to a rather obtuse group of students something that should have been simply grasped, "Adolf Hitler's remains were safe where they were. War is coming. Why risk their destruction? Unless there were something positive to be gained. And, because of the work which I accelerated in order to effect the operation on Sarah Rourke, saving her life, and Generaloberst Mann, in order to control him, I now have the ability to utilize the Führer's remains to fulfill his dreams."

"Some would call them nightmares," Rourke supplied.

"Many great prophets have been destroyed by those whom it was their intention to help, to save Jesus, the—"

Paul took a step closer to Zimmer. "As you pointed out, I'm a Jew. But what you're about to say is still a sacrilege."

Zimmer shrugged it off, went on. "As you will. With the Führer's DNA, and thanks to the surgical skills I have at last perfected, I can complete the work which I have already begun on Martin, altering those aspects of him which I could not have hoped before to alter. He will not just bear some few of the Führer's genes, distilled and weakened over the centuries, but he will become the Führer. Adolf Hitler will be reborn. You will see to that or Sarah Rourke will be treated very badly indeed." And Zimmer looked back toward his vehicle. "Projector!"

John Rourke followed Zimmer's eyes, Rourke's hands reaching toward his guns as a panel within the front of the vehicle opened.

"Watch out, Annie," Paul snapped, pushing Annie behind him, moving the muzzle of his submachinegun toward Zimmer.

"No, Paul," Rourke said, then looked back toward the opening in the vehicle.

Then there was a flicker of light, but not like that of an energy weapon. And then, there in the air, as if floating, John Rourke saw his wife, in perfect dimension. She was as he had seen her in cryogenic sleep, at peace. There was a flicker, and he saw her from the waist up, tented from the forehead down. Another flicker.

What he saw was inside her brain, microsurgery in progress.

And there was a flicker again. And Sarah lay in a bed, a portion of her head bandaged, but her eyes open, as though looking at him.

Her lips moved.

Although there was no sound, he could tell what word she spoke. His name.

"A hologram," Natalia whispered, stating the obvious.

"You see, I do not lie to you. Sarah Rourke lives." Zimmer said almost cheerfully. "And thanks to me alone. Whether or not she continues to recover— and she recovers well—is entirely up to you. A small unit of men will be dispatched with you, to obey your orders to the letter until the remains of the Führer are brought to me here. The traitor Mann is yours, to accompany you, whatever. I have no further use for him unless you elect that following the return of the

Führer's remains I should remove the control device within him."

Zimmer walked toward Mann, stared at him, but addressed what he said to John Rourke. "I can, always, order him to kill himself. You might like that, Herr Doctor. I understand the man is in love with your wife. If he kills himself, and if you succeed, of course, you can have her all to yourself. Whatever you wish. You will find me very much the romantic. Perhaps you still secretly yearn for this Russian woman, or that American pilot. We have spies who—"

John Rourke was already moving, grabbing Zimmer by the shoulder, twisting him around. There was the clicking of energy weapon safeties. Zimmer shouted, "Nicht!" Then he looked John Rourke in the eye. "Strike a nerve?"

"You think you've won."

"I have. I have read everything there is to know about you, Herr Doctor. Despite all your abilities, you are a slave to your emotions. You will get me my prize, you will return Wolfgang Mann to me in order that I may effect his salvation. You will hold out hope that I will restore both your wife and Mann to you, knowing full well that you perhaps destroy what little happiness might remain to you before my forces crush the Trans-Global Alliance and lay waste you and everyone like you. You are hopeless, Herr Doctor.

"Brave, resourceful, but pitiably predictable. You will adhere to an abject moral code of right and wrong, no matter how ludicrous the application of that code, nor how self-destructive—you will not deviate from it. The troops I send with you are not to ensure your cooperation, but merely to assist you. Your cooperation is already assured.

"I have won, and you would be a liar if you said otherwise."

John Rourke said nothing.

Twenty-Five

Her "Blackbird" shrieked over the confluence of Gulf and Atlantic waters where six centuries ago there had been peninsular Florida, before the earthquake following the Night of the War had severed it from the rest of the continent, and dropped it into the sea. Water rose on either side of her slipstream in whitecapped waves of enormous height, a deep trench opening below her fuselage. Her aircraft did not summon the Hand of God to part the waters, however; it only displaced the waters.

Land now, and terrain following here was not nearly so beautiful, so spectacular, but terribly more dangerous. She was roughly equidistant between what had been Tallahassee and Jacksonville, but was now only among the most jagged coastlines she had ever observed. Early warning systems required her to climb ever so slightly, then bank almost into a right angle to the surface, flying nearly perpendicular in order to minimize her aircraft's profile to computer-linked sensors.

Emma Shaw actuated her holographic targeting headsup, the display appearing in her windscreen. Plant 234, where Eden City under the direction of its Nazi masters used human beings as quality control test subjects in the fabrication of poison gas, was clear in every detail, however minute, looking exactly the way that it would when she overflew the real target.

She would be killing some innocent people, she knew, those test subjects that the American agent James Darkwood had not freed, or those new test subjects brought in since his daring escape. And, doubtless, some of the personnel at the factory worked there involuntarily.

But the mission had been designed, at greater risk to pilots like herself, in order to minimize civilian casualties.

Eden pilots would not, at least officially, care.

Emma Shaw had never ascribed to the philosophy first espoused by a Catholic bishop during the Albigensian Heresy in the Thirteenth Century: "Kill them all; the Lord will know his own." Or, its more vernacular equivalent, "Kill 'em all; let God sort 'em out."

She was past the early warning sensors and returned to standard horizontal flight, approaching from the southeast toward what had been Montgomery, Alabama, almost to what had been Birmingham before she realized it at the classified speed at which the Blackbird flew.

She punched up the course correction, vectoring through a steep bank to starboard toward the water-filled crater lake which had once been Atlanta.

At Atlanta, she would dogleg the Blackbird almost

154

directly south toward Eden City. Her wing consisted of nine pilots beside herself, each flying his or her own course to the objective. But only three of the aircraft—hers was one of the three—were set to penetrate within Eden City defense systems and strike Plant 234, the remaining seven pilots attacking those defense systems themselves.

Plant 234, of course, was set in a residential area, the other factories in its immediate vicinity producers of innocuous necessities—processing milk, baking bread, one even engaged in the legitimate manufacture of pharmaceuticals.

Lake Atlanta was nearly upon her, and she began the dogleg, paying scrupulous attention to course coordinates on the penetration program. Passing over the lake, once again white-capped waves rose in her aircraft's wake, as if somehow she flew between two magnificent waterfalls which were able to defy the force of gravity and flow upward.

She backed off a little on the Blackbird's speed, so she wouldn't outrun her missiles should Eden City get up fighter aircraft after her—because, despite her stealth capabilities, Eden City defense systems would acquire her in—she ticked off seconds—five, make that four.

There were the remains of what had once, she recalled from her topographic briefing, been a great civilian airfield, just south of the crater lake. A few isolated patches of runway surface were visible in strips among the mounds of wind-driven snow and sparse wintry vegetation and just before she blinked she thought she detected a few isolated framing ribs from an aircraft, lying there like the bones of a dinosaur.

She was into the approach to Eden City's Plant 234.

In the same instant, her incoming alert buzzers started going off. Eden City had aquired the Blackbird sooner than she had thought. The irony of a United States Navy pilot flying a combat mission over enemy territory in Georgia, what had once been part of the United States, did not escape her.

The voice of her battle computer was speaking through her helmet's integral headset, its voice annoyingly calm. For female pilots, the voice was synthesized into sounding male, for male pilots the opposite. Perhaps that was to prevent chattiness, keep a certain edge to the discourse. If she had not known that the voice was not real and never had been, she could have fallen in love with it. "Commander Shaw, we have thirty-three seconds on my Mark to impact from the first incoming Spider Seven. I recommend evasive—"

"Out-thought you again, Gorgeous." She banked to starboard, rolled and started climbing. She could outfly her own missiles and she could outfly the Spider Sevens. Spider Sevens, possessed of eight (same number as the legs of a spider) multiple independently targeted warheads, surface to airs, were principally dangerous in the fact that their individual warheads functioned independently, and it seemed (in virtual reality computer simulations, at least), erratically. In order to successfully defeat a Spider Seven, one had to dive into it, bypassing the main body of the missile and threading one's way among the eight warheads at almost the precise moment of release.

Her aft video—she was climbing nearly vertically—displayed what she had feared, a second Spider Seven. The odds of defeating a single Spider Seven in an aircraft as fast as this were basically on her side. With two, however, if the Spider Sevens fired their warheads synchronously, the odds were suddenly and radically skewed the other way. Intentionally, she avoided calling up the numbers from Gorgeous. She didn't need to know them in order to know that she was in trouble.

"A second Spider Seven missile—"

"I know, Gorgeous. You just relax and let me do the flying."

"Commander Shaw, I am required to inform you that the odds—"

"Either shut up or shut down, Gorgeous."

"Yes, Commander."

She wouldn't have liked a flesh and blood man that she could tell to shut up like that and he would do it.

The Blackbird reached one thousand feet under operational ceiling, her hands torquing the yoke, her heart praying that the Blackbird's hydraulics wouldn't spasm, would respond. Out of the climb, now, almost into a flat spin, Emma Shaw throttled out into a full power dive.

Gorgeous was saying, "Spider Seven One and Spider Seven Two in process of releasing independently targeted warheads, Commander Shaw."

"No shit, Sherlock—hang onto your microchips."

"I am monitoring, Commander."

"Don't talk to me like that; you know it gets me all wet." Despite her pressurized flight suit and the cabin's engineering, sheer speed drove her lips back from her clenched teeth. Over the red-glowing nose of the Blackbird when the wisps of cloud parted for an instant, she could see two shapes suddenly turning into

157

more shapes than she could count.

"You are at thirteen percent over recommended maximum speed for—"

"You know I'm slightly triskaidekaphobic—shut up."

"Yes, Commander."

Emma Shaw murmured the word *wimp* under her breath, but not so loudly that Gorgeous would hear her; after all, computers had feelings, too.

The crew of an entire submarine could not be risked. With three volunteers, instead, Thorn Rolvaag descended over the subsurface volcanic vent in what was the world's most high-tech state-of-the-art deep dive submersible, the Bathyscaph Woodshole named after the scientific center in Massachussetts which, centuries ago, had served as home base to what were then the best of the best in diving bells. An ordinary submarine could now descend to those earlier depths with relative impunity. But the pioneering efforts of the early explorers of the deep sea were undiminished.

Thorn Rolvaag was reminded of the expression so popular among young people centuries ago (he had first encountered it in a sociology course he had not wished to take): "Bummer, dude!" This was, indeed, the very essence of the phrase; he was several thousand feet down within a trench unknown until recent decades and he could only see by means of video. No transparent material—even the best of alloy infused resin synth—could be trusted to withstand the pressures here, their per square inch rate almost incalculable in numbers that meant anything.

But from his seat, he could summon up video from almost any possible direction. And it was what he saw below him, running through the center of the trench and almost due eastward with an almost negligible northward cant along the tropic of Cancer, which obsessed him.

It was a volcanic vent, glowing so brightly that the video persistently flared white.

An enormous crack, extending as far as the video eye could see.

The Spider Sevens were in full release. Emma Shaw ignored Gorgeous as he ignored her. She kept telling him to shut up—maybe he had guts after all—and he kept telling her that she was redlining and that the odds against pulling out of her dive were growing exponentially.

Her fists were locked onto the yoke, knuckles pounding within her pressurized gauntlets, heart pounding within her chest, her chest feeling the weight of the fast-approaching earth crushing in upon her. She would auger into the icy ground in under fifteen seconds at this rate of speed.

In three she would be into the cluster of warheads.

She'd rehearsed it in her mind, even done it once in a simulator (and racked up the simulator for three days), but there was no guarantee—

There was a crack as she pulled up the Blackbird's nose, airbraking, the aircraft shuddering around her.

Through it, climbing the shockwave she'd made as she changed course, rolling away from her in a wave. Levelled off. "Hang on, Gorgeous!" Full throttle.

The warheads which had surrounded her at the instant she airbraked were detonating now from the shock wave.

All she had to do was outrun the explosions. By then, she'd be back over Alabama and have to start the run on Eden City over again.

Twenty-Six

John Rourke walked slowly, evenly.

The corridor here was of polished synth-marble, the floor, the walls, the ceiling, black, marbled in white and in various shades of grey.

As he passed them, black uniformed guards of the SS saluted him.

The junior officer who walked at Rourke's side remarked, "The Herr Doctor General must realize that rank, regardless of whether or not the man holding it is the enemy, is to be respected always."

Rourke glanced at the man and smiled, the smile a humoring one, not because there was anything about which to be happy.

John Rourke's right fist was on the butt of the gun he had borrowed from Paul Rubenstein. The gun had an interesting history. It was an original German MP-40 submachinegun, evidently brought to the United States as a war trophy by a returning World War II GI. Whether or not the gun had ever been made legal was another question, but a moot point more than six and one-half centuries after the fact.

It was taken from among the weapons belonging to the Brigand bikers who had attacked the surviving crew and passengers of the jetliner aboard which he and Paul had spent the Night of the War. Aside from considerable wear on the finish, both gun and magazines were in pristine condition, not only well cared-for but very recently checked with the very latest analytical equipment for any sign of metal fatigue, stress fractures, etc. During World War II, considerable numbers of Nazi weapons were turned out in inferior condition, because of the exigencies of the struggle. This gun, however, was as perfect as if it had been made commercially. And MP-40s were among the finest submachineguns ever designed.

Made for the Nazis, the property and fighting companion of a Jew for more than six hundred years, it now guarded John Rourke as he entered the sanctum sanctorum of the new Nazi power which threatened the Earth with a war which might well be the last.

At close range, it could spray more lead than any other weapon Rourke had at his disposal. He had left Paul with his Heckler & Koch rifle in temporary trade.

"Not that I'm concerned about you, John, of course, but I've really become attached to this gun," Paul had told him as they clasped hands.

"I never thought otherwise," Rourke told his friend, that time the smile genuine.

The purpose of this visit under flag of truce was two-fold: to see Sarah, making certain she was well; to be briefed on the details of Deitrich Zimmer's mad bargain for her life—the retrieval of the remains of Adolf Hitler.

162

There were identical doors at the end of the corridor, black enameled with brass handles and hinges. Of the inverted Christian door design the larger, upper panel of each had inset at its center the swastika, surrounded by a circlet of oak leaves, both in brass, gleaming.

The junior officer at Rourke's side knocked on the door at the left.

From within, the voice of Deitrich Zimmer responded, "Yes!"

The junior officer opened the door inward, Rourke stepping past him and inside, Rourke's right fist tighter on the butt of Paul's Schmiesser than before.

"So, Herr Doctor General! You trust me!" Zimmer stood at the center of a large conference room, the walls and floor and ceiling of the same synth-marble, in the same glowingly dark pattern. His hands rested on his hips and, as if costumed for some theatrical production, he wore riding jodhpurs above high, brightly shined boots. The trousers were black, the shirt which covered his upper body, white. Despite his age, Deitrich Zimmer was physically impressive in the extreme. "Welcome!"

"Trust you? Hardly. Where's my wife?"

"Ahh, but first things first." Zimmer was so far away that he needed almost to shout, Rourke the same. Zimmer started walking toward the furthest wall, Rourke—almost ambling—moving after him. "Your choice of antique firearms is interesting, Rourke. German, isn't it? From the Third Reich?"

"You Nazis did build to last—in some things."

Zimmer laughed, stopping before a small panel in the wall, folding it out. Within it was a console, and Zimmer was already working switches and dials as

163

Rourke stopped to stand beside him. Their eyes met, and Rourke was at once surprised to see that, indeed, Zimmer had two eyes. One had been sacrificed in order to make it appear that he had died instead of his brother. But the second eye seemed real enough. Rourke didn't really want to know how it had been obtained.

The wall here was opening, huge panels—synth-marble was amazingly strong and could be plate-glass thin—pulling aside to reveal a video screen of vast proportions. Already a picture was appearing on the screen. "You will see your wife, Frau Rourke, very shortly. And, to show that I am not without feeling, I will afford you a few moments alone with her, more I daresay than you would afford me with my son, Martin. Cyanide gas! I would not have thought you so diabolical, my old adversary."

"My son thought of it," Rourke said truthfully, smiling.

"Perhaps he does not embrace ideals so lofty as your own. A Rourke, a realist. What a disarming thought."

"He's just less trusting," Rourke told Zimmer.

Appearing on the video screen—John Rourke stepped back in order to see it more fully and in better resolution—was a mountain chain, the slopes, the peaks, the valleys within, all snow-covered. "It is perpetual glacier here."

The screen, once fully exposed, was nearly the size of the original Cinerama screens John Rourke remembered from his youth. In those days, of course, three projectors, working in crossfire side to side and down the middle for the center screen, operated in synch in order to give a motion picture size wider than any film stock. Rourke recalled thrilling to Lowell Thomas travelogues, promising himself that someday he too would see the exotic places of the world, never realizing what that promise would be like when it was fulfilled.

"What is it you really want, Zimmer?"

Zimmer laughed. "I am that transparent?"

"No, just the situation. If this is such an easy trick, why don't you send some of your Alpine troops in there and just get the body out of cold storage and bring it back and start whittling? Figuratively speaking, of course."

Zimmer laughed again, almost sincerely it seemed. "There is a problem, potentially, with which none of my men can effectively deal. There is a society within the mountain."

"A society," Rourke repeated. "And?"

"The remains of the Führer are within the mountain complex, but I do not know where. Hence, I cannot blast my way inside with a large force, because the result might be the very destruction of that which I seek. For six hundred and twenty-five years, what might be a very American civilization—in the sense of your age—has survived, and, it would seem, flourished in almost total secrecy within. The only hope for discovering the location of the Führer's remains, then safely getting them away, is likely to be blending in with this society. My men, unaided, cannot do that. You, on the other hand, and even the Jew, Rubenstein, are the most ideally suited men on the face of the earth." And Zimmer laughed again, clearly struck by some irony. "I am giving you the trump card, as I believe it is said, in the trade for your wife. You will have not only my son and heir, the future leader of the world, but the man whose remains are to me the single most important thing on the face of the Earth."

John Rourke, as his eyes surveyed the aerial video of the glaciated mountain range—forbidding was too mild a word for it—realized that Zimmer, with his proposed unholy bargain, had perhaps given him more than a trump card, the proverbial Ace-in-the-hole. If Zimmer discovered that Martin was, in fact dead, there would still be a chance to get Sarah alive without losing Michael.

The mountains, weathered by six more centuries of unremitting natural assault, were less soft in shape than their origin would have suggested, craggy and rugged in the extreme. Already, Rourke had picked what he thought might have been the logical location for the original entrance, but it was only a guess. "I'll need all the intelligence data you can get me. Everything. Nothing held back. And if you insist on dispatching your own troops, they will have to be under my orders. If they are not, they can't kill me—you know that—or you'll never get what you want. But, I can kill them. We won't be going into that mountain for a bloodbath, merely to get the job done. Understood?"

Deitrich Zimmer smiled again. "I might grow to like you, Herr Doctor General."

"I sincerely hope not."

Zimmer shook his head, laughed almost good-naturedly. "You must understand, of course, that when this temporary alliance of ours has served its purpose, the truce is over."

"This isn't a truce, Dr. Zimmer; it's merely the blink of an eye. I never fancied selling my soul, nor even loaning it out. I'll see you dead if I can."

"I admire your candor, Rourke. You know that my feelings are the same."

"We'll need to preserve the body. After so long, exposure to the elements might cause instantaneous disintegration."

"Indeed," Zimmer nodded, stroking his chin as though he wore an invisible beard. "I have planned for that. I have planned for everything. Any weapons, equipment, whatever—personnel!"

"An expert in cryogenics, I should think, would be in order, and an ordinary mortician. And a doctor, besides myself. Those personnel and whoever else you feel you have to send along to watch."

"My entire resources are at your disposal, Rourke." And Zimmer extended his hand.

Rourke didn't take it.

Zimmer didn't move his hand. "Not to friendship, but to a gentleman's agreement."

"Not that you're a gentleman," but John Rourke, shifting his left hand to the butt of one of the Scoremasters he had cocked and locked—faster but not his usual carry—released his grip on the pistol grip of the submachinegun. "To your honoring the bargain."

"To that, then. And now, you would like to see your wife. We can resume with the details later."

"Yes. Later," John Rourke almost whispered.

Twenty-Seven

Greater love had no man for another, Annie realized. Paul, as her father had left, merely said, "If we must do this thing, we will do it."

She put her arms around him, held him, let him hold her.

Her husband would, with the enlightened self-interest of a man who valued friendship and honor above what was to him personally despicable, go forth to rescue the body of the man who had nearly been the executioner of his people—had caused the deaths of six million Jews, some perhaps his relations, however distant—the man who would have exterminated every Jew on the face of the Earth had he triumphed.

Paul would do this because Paul was John Rourke's friend.

Annie Rubenstein stood silently at her husband's side, waiting for her father to return. And her right hand held tight in her husband's left, she clutched the hand of a man who defined to her the heroic and the good . . .

169

*   *   *

Natalia Anastasia Tiemerovna lit a cigarette.

It was amusing to her that the lieutenant who had been left in charge of the Alpine troops seemed so fascinated with her. Yet she knew it was not her beauty—to have denied that she possessed beauty would have been fatuous—but rather her sex. Nazis believed that women were inherently inferior to men, of course. In that way, the Communist regime in which she had risen to the rank of major, had been little different. Women were treated as inferiors. Her own successes—those not attributed to the devil incarnate who had been her husband—were the stuff which would have made a man a colonel at the very least. Until the Night of the War, she had been a captain only, and that in all probability as a sop to her uncle, one of the Soviet Union's most powerful generals.

She had watched her uncle, Ishmael Varakov, as he watched the dissolution of the Soviet Empire.

The disastrous warfare with Afghan rebels—the Soviet Viet Nam—and the economic crises which followed, then the revolution, growing, unstoppable, except by men like her husband, Vladmir Karamatsov. He had the formula: death.

Then the rising tide of the independence movement within Turkmen and Uzbek, and the weapons and munitions and medical supplies and food which fed it from Afghanistan. Then—

Natalia flicked ashes from the tip of her cigarette.

Who had precipitated the missile strikes that Night of the War so long ago which changed everything for ever?

170

Would she ever know?

Natalia inhaled, exhaled quickly, stared back at the young lieutenant who marvelled at her so.

The Blackbird was invincible now.

A half-dozen men with assault rifles firing full auto in a random pattern from the street below her might kill it, but no missile could. The Spider Sevens could not be used at this altitude, nor could any conventional antiaircraft system, missile or shell, touch her. Of course, after she got her missiles delivered over Plant 234, she would have to try to make it out alive. That would be tricky.

She flew mere yards over the rooftops of Eden's skyscrapers, her avoidance scanning systems on alert for the mundane things which could destroy the Blackbird—a radio broadcast tower, a satellite-receiving array, a rising spire. Well away yet, using magnification on her forward scanning video, there was a vast parking lot visible. There were loading docks.

Emma Shaw's headsup before her was flashing the primary target entry points.

Gorgeous announced, rather sanctimoniously she thought, "Commander Shaw, missiles are armed for firing at pretargeted coordinates and coded launch sequence program has commenced."

"Keep me informed, Gorgeous."

"Yes, Commander."

These days, being a fighter pilot was like being a delivery driver with a dangerous route. An entire pod of missiles was pretargeted to the coordinates they needed to strike. Laser guided and video monitored, all she had to do was get their launching pad, her Blackbird, into exactly the right position for launch and they would do the rest themselves. It would have been possible to autopilot her way from this point, but it went against her grain to do so, any implication that a machine was somehow more judgementally capable than a human being offensive by its very nature.

Seconds only until target positioning.

"Final stage of firing sequence ready to commence Commander," Gorgeous told her. "At your mark."

If she'd machined it in, the thing wouldn't have been at her mark, merely when the navigational computer, and the weapons computer got their "heads" together. But that was so sterile. Some pilots, of course, preferred it that way, easing their consciences when it came to the responsibility for the missiles their aircraft launched.

Emma Shaw didn't like death on her hands, but there was no sense in playing morality games, either.

She brought the Blackbird's nose up, on perfect level for the preprogrammed altitude the weapons would require. Far below and to her left, off the portside, lay Plant 234.

A glance to the headsup, Gorgeous almost panting in her ear, Emma Shaw intoned, "Five . . . four . . . three . . . two . . . Mark!"

Firing was instantaneous, the video display at the center of her headsup activating in the same microsecond. She watched, because that was the prudent thing (and, of course, what she was supposed to do). The video display was off the lead missile, whose function was to blow a hole in the target, the principal damage to the site to be done by the follow-ups. The video display from the first missile automatically cut off just prior to detonation, the display picking up video signals now from the last of the missiles.

The first missile detonated, blowing out a segment of Plant 234's roof and west wall. Contrails from the following missiles were lost inside the smoke and dust cloud. Then, one after the other, in perfect series, explosions began rocking the structure, to its very foundations, it seemed as, one after the other, the missiles impacted.

Had she blinked, she would have missed the final seconds of video as the last of the missiles closed on Plant 234, or what remained of it. The building was folding in on itself, great billowing mushroom-shaped clouds of black smoke rising, enveloping it.

Video display was gone and, in the same instant, Gorgeous announced, "Firing sequence complete, Commander," and Emma Shaw banked the Blackbird into a steep rolling dive to starboard.

Twenty-Eight

There were no obvious observation devices in the spacious, windowless sickroom. The room was pleasantly lit, the lighting's source hard to determine. For a moment, John Rourke intentionally observed these little details, avoiding looking at his wife there on the bed.

But he turned to look at her.

Sarah Rourke was five foot seven, not extraordinarily tall for a woman of these days, yet tall enough, and definitely tall for a woman born more than six and one-half centuries ago. But she looked very, very small, very fragile, covers—a white sheet and yellow waffle-knit blanket—pulled up to just under her little chin. Her chest rose and fell regularly, evenly. John Rourke walked over to the bed, let Paul's Schmiesser—Paul had called the MP-40 that for so long, Rourke subconsciously thought of it by that name himself—fall to his side on its sling.

Sarah's head was bandaged near its crown, her auburn hair—very long and still possessed of the three gray hairs she had almost always had—visible beneath and in stark contrast to the white bandages.

Her eyelids were closed and she looked either very peacefully asleep or drugged, because they did not flutter. She was, Rourke knew, the latter. Deitrich Zimmer, her physician, had told him so and there was no reason to doubt that.

There was a solitary tube up her left nostril, and there was a solitary IV tube connected to her left arm.

"Sarah."

There was, of course, no response.

John Rourke sat on the side of the bed, reached beneath the covers and held her left hand. Her pulse was regular, strong.

He whispered hoarsely, "I'll always love you," as he closed his eyes against the tears which came now so uncontrollably . . .

Deitrich Zimmer would have considered himself inhuman had he not been moved. The optical fibers built into the very walls of the room allowed him to select any of various angles from which he could observe John Rourke sitting beside Sarah Rourke holding her hand, weeping.

Zimmer whispered to the vid-screens, "Soon she will be restored to you, my old enemy, as healthy and well as she ever was, only more so. Your wife will be perfect in every way for you and for me, but even more so for me." And then he laughed. "You'll find her a new woman."

Twenty-Nine

The Eden fighter aircraft were upon her almost before Gorgeous was able to announce them. But in combat, one didn't stand on protocol. Emma Shaw banked the Blackbird into a barrel roll, the three leaders—they were the only ones of the enemy squadron close enough to get at her for the next couple of seconds—overflying her. "Give me manual on my guns Gorgeous," Emma Shaw hissed through clenched teeth as she pulled the Blackbird so rapidly out of the roll that for a split second she almost wondered if her kidneys would continue on down to the deck.

She had the nose of the Blackbird up and the furthest away of the three Eden fighters which had overflown her targeted in the same instant that Gorgeous announced, "You have manual control, Commander."

She'd given over control to the weapons computer because as she flew out of Eden City, she'd spotted a convoy of trucks loaded with munitions and laid some missiles on them. Now, Emma Shaw activated fire control, the safeties off even before Gorgeous had

... of High Explosive Anti-Armor
... the Eden fighter and laced across its
... ng igniting the synth-fuel tanks. Emma
... ght of the fireball.

"... ive more Eden fighters approaching from—"

"Never mind, I've got 'em, Gorgeous."

"Yes, Commander."

She had them but she'd worry about them in another
few seconds. For now, the two remaining fighters out
of the original three were coming onto her in a big way.
She pulled out of the bank and climbed, outdistancing
them easily, levelling off, then diving down onto them
while they still climbed after her, the G-forces making
her regret the small meal she'd consumed before
embarking.

She saved her missiles, these two in gun range and
handily so. As the two Eden fighters started their
predictable peels away from her trajectory, Emma
Shaw let the one on her right have a burst, knowing she
would miss, then banking after the one on her left. She
came out of the dive just under him and about two
hundred yards back. She fired.

The Eden fighter's exposed fuselage underbelly took
a string of hits, the plane seeming to skip across the
clouds as if it were airbraking. Instead, it spun to
starboard and the portside wing sheered partially
away.

One of the three originals to go. Emma Shaw didn't
even look, which was dangerous but there wasn't any
time for looking. Instead, she dove, knowing that the
Eden fighter would expect her to use her aircraft's
superior speed and climb away.

He was already climbing in order to intercept her.

Wrenching her body into near nausea, Emma Shaw brought the Blackbird out of the dive and looped upward. Buzzers sounded from her computer systems, Gorgeous announcing, "This aircraft has been targeted. There is lock on by incoming enemy missile. Impact in thirty-eight seconds, Commander."

She snarled under her breath, locking her gunsights on the third aircraft as it started levelling out. She fired, fired again.

"Thirty seconds."

Emma Shaw banked to port and away from the fireball and burning debris of the third Eden fighter.

"Twenty-five seconds."

The buzzers persisted. These were not Spider Sevens after her, the Spider Sevens surface-to-air missiles. Instead, these were laser-locking Penetrator Twos, air-to-air combat missiles which doubled as tank killers. Once fired, they were independently guided, like torpedoes, homing in regardless of the distance involved until they ran out of propellant.

Her only hope was to outrun them.

Climbing as she was now, she levelled off and, in the next instant started the Blackbird into a full power dive. The leading edges of the Blackbird's wings glowed red.

Twenty-seconds until first impact.

Emma Shaw brought up the Blackbird's nose and banked to starboard, throttling out.

"Enemy missile falling back. Second and third enemy missiles fired on vectors—"

"Shut up, Gorgeous! You're depressing me."

The Blackbird's top speed was so classified that only the program test pilots knew the top end. Although she'd flown in some of the testing, she'd never been involved in speed trials.

Mach Nine and past it.

"Alert, Commander. Spider Seven surface-to-air missiles have acquired the aircraft."

"Shit."

Below her, barely visible and well off to starboard yet were the contrails of three—make it four—surface-to-air missiles.

"Additional incoming Spider Sevens have been launched, Commander Shaw. They are on intercept trajectory with this aircraft's current flight path."

Below her, there was nothing but snow, ice.

"Gimme my position on headsup and calculate position with continuous updates, Gorgeous."

"Yes, Commander Shaw."

The headsup display in her windscreen showed Tennessee rolling away beneath her. The Blackbird's speed was still increasing. The red coloration on the leading edges of the wings was bleeding back across the surface. Friction was giving her the effect of turbulence, the Blackbird becoming more difficult to control by the second.

Kentucky would be under her soon.

"A total of nine Spider Seven surface-to-air missiles have locked on to this aircraft as target, Commander Shaw. Impact will begin in exactly thirty-four seconds. Probability of evasion zero per cent."

"Fuck off, pal!"

But Emma Shaw knew that Gorgeous, however reserved he might seem, wasn't an alarmist. This was it.

She congratulated herself for getting Eden Plant 234 blotted off the map. She congratulated herself for John

Rourke's almost loving her.

There was one possible textbook solution to her dilemma. That was to launch all aft firing missiles in unison, thus giving her aircraft a speed boost and providing multiple targets for the incoming.

Also according to the manuals, to do so had a better than ninety percent probability of ripping off the aircraft's wings.

"Gorgeous, two things. First, you're a hell of a guy and if I fly again, I'll get your program, honest."

"Thank you, Commander Shaw. It has been a pleasure working with you."

"Second thing, Gorgeous. On my mark, computer fire all aft firing missiles and jettison forward firing missiles to reduce friction drag and lighten the aircraft."

"As you order, Commander Shaw. I am obligated to warn you however—"

"I know the odds. Sorry I got kinda gruff with you."

"Good luck, Commander."

Emma Shaw only nodded, as if he could see her somehow. "Four . . . three . . . two . . . Mark!"

There was a roar so loud that she screamed and the Blackbird's controls suddenly died, but the aircraft shot forward, its airspeed indicator going wild. Every alarm system in the aircraft went off, buzzers buzzing and bells ringing, systems overload announced by Gorgeous, then the plane went banking off steeply to starboard, northward.

Emma Shaw forced her right hand to move, her gloved fingers arming ejection control. First there would be cockpit separating, then retro firing, then canopy ejection and, if everything worked, maybe she wouldn't be torn limb from limb by the G-forces and her chute would open.

Maybe.

Behind her, in the aft view display, she could see the enemy missiles fizzling out, falling away.

The needle of her airspeed indicator was stuck all the way to the right. The starboard wing was vibrating, tearing away.

She folded back the firing panel.

The first finger of her right hand poised over the fire control button. She ran a mental checklist. She had both pistols, her survival knife, survival kit maps. Shit. Emma Shaw closed her eyes and pushed the button. No one had ever reported on ejection at this speed because the crash test dummies couldn't talk and, even if they could they were ripped apart.

There was a roar almost as loud as the roar when all aft firing missiles went, and a pressure in her ears that even screaming didn't help. Automatically, a distress signal would be sent out, if the equipment hadn't failed. The United States was very good about going after pilots downed in enemy territory, she reminded herself. She spoke the language, could pass—if she made it to the ground at all.

Canopy separation.

"Ohh, Jesus!"

The rush of wind against the few exposed patches of facial skin was bitterly cold.

There was a roar and she felt herself shooting upward, her body molding into the contours of the cockpit seat.

The roar stopped and there was an instant of total deathly silence.

Now there was a new roar, the roar starting as a hiss, the hiss becoming a wail, then a scream, then so loud that again she screamed to protect herself from it but she couldn't hear herself screaming at all.

The seat restraints would release her automatically if everything worked right. That would be in seconds.

Below her and far to the northeast she saw the Blackbird, the starboard wing breaking off, the aircraft bouncing through the clouds as if it were rolling over obstacles, then the wing totally gone. Now the Blackbird flipped left, the portside wing snapping away. The fuselage began to tumble then, end over end, cartwheeling, then just exploding.

Emma Shaw's main chute billowed out but did not open and in the pit of her stomach she had a sinking feeling like she'd had when her mother died. The seat restraints had not released her and her chute would never open.

Falling. She was falling and she was trapped in her damn cockpit seat and she was going to die. No!

Falling, spinning, then tumbling head over heels her stomach churning, the blood racing to her head she groped for the knife that was her one hope. Her survival knife was impossible for her to reach. But there was a little knife she always carried in her flight suit, a little knife she'd found in Lancer's once. Just recently, and years after she had purchased it, she'd discovered John Rourke had one just like it only his was an original. It was a B&D/Executive Edge Grande. The size of an ordinary pen, it locked open to a full length scalpel-sharp blade of 420 stainless steel. It was clipped, like a pen, into one of the little pouches on her sleeve.

She had taught herself to open it one-handed, but wouldn't risk that now, couldn't, her body still rolling head over heels.

Emma Shaw was close to blacking out.

She had the Executive Edge Grande open, slipped it under the seat restraint near the edge closest in to the seat, but still accessible. There would never be time to cut the *X* of harness fully apart, but she was small enough that if she could just cut this one segment, she might be able to wriggle free under the harness.

Then, if the chute she wore on her body would work—if there was enough time—she could—

She had it, almost.

The Executive Edge Grande sawed through the last portion of the webbing and immediately the seat was out of balance and the spinning turned to radical tilting and lurching and she thought for an instant that her body would be ripped to pieces, like the test dummies had been.

There was no time to close the knife. She threw it away promising herself that if she made it she'd buy another one. Her body was already slipping out of the chair and she lurched downward, the *V* which formed the uppermost portion of the harness *X* fouled in her oxygen mask. She was slipping still further, choking now. Her hands fought the webbing, twisting, tearing at it, all futilely.

The chair flip-flopped and suddenly she was free of the rigging and she was tumbling. She forced apart her arms and her legs, trying to stabilize herself, spread-eagling, like a snow angel in the mountains that rose above her little house. If she tried opening her chute now, it would foul and never open at all.

The ground was racing up toward her so fast that there would never be time for the auxilliary chute, maybe wasn't time for this primary chute either. But to give up was the ultimate sin. There was an automatically activated altimeter on Emma Shaw's chest pack, but there wasn't the time for her to look at it.

She was stable.

She flipped the release for the safety. She pulled the cord.

Emma Shaw was snapped upward, shoulders wrenching, neck aching, her back on fire with pain for an instant.

Her hands reached up, to grab the shroud lines.

She was slowing.

Her chute was fully opened and she swayed sickeningly over the snowfield below.

Emma Shaw breathed.

It was likely that she had been picked up on some aircraft sensing device employed by the Eden forces. And that would mean the bad guys would be looking for her sooner than the good guys. She would have to move. But as her eyes surveyed the unrelieved whiteness below her, Emma Shaw had no idea which way to go.

Thirty

There was nothing for it but to leave Annie and Natalia behind to protect Michael's cryogenic chamber from Zimmer's Nazis.

John Rourke knew that, but as the Nazi aircraft which he had just boarded—a V-Stol that was identical except in its markings to the state-of-the-art models of New Germany—went airborne, he looked past Paul's shoulder and honestly wondered if he would ever see his daughter and his dear friend again.

Hauptsturmführer Gunther Spitz called to him from the other side of the fuselage, "Herr Doctor General! What is your first order?"

John Thomas Rourke looked at the man and smiled. "To stop addressing me as 'Herr Doctor General.' Doctor or just Rourke will be fine. And my second order is that you remember one thing: Anyone who doesn't do exactly as Mr. Rubenstein or I say gets killed. If you or your men try anything after we have recovered the remains, they'll be of very little use to Dr. Zimmer because they'll be destroyed. And my third order is just as important. Centuries ago, there was a wonderful television series and subsequently there were movies as well; they dealt with a group of men and women going off to explore the stars. They had what was called a 'prime directive' which had to be followed at almost any cost. This is yours: Don't go into this thinking that we're going to kill everyone who happens to get into our way. Judging from what intelligence data I was given by Dr. Zimmer, the society where the remains you seek may be hidden has been unmolested by outside influences for more than six hundred years. There is no reason to destroy it. We'll do what we must in order to achieve the objective and nothing more. The first man of you who violates that dictum will pay with his life in the very next instant."

Hauptsturmführer Spitz leaned back in his seat, drumming his fingers on the table near him. The interior of the aircraft was luxuriously appointed, much as then-Colonel Mann's craft had been more than a century ago. It was designed to be a highly mobile office, an "Air Force One" as it were.

John Rourke looked at Wolfgang Mann now, the Generaloberst sitting alone, staring off through one of the windows as the aircraft climbed. Rourke knew the feeling of disorientation Mann must be experiencing only too well. One closed one's eyes in one era and opened them in what could only be viewed as the distant future.

And, this future was hardly appealing.

The last coded transmission Rourke had seen from the deep dive mission assisting Thorn Rolvaag before embarking, indicated that Rolvaag had discovered a previously undiscovered suboceanic trench of incredibly vast proportions.

Nothing needed to be said further. With the suddenly heightening volcanic activity in the Hawaiian islands, and the discovery of a new El Ninio well off what had been the coast of Ecuador, this new trench might indeed be the harbinger of the end, not manmade this time, but certainly man assisted.

And, here he was, going in search of the remains of the body of Adolf Hitler, an unholy mission in a wholly selfish cause.

And nagging at John Rourke still, was a question the answer to which he might not realize until it was too late: Why had Doctor Zimmer returned Wolfgang Mann and why—certainly not out of any desire to do the decent thing—had Deitrich Zimmer performed the life-saving surgery required by Sarah?

Although he had been at the top of his class in medical school more than six centuries ago, John Rourke's skills by comparison to medicine of today were more analogous to those of a crafty tribal shaman. But could it be possible that in the very act of restoring Sarah Rourke, Zimmer had done something even more despicable than when he had originally shot her one hundred and twenty-five years ago?

John Rourke clapped Paul Rubenstein on the shoulder, unbuckled his seat restraint and left Paul, walked aft along the fuselage and sat down beside Wolfgang Mann. Paul looked back once, then took out his diary.

Before Rourke could speak with Mann, Gunther Spitz called out to Paul, "And, what is it that you do there, Jew?"

The muscles around Paul's eyes tensed slightly, but

189

Paul smiled as he responded, "Well, damn Nazi, I tell you—"

Hauptsturmführer Spitz's entire body seemed to tense. Paul's left hand was under the table, near the butt of his second Browning High Power.

Paul continued to speak. "I'm writing a log, as it were, a diary but, more than that, a history. After a section is filled in by hand, it's transfered to a universally translatable hard disc. Someday, there'll be a record of what has happened since the Night of the War. A personal record. Documents such as this can be invaluable to the historian. I began it after our airliner crashed during the Night of the War, before your great-great-grandfather was a tickle in his father's pants." And Paul smiled broadly. "And, as to being Jewish, I am. And proud, too. We survived, despite what your spiritual antecedents tried doing to us during World War II. We helped to build a better world. We helped to promote understanding. You did nothing but destroy. To the enlightened man, Jew, Christian, Moslem, the label doesn't matter, really. It's what a man or woman does, who they are as a person, not anything else that truly matters. I'm sure, for example, that if I looked really hard—although admittedly it would be challenging—I might even be able to find a Nazi who didn't deserve to be exterminated from the face of the Earth."

Spitz nearly tore away his seat restraint, rose abruptly from his seat.

John Rourke's hands were near his waistband, ready to touch the two Scoremasters there. But, this was Paul's play and Rourke would only interfere if his friend needed him.

As Hauptsturmführer Gunther Spitz stared across the aisle, Paul—looking for all the world like a gunfighting gambler from a western movie—moved his left hand forward under the table. The second Browning High Power was tight in Paul's fist, the hammer back. "To keep from punching a hole in the aircraft, I'll keep all my shots in your chest. Your move."

Gunther Spitz just stood there, limbs shaking with rage.

His men, collecting around him, were ready to follow his lead.

Paul said nothing, merely kept the pistol still under the table—aimed at Hauptsturmführer Gunther Spitz's center of mass.

Gunther Spitz snarled, "Our hour will come, Jew."

"Any time, Nazi."

Gunther Spitz nodded to his people and sat down again, rotating his chair in order to put his back to Paul, perhaps as a show of defiance.

When John Rourke looked back at Paul the High Power had already disappeared.

Rourke turned to look at Wolfgang Mann beside him. They sat on a U-shaped couch much like a conventional Twentieth Century sectional sofa, positioned just forward of the aft bulkhead, behind them one of the lavatories, the galley area and some storage space. Since John Rourke cared nothing for the company with the exception of Paul and Wolfgang Mann, and he knew that neither man was bothered by cigar smoke, Rourke took one of his thin, dark tobacco cigars from the outside patch pocket of his bomber jacket.

The jacket had recently been cleaned, and rapidly so after being impregnated with volcanic ash during the abortive attempt to rescue young Martin, an affair which had resulted in his son's death. Rourke shook his head in disgust. The tip of the cigar was already excised. Rourke placed the cigar between his teeth and flicked open the cowling of his battered old Zippo windlighter. He rolled the striking wheel under his thumb, the lighter's blue yellow flame rising at once. Rourke held the flame beneath the cigar, drawing the fire up into it. Once the cigar was lit he exhaled, then rolled it to the corner of his mouth. "It is good to see you again, Wolf."

"And you, John."

"Tell me, Wolf, what do you remember concerning the time after you were awakened."

"Why do you ask? Surely, you have experienced the same sensations."

"Curiosity. Please, indulge me."

Wolfgang Mann cleared his throat, lit a cigarette. "It was very bewildering at first." And then he laughed a little. "I was thirsty and, no matter how much water I drank, I could not slake my thirst."

"Are you thirsty now, Wolf?"

"No; I am fine. Why do you ask?"

"Curiosity. Cryogenic sleep affects every person differently. I felt terribly stiff."

"I did not, oddly, but I would have thought that I would."

John Rourke merely nodded, then closed his eyes. Thirst, beyond wetting one's mouth, was not really a problem after cryogenic sleep. Neither of the children—they were adults now, of course—had ever

192

complained of it, nor had Sarah, or Paul or Natalia. Rourke had never experienced it either. On the other hand, thirst was common after some types of anesthesia. And muscle stiffness—from the inactivity—was intense. One felt weak as the proverbial kitten following awakening. Yet Wolfgang Mann had not experienced this and, indeed, the Generaloberst's walk as he had approached their aircraft earlier had seemed more or less normal. Yet Mann had been decidedly fuzzy-sounding, as if drugged.

One of the keys to Deitrich Zimmer's successful microsurgery was the appliances he constructed, then used—surgical tools of his own creation.

John Rourke respected that rare thing known as genius wherever he happened to find it, and Zimmer possessed it. Had Zimmer somehow found something else to do with his tools?

John Rourke opened his eyes.

Wolfgang Mann had returned to gazing out the window. There was nothing to see but clouds, beautiful to be sure but repetitive, always the same.

John Rourke flicked ashes from his cigar into one of the ashtrays permanently set into the coffee table, anchored to the floor in front of him. He took from his clothes the primary map he would use of the terrain surrounding the mountain enclave. It was an aerial recon photo transposed over a topographical map. From the look of things, it would be an easy enough climb to the presumed site of the main entrance, but that would not be the way to get inside, a fact which no doubt had not eluded Deitrich Zimmer. One could not, after all, just knock, then announce, "I'm sorry to bother you, but I've come to pick up something you

193

probably don't know you have—the remains of Adolf Hitler?"

No, Rourke almost verbalized. Entry to the facility would have to be through some more subtle means.

He was experienced with this sort of arrangement, of course. His own Retreat (now a museum in Eden), the Soviet Underground City in the Urals of more than a century ago, New Germany's heart in Argentina.

All of these facilities, including his own, had one central theme, that the outside and the inside were hermetically sealed away from each other, at least to begin with. That this civilization had not come out onto the surface again either meant that it—the civilization itself—had collapsed or that their system was so efficient as to preclude any necessity of venturing onto the surface. A true underground city, as the Russian and German facilities had been until the atmosphere outside was sufficiently restored.

Perhaps, although that seemed incredible, these persons had no idea that the surface was, at least for the moment inhabitable, had been so for well over a century and a half.

If the entire facility were sealed and there was no interchange between the inside and the outside world, then the only means of access would be explosives. John Rourke had planned ahead for that.

But what he hoped to find instead, was some sort of service entrance, perhaps for the removal of waste gases, but for whatever reason a connection between the outside and the inside.

And the heat signature near the very top of the mountain well to the north of what appeared to be a vast, gently sloping plateau, suggested just that.

194

He hoped.

If the society within the mountain had grown, progressed, if for nothing else than the cleaning of their environment, they would have such a waste gas cleaning vent. There was no data to support Rourke's theory beyond the suggestion of a heat signature but he clung to that nonetheless, his best hope.

Thirty-One

According to technical specifications, her flight suit would protect her, keep her comfortable to temperature extremes to twenty degrees fahrenheit, and was windproof, of course.

Evidently the temperature was lower.

Emma Shaw was cold.

She wasn't freezing, yet. But, she wasn't comfortable either.

Nothing but snow and ice.

Her primary chute was folded and partially stowed in its pack. The high-strength windproof synth-silk could be utilized for a variety of purposes—she might make it into a coat in a little while—and the paracord could prove useful as well in a survival situation.

Her Lancer pistol was still in the issue holster, but the Government Model .45—she'd been hanging around John Rourke too long, and her father too, Emma Shaw thought—was in her hand, chamber loaded, cocked and locked. Emma still wore her helmet, as it would protect her head from the effects of the cold, and the oxygen mask was still in place, but switched from the oxygen supply to filtering environmental air. This warmed the air a little before she breathed it.

Snow crunched under her flight boots as she traversed what seemed to be a vast, featureless plain. By her survival compass, she was moving northward, only because according to her escape map—it was printed on synth-silk and tied around her throat now for warmth—there were human habitations to the north that were not under control of the Eden government.

She could survive a few nights out here if she had to, and as it appeared now she would probably have to do just that, but eventually Eden forces would track her down, before her own people could get there to extract her. Alone, here in the wilderness, her grey flight suit sticking out like a sore thumb against the whiteness of the landscape, she could not help being discovered.

At last, after walking for what she judged was four miles or so, Emma Shaw stopped. She shouldered out of her flight harness and began to utilize the parachute. Using her survival knife she cut a neck hole and two wrist holes in double thicknesses of the synth-silk parachute. In this manner she would be warmer and less visible from the air. She wore a transponding device which would home in rescue forces, so she didn't need to be observable. And the parachute would still be large enough to utilize as a shelter, if it came to that—the tube shelter in her survival pack somehow was probably not warm enough. In order to have ready-made guys for the shelter, she cut off only a portion of the paracord, weaving what remained attached into modified hangman's nooses. The rest of the cord she coiled and stuffed into her harness pack, out of which the chute had originally come.

When she cut the holes in the synth-silk chute she did so in such a manner that nothing was excised. Therefore with the emergency sewing materials in her survival kit, she could close any holes if need be, should the weather turn really severe.

Emma made herself a cold meal using the rations sparingly. She had a four-day supply, but how was she to know if that would be enough?

Eyes casting down to glance at the radiation counter in her chest pack, she trudged onward again warmer somewhat (once she got moving again) with her synth-silk poncho. From above she might look like some giant, mobile mound of snow.

After what she judged to be another mile the terrain started to break up and simultaneously rise. And there, ice was more prevalent than snow. She was deep into the glacier now.

Another mile onward—she was becoming very tired and needed to rest, perhaps eat again, the cold multiplying the effect of the exertion—and the land just stopped. Before her lay a chasm, incredibly wide and more importantly, seemingly impassable.

At its center, perhaps two hundred yards below, coursed a river, blue and silver like a ribbon.

Emma Shaw was beginning to worry that sometime during the various twists and turns and bumps and jars her body had endured, she might have done some real damage to herself. Her head ached. That could be shock, even a mild concussion, or maybe a compression fracture.

At least, as best she had been able to discern before picking herself up off the ground, nothing seemed broken.

What to do, she wondered.

And then, as she scanned the far wall of the chasm in detail through her small field glasses, she realized what her best chance might be. If she could take the near wall downward, perhaps here, as in the far wall, there would be caves. If she could rest, perhaps for the night, she would feel better, warmer too. A fire might even be possible.

And the river itself might be her way out. It seemed free flowing enough. As a part of her standard kit there was a single-person inflatable life raft. The things were cramped and not the sort of boat one would use for a pleasure cruise. But she might be able to use the raft to carry her downriver. This river eventually would flow to the sea.

Once she located a port of some sort, it wouldn't be that hard to find the local anti-Eden forces, or she could just connect her emergency beacon to a satellite dish and bring in the troops.

Of course none of these ideas might work at all but convincing herself that they would, Emma Shaw began to climb very carefully downward along the chasm wall in search of a cave in which to spend the night.

Thirty-Two

The Nazi V-stol touched down with amazing delicacy.

Immediately, the fuselage door was opened and Hauptsturmführer Gunther Spitz's personnel exited into the snow. The last of them was the mortuary sciences specialist, a man named Krause.

Snow was heavy here and deep in the niches and depressions, but the rock face itself was smooth and reasonably level, blown clean of snow in the nearly gale force wind. The wind was a further tribute to the pilot's skills.

The glacial ice was far below them now. Here at the summit of the mountain they could see literally for miles. The only hint of civilization was the thought of that which might have survived within the mountain beneath them. If it had, it had remained untouched for six hundred and twenty-five years.

John Rourke, in his black arctic parka now, but the snorkel hood down and the front of the coat open so he could access his pistols, despite the cold, jumped down from the V-stol. Unslinging his HK-91, then loading the chamber, Rourke started ahead, bending his frame into the wind as he trod over the plateau and toward the ultimate summit. The men fell in around him, Paul close beside him.

"There wasn't anything at all?"

"Not a thing showed up on the aerial photography, nothing showed up on the aircraft's sensors. Overflew it three times, then twice more for good measure, as you know." Rourke shrugged his shoulders. "If they've got anything, it's more sophisticated than anything anyone's operating with, more sophisticated than anything we could imagine."

"That's crazy," Paul observed. "No defenses, no detection devices."

"Could be a community of pacifists," Rourke noted, but not quite convinced that this was the reason for no apparent defenses, no radar or any sort of sensing equipment. "After the Night of the War and the Great Conflagration, God only knows what people who survived might turn to. They might view something as basic as self-defense as an intrinsic evil. Many persons claimed to believe that even prior to the Night of the War; and, of course, there were some very sincere Christian religious sects which held those beliefs. I always believed that brotherly love was something certainly to strive for, but that making self-defense moral anathema was tantamout to suicide."

"And you think there's a vent up here, for getting rid of poisonous exhaust gases? And that's it."

"Maybe. Either that vent provides us the access we require or we plant explosives and then have the

V-stol's missiles or plasma guns detonate them. But that could cause a lot of death and destruction inside. So, hope there's a vent, Paul."

The younger man nodded.

Snow crunched under Rourke's boots as he dug in his heels against the gradually steepening grade. The wind which blew here on the mountain top was bitterly cold, but somehow very clean, refreshing, and because of that almost pleasant. The V-stol's overflights had confirmed what the intelligence data had suggested very strongly—that there was no radiation danger here, that the air, despite its natural thinness at this latitude and elevation, was perfectly breathable.

In fact, it smelled fresher than he had remembered air smelling for a very long time.

But then John Rourke shouted, "Fall back! Fall back! Gas!" John Rourke turned, ran, Paul beside him, the younger man already staggering. One of the Nazis, the medical doctor, who was also a specialist in cryogenics, collapsed. And John Rourke would need him very desperately. Besides that, Nazi or no, the fellow was a human being. Rourke shoved Paul Rubenstein toward Gunther Spitz shouting, "Care for him or die!" Then inhaling deeply of what he hoped was good air, Rourke raced back.

If this were nerve gas, Rourke and everyone with him was close to dead already. Rourke grabbed up the doctor, hauled him into a fireman's carry and turned, nearly stumbled, light-headed, then threw himself into a lurching run.

Paul seemed all right, from ahead started running back to join him. They met, Paul grabbing the man from Rourke's shoulder, taking the doctor over his shoulder. Rourke stumbled. Paul reached for him. Rourke shook his head, waved Paul ahead. Rourke pulled himself to his feet, then ran on.

The others were huddled about the aircraft, coughing, but apparently unharmed. As Rourke joined them, he sagged to his knees in the snow, breathed tentatively. The air smelled normal not sweet. "Back into the aircraft. Seal everything. Hurry!" Paul was the first up, the Nazi doctor over his shoulder still.

And John Rourke cursed his carelessness. He was, after all, looking for an outlet vent where poisonous gases generated by industry or waste management could be purged from within. Perhaps this was a defensive system, perhaps not. Either way—it had achieved the same purpose.

And he had found what he had detected from the photo reconnaissance. "We suit up before we venture out again. Come on," Rourke ordered.

He could have gotten them killed.

They hurried into the aircraft, John Rourke suddenly realizing that his face was beaming with a smile. On the floor of the aircraft, in what formed a center aisle between the comfortable lounge chairs and the small work tables, Paul had the Nazi doctor lying flat and was administering coronary/pulmonary resuscitation.

Hauptsturmführer Gunther Spitz just stared in amazement . . .

Emma Shaw's eyes squinted against the darkness. At

204

last she closed her eyes and counted to ten, then opened them again. The .45 in her hand felt as comforting as the teddy bear she'd slept with as a little girl. But when she was little, she never let teddy go first. She let the .45 go first, holding it out ahead of her as though it were some sort of magic talisman, very much like a teddy bear, and would keep the evil of the darkness away.

But unlike when she was a little girl, it wasn't imaginary monsters of which she was afraid, but men or animals. She'd heard that bears and wolves had been released into the countryside by the Eden City officials, to restock nature. That was fine, but she didn't care to have a chat about ecology with either. And because the government of Eden seemed almost intent on disaffecting the population, large numbers of persons had either formed independent and sometimes quite primitive societies outside Eden's direct sphere of influence and gangs of Land Pirates and solitary roving thugs roamed at will in the wilderness areas. These latter might be worse than wolves or bears.

Some things had not survived the Great Conflagration, and as best she could tell among those were bats. She realized full well that the majority of these flying mammals were thoroughly harmless creatures but she wouldn't have enjoyed finding this cave to be full of them. Their very representation in an old book or in some of the vid films from the twentieth century made her skin crawl.

But the cave, more of a deep niche in the rock, seemed uninhabited.

Emma Shaw shone her handflash and inspected the cave in greater detail. There was no debris to show that wild creatures had used this as a home. And she could see why. It was a little cramped. She could stand up, but only barely. Someone the height of John Rourke would have been forced to stoop over.

There was a solitary rock, almost inviting in its way, begging her to be seated on something besides cold snow and ice. She accepted the invitation and sat on the rock. It didn't feel half bad. Her .45 was in her right hand, the flashlight in her left. If she got out of this—
WHEN! Emma Shaw reminded herself—she might decide to come back here someday and take the rock back and put it in the living room of her house.

She could always paint it, stencil it. Some women did that sort of thing.

Most women didn't do *this* sort of thing. She sat on the rock, exhaled.

The cave would have to do.

The first order of survival after remembering not to panic was to keep one's body in shape, whether that meant food or water or warmth or shelter. She had everything for that.

She took a swallow from her emergency water ration but only a small one, then took out a partially eaten high energy bar, slowly, almost savoringly consuming the rest of it. And she thought.

Over the course of her several miles of walking, she had considered just where she might be. The Blackbird's airspeed indicator had gone off the gauge when she activated the rear firing rockets. And she had already been at maximum, the aircraft's wings glowing red from heat despite the frigid air temperatures. It seemed clear that she was exceeding what the aircraft was built for, and the classified maximum speed was staggering to contemplate. She read a story once about a pilot who so exceeded the speed of ordinary aircraft that he travelled through time. That was impossible at least as far as she knew. But she had travelled through a considerable distance.

The terrain feature beside which she rested in this nichelike cave was not on the map—at least not the map of the southeastern portion of the North American continent.

Had she overflown her area of operations by such a considerable margin that she was in what had been the Northeastern United States?

She was beginning to think so.

And these days, this was essentially uncharted territory.

Some settlements were here, and there were supposedly some few gangs of Land Pirates. That was all. The land was too forbidding for anyone to wish to claim it, although it was—technically speaking—under the control of Eden.

She wished she'd studied geography with more enthusiasm when she'd been in school. Perhaps she would have been able to recognize what river this was which flowed outside. And through what area it passed.

Mentally Emma Shaw stuck to her plan, however, holding fast to its eventual efficacy. Even in the harshest of climates, where a river met the sea there was at least some sort of settlement, however small. If she followed this river long enough she would reach the sea, reach that settlement. Then she could effect her own rescue.

Failing a belief in that, she was stuck.

There was no sign of game, a fact which at once both heartened and dismayed her. In the absence of game, there'd be no predators. But without game she would run out of food all too soon. Then what, she asked herself?

Stuck. No food. No hope.

Her best chance would be that the Land Pirates got her, and decided she was too pretty to kill—and Emma Shaw smiled thinking there was a fat chance of that.

Thirty-Three

The V-stol, on Rourke's orders, went airborne again, moving back several miles distant from the mountain top. With the help of the restored Nazi doctor, a man named Mentz, John Rourke took blood samples from each of the men of the party, himself included.

John Rourke had planned ahead. In order to preserve the cursed remains which they sought, it might be necessary to have chemical analysis equipment. For that reason, among other items, there was a computer, which was designed to sniff and otherwise scan trace elements and identify their nature. The blood samples were run through the computer, its monitor flashing up the entire chemical composition in less time than it took Rourke to light his cigar.

"What is this?" Mentz began. "These elements—"

"It's just what I thought it would be, at least in part," John Rourke said very slowly, his voice almost a whisper. "Paul? Take a look, will you."

After a second, Paul Rubenstein was beside him.

Rourke vacated his seat before the terminal and Paul slid in. "Look familiar? Think 1960s."

"LSD?"

John Rourke smiled. "Not in the traditional formula, but evidently gasified and with carriers. Yes."

Doctor Mentz asked, "You mean the halucinogen?"

"Yes. Apparently, unless there's some other reason for it that I can't begin to comprehend, somebody down inside the mountain likes to keep people happy—whether they like it or not—and kill them at the same time. Other elements of the formula were clearly poisonous, and lethally so."

John Rourke called forward to the pilot, "Captain—have your copilot take over. I need a conference." He might need more than that . . .

Wearing a chemical decontamination suit with full self-contained respiration was rather like wearing scuba gear, but on land it was grossly uncomfortable. It was light in weight, to be sure, but one was forever conscious of wearing it.

Paul Rubenstein didn't like it.

It was toward dusk when the V-stol touched down again and they disembarked, their weapons at the ready, the pilot ordered to go airborne and select a suitable safe landing site, then wait there to be contacted or return in twenty-four hours.

This time they were more careful in approaching the site of the supposed vent.

Various members of the party were equipped with everything from heavy weapons to ultrasensitive devices for sensing everything from radiation to gas to high frequency sound or light.

There was a great deal of chatter in German going on in his ear through the helmet mounted radio. Paul Rubenstein could not understand it, but he knew that John could, and perfectly (although John did not speak German as well as Natalia). Natalia was a veritable polyglot, naturally gifted in languages, with the accents to match.

They passed the point where the gas had overtaken them the first time and Paul Rubenstein could hear the voice of the Doctor, Mentz, saying in English, "My corpsman reports that we are in a cloud of gas identical in composition to that which we identified before. It is becoming more dense."

"Thank you Doctor." John Rourke answered. "Please maintain the English language updates for the benefit of Mr. Rubenstein."

"Of course, Herr Doctor."

Beside John, Wolfgang Mann walked along, spryly enough, Paul Rubenstein supposed. Yet there was still something odd about the once Colonel, now General-oberst. Perhaps it was muscle or joint stiffness, after the cryogenic sleep, but his mannerisms held the hint of almost mechanical detachment.

Why?

John's voice came again. "We're approaching a slightly visible concentration. Can you confirm that as the source, Dr. Mentz?"

"A moment, please, Dr. Rourke." There was a pause, Rubenstein hearing the mortician Krause, saying something which sounded disagreeable, even

211

without translation. Then Dr. Mentz's voice returned, "That is the origin, Herr Doctor."

"All right. Everyone on alert," John cautioned, then, presumably, repeated his warning in German. The officers spoke perfect English, but the enlisted personnel did not, although most of them understood well enough, Paul deduced.

The party had reached the very pinnacle of the mountain top, and indeed there was a crack in the face of the rock, from below which gas emerged in a cloud just faintly visible dissipating almost immediately in the wind. "Scan this, gentlemen," John ordered.

Hauptsturmführer Spitz said, "It is not natural in formation, but made to appear so, I think—some type of metal framework within and stretching downward until it is beyond the range of the instruments. The material above it is a form of synth-concrete, or something very similar. The metal is an alloy with which the scanning device is not familiar."

"So, they do have technology," Paul observed, forgetting that everyone was able to listen.

"Indeed," John remarked, "And it would seem they haven't stagnated over the intervening centuries, either."

"And now what, Doctor Rourke?" Spitz asked after a moment.

John Rourke answered him very quickly, evidently already decided upon a course of action. "This doesn't appear to be in place for defensive means, so it may still be reasonable to assume that the people down below don't know we're here. Dr. Mentz?"

"Yes Doctor Rourke?"

"Would you concur that the suits and equipment we wear should protect us from this gas, no matter what the concentration in parts per million?"

"I should think so sir."

"Good. Spitz, get your people to take this cap off the outlet vent and do it as neatly and quietly as possible. The gas must be bled off because it's too dangerous to try to clean from the atmosphere. This appeared to be the only heat source in the aerials. That might mean that this is the only chink in their armor. We have to exploit it."

"I am in agreement Herr Doctor," Gunther Spitz answered.

John Rourke nodded.

Paul Rubenstein was beginning to picture what they might find below, and he didn't like what he saw . . .

Darkness had fallen so abruptly within the gorge that it was, almost literally, as if someone had dropped night's curtain on some sort of stage play.

Emma Shaw had a fire going, a small one, and it was necessary to waft the smoke away toward the mouth of the cave, and even at that, there was still an acrid smell. Her emergency gear had battery-operated heating coils and she would sleep warm in the night without the fire, but for now she used it to ward off the feelings of aloneness. Somehow her flashlight just didn't make it in that department.

After heating a small amount of canteen water and mixing it with a soup packet—the result was something thick and yellowish and gluey tasting but supposedly terribly nutritious—she had set about checking the raft that would be her ticket out of here, she hoped.

The raft's inflation directions were something every pilot had memorized, but she read through them again just to be on the safe side.

Then she lit a cigarette, rationing these as well. She had a pack with fifteen remaining in it and a fresh, unopened pack. She lit the cigarette from the fire, not willing to waste a lifeboat-style match on it.

In the morning, before she set out on the raft (and after she found a safe way into the bottom of the gorge), she would check the river for radiation levels and, assuming they were satisfactory, do some fishing. Some rivers in the North American continent had been restocked in the early days after the return of the Eden Project and a precious few had somehow retained a modest level of life, even after the Great Conflagration. If she could supplement her food supply, that would be helpful. As a little girl, she'd gone fishing in the ocean with her dad and her brother quite a number of times and she wasn't half bad at it.

There was always the faint possibility—at least she hoped it was no more than that—that the river would be too hot in radiation level and then not only would she not be able to fish but she would not want to risk using the raft, either. If that were the case it would be better to climb up the other side of the gorge (once she figured a safe way across the river) and then continue northward.

Before lighting her fire, but after making certain that she was in a defensible position, she used her radio compass and got her position off one of the satellites.

They were not all in place yet and so it was only possible in this general geographic area to tap in between the hours of six and nine, roughly speaking. By comparing the coordinates that her instrument was passively fed with—her pocket navigation computer— she had her position to within a quarter of a mile.

Actual position, however, told her little. She knew where she was, but not what was where she was supposed to be. She was south of Lake Ontario and east of Lake Erie at roughly 42 degrees north latitude and at 76 degrees west longitude. If she headed straight east she would eventually bump into the Atlantic Ocean sooner or later. And the river flowed generally south and eastward.

It was the "eventually" part which worried Emma Shaw, and all the little things along the way.

If the river proved exceedingly navigable, it might be that the Land Pirates used it as well. Supposedly, Eden forces and their Nazi allies periodically swept these areas, and occasionally used them for cold-weather training exercises. That might be another problem.

At last, Emma Shaw put out her cigarette, then began to put out the fire.

The paper-thin sleeping bag was already prewarming as she tested it with her hands. A good night's sleep would give her a fresh perspective on her plans. Why had she not begun to execute them earlier? If the enemy were on her trail, she wouldn't get away from them on a little raft on the river anyway.

Emma Shaw took off her boots then slipped inside the bag. Once inside, she skinned out of her flightsuit, leaving the one-piece outfit inside the bag just in case.

Before settling in, she removed the magazine from her .45, cleared the chamber, replaced the once-chambered round into the top of the magazine then reinserted the magazine up the well.

Emma Shaw had no desire to shoot herself accidentally during the night, but she wanted to be as ready as she could—for anything.

With her right fist closed on the butt of the chamber-empty pistol, she closed her eyes and hoped she could make herself go to sleep.

Thirty-Four

Tim Shaw's driver, Bob Bilsom, left the car on auto-control too much for Shaw's tastes, but Tim Shaw had learned long ago that a sideseat driver was a pain in the ass. So he said nothing.

It was almost four in the afternoon, a rainy day in Honolulu and the skies already dark from the rising plumes of volcanic ash and the permanent clouds they made. It was, in a way, nearly as black as night.

His attention was divided, split between the job at hand and thoughts of his daughter, shot down over enemy territory. A friend—Commander Washington to be precise—had sneaked the news to him, telling him that even though the top-secret aircraft Emma had flown was down, there was no reason to suppose that she was dead, or even injured. She was as good as they came in pilots—Tim Shaw already knew that—and the aircraft type she flew had state-of-the-art pilot-escape devices incorporated into its design. Washington's encouragement and Shaw's own innate confidence in his daughter's abilities didn't make it easier to accept.

He was relatively safe, playing cops and robbers with a bunch of Nazi terrorists in Honolulu, and Emma, if indeed she was still alive, was stuck in the middle of God-only-knew-where with the Eden Forces at her heels.

"Shit."

"Whatchya say, Tim?"

"I said, 'shit,' Bobby. That's what I fuckin' said."

"Hey, Emma's got balls, Tim, ya know."

Under some circumstances, Tim Shaw would have considered the remark a veiled request for a punch in the mouth, but he knew Bob Bilsom considered it a compliment, words of encouragement, "Right, but I still say 'shit,' Bobby."

"Yeah."

Shaw shook his head and folded out the dashboard computer console, flashing up the street map and acquiring the overhead video monitoring position of the truck convoy then putting the position into the map. The convoy, three blocks up and two blocks over on James Madison Way, was moving right along, no sign as yet that it had attracted the Nazis.

But logic said that it had to.

The terrorist band which had launched the hit against Emma's place in the mountains was the same group which had hit Sebastian's Cove Country Day School. Tim Shaw and his son Ed's SWAT Team had hit them where they were in hiding and knocked out a half-dozen members of the team, found weapons, explosives, maps showing targets, the whole nine yards.

218

But all of the targets would have been changed, and the terrorists had evidently made contact with local Fifth Columnists to supplement for the manpower loss.

And this was only one group. How many Nazi units were in the Islands was anyone's guess with Eden on the verge of attack.

So far, however, this was the group that was making the most noise and, for a variety of reasons, Tim Shaw wanted them. He could live with the volcanic ash, he could live with the rain, he could live with the threat of more vulcanism and war. In a way he could even live with Emma's being shot down, because she did have balls, real hang-tough-when-it-counts guts. If anyone could make it back out of enemy territory, Emma could.

But these guys, the Nazis he was trying to lure with an irresistible (but not too irresistible) trap, had killed children. For that they'd die.

He switched the console so it would superimpose the map image over the actual video image of the truck convoy. The image was blurry because of the rain, and grey like everything else.

"Think they'll tumble to this, Tim?"

Tim Shaw stared hard at the computer screen's video display. There was a blue van perfectly matching the speed of the convoy, about a hundred yards back from the rear vehicle, the one with the Shore Patrol in it.

"Tumble to it, Bobby? Yeah, I think they did. Here." And Tim Shaw reached over and grabbed for the radio set on the driver's side of the dashboard. This radio was linked to the Shore Patrol, the one on Shaw's own passenger side linked to the police units that were part of the setup. "Watchdog to Lamb, Watchdog to Lamb. You're waggin' your tail. Over."

"Read you loud and clear, Watchdog. Lamb standing by and out."

Shaw plugged the handset back into the dashboard then grabbed the second radio. "This is Shaw. We got some action. Nobody fuckin' moves till we got 'em ready for the bag. Stand by your radios. Shaw. Out." He reached under his raincoat and the suitcoat beneath it, grabbing the Colt auto. He racked the .45's slide, then upped the safety. Shaw returned the gun to his waistband; carrying it cocked and locked so near to his crotch, even though he trusted the gun and always had, gave him the creeps. He reached into the right pocket of his raincoat, snatched out the three-inch barreled Centennial, gave the cylinder a good luck look and a spin, closed the cylinder, then dropped the little hammerless .38 Special into the left outside pocket.

The video display—it was fed to the computer as a regular video, then digitized for added clarity—showed the blue van still dogging the Shore Patrol.

Because of the way the drone was vectoring over the shops and businesses in order to be out of direct line of sight with the street, therefore less easily noticed, Shaw couldn't see the entire convoy of three trucks and a lead car. The trucks were the Real McCoy, a shipment of surface-to-air missiles for the shore batteries guarding Pearl Harbor—just the sort of target the Nazis would want to take out preparatory to an attack.

His eyes stayed on the blue van. There was no way of telling who or what was inside. Only amateurs would have tried to explode the van near to the convoy and precipitate a mass explosion of the missiles, because the warheads would not be armed and nothing would happen. But if enough explosives were used, the missiles could be destroyed, rendered into high-ticket junk that would be useless.

Or the trucks could be hijacked with the intent of arming the missiles and then either using them or detonating them.

"Lots of cheerful possibilities," Shaw said aloud.

"What was that, Tim?"

"Just wonderin' what these guys'll try if they go for it."

Bob Bilsom was grinning when Shaw looked over at him. "I bet they stop the convoy, put a truck full of explosives at either end and maybe one in the middle and blow the whole friggin' thing to junk, and trash James Madison Way at the same time."

"Ya could be right, Bobby." Bob's theory was as good as any, Shaw reflected.

Such an explosion would destroy both sides of the street for at least a block in either direction, probably knock out the power grid, communications, not to mention cause a lot of deaths. Tim Shaw still had the radio on the seat beside him. He pushed to talk. "Eddie. Talk to your father. Over."

"What's up, Dad? Over."

"Bobby's got an idea, might be a good one—but with Bobby hey, who can tell? Listen, can you get up a video remote?"

"From the street?"

"Yeah, from the street. I need one you can coast in

221

over the front of the convoy."

"I gotta clear it with—"

"Fuck clearin' it—launch it. I need to see if the bad guys got the front end of the convoy tapped. Do it now and get back to me. Out." Tim Shaw smacked the handset he'd used for talking with his son into the dashboard nest, then reached across for the one nearer to Bob Bilsom. "Watchdog to Lamb. Over."

The by-now-familiar Shore Patrolman's voice came back. "This is Lamb, Watchdog. Over."

"Both you guys on radio?"

"Affirmative, Watchdog. Lead and drag car. What's the problem, Watchdog? Over."

"You got one in the front like you got in the back? Over."

"Say again Watchdog. Over."

"You're waggin' a tail. You shakin' a dick too? Over."

"Negative, Watchdog. Only the tail. Over."

"Stay cool; you might be wrong. Watchdog Out." Shaw put the handset back into its receptacle. His eyes went back to the video display on his computer screen.

The radio set linking him to the SWAT Team started crackling, "Watchdog Two to Watchdog One. Watchdog Two to Watchdog One. Come in. Over."

Shaw had the set in his hand. "What's the story, Eddie?"

"Got a problem. The probe can go up, but we can't control it. The magic box's broken. Won't switch on. So, we can't launch it."

"Shit. Anybody can fix it?"

"Negative on that, Watchdog."

222

"Wonderful—" Before he could say anything else, the probe that was already up picked up something it digitized into the far lower right corner of his screen. "Hold tight, Eddie." Tim Shaw threw down the handset and started fiddling with the computer controls, getting the machine to pick up the image from the lower right corner and move it to center screen, then fill in the rest of the image based on data in its memory. What was taking shape was an armored delivery vehicle, the kind used for gold and diamond shipments. "Eddie—still there?"

"Right here."

"Get on the radio telephone and check with the armored car companies quick as you can. See if they got anybody toolin' down James Madison about a half-block behind the convoy. I'm gonna check with auto theft. Call me back." Tim Shaw flicked off the localized frequency and into the police emergency band. "This is Tim Shaw. Get me Phil Zimowitz in auto. Quick as you can. I'm holdin'."

The operator acknowledged, saying, "Put you through right away, Inspector."

It was a bad patch, but Zimowitz was connected in under thirty seconds. "Tim, what's happenin'?"

"You got any reports on an armored car getting boosted lately?"

"How'd you know? You find it?"

"Yeah. I found it. I'll get back to you." Shaw cut frequencies and back to the localized band. "Eddie. Whatchya got?"

"Two of the companies down, one to go. Nobody should be on this route, but the guys over at Blackstone

Protective wanted to know if we found the car they lost."

"Make that third call as you close in. We cut off the van that's following the drag car and then we block James Madison Way, completely. Sidewalks and everything."

"This it?"

"Damn right," Tim Shaw said.

Thirty-Five

By using muscle rather than technology, the protective cap of something like synth-concrete out of which the gas escape vent emerged was broken open in large sections. Then the sections were set aside for possible replacement. There would be no way in which they could ever hope to have the fact that they had disturbed the cap pass detection in close inspection, but from a distance at least, things might well appear normal.

Below the cap was a funnel-shaped feeder leading out of a sixteen-inch diameter pipe. The sensors which read the gas content went wild at the volume.

John Rourke stepped back in order to consider the problem. He wanted a cigar, very badly, but under the circumstances that would be impossible. "I hate to say this," Rourke at last announced, "but in one way at least, we've wasted our time and our energy, gentlemen. This pipe is too narrow, at this end at least, for us to use it as a means of ingress. We'll be forced to blast our way in. And not from here. On the plus side, the volume of gas indicates that it is being evacuated from a substantially sized chamber below us." Almost in the same instant that he said that, the sensors reading the gas began to show that its flow had ceased. There was no visual confirmation.

John Rourke considered that.

"What do you think it is, Doctor Rourke?" Dr. Mentz asked him.

"The reason for the gas?"

"Yes."

"I hate to make a judgement based on so little hard data, but it seems quite likely that lysergic diethylamide acid in a gaseous state occurring simultaneously with what appears to be a synthetic form of some cyanide-based compound would indicate that the gas is perhaps used as a means of execution where it is, for some reason, necessary that the victims are in a euphoric state while they die. Hence, this isn't for extermination of vermin or anything like that, but rather sentient beings. I'd say that below us, wherever this pipe ends, there is organized death."

Paul looked up from the vent. John Rourke saw the tilt of his friend's head, although he could not see his face. Rourke had come to understand every nuance of the younger man's body language over the years, just as Paul, it seemed evident, had learned to read him. It was a natural result of fighting side by side, a natural defense system. The body language told Rourke more than language could have at the moment—that Paul was at once shocked and wary. John Rourke, for the benefit of the others, said, "Our experience in earlier days with the ill-fated survival colony from which my son's late wife originated would be ample precedent for such a thing. The society from which Madison Rourke was rescued by Michael was predicated on a static population figure which could never be violated. Such is the fate of a closed world.

"It might not be imprudent to infer," Rourke went on, "that the methodology is to some degree or another ritualistic. Ritual takes on great importance in closed societies as well, without the outside influences by which it can be judged."

"This sounds like a lecture in basic sociology, Herr Doctor," Hauptsturmführer Gunther Spitz announced.

"Perhaps it's their basic sociology; but I hope I'm wrong."

Thirty-Six

On Ed Shaw's signal, the pursuit cars converged on James Madison Way simultaneously with the convoy that was increasing its speed in order to distance itself from the grey van and the armored delivery truck. The armored truck was massive, not powered by electricity but by internal combustion, powerful enough to punch through most obstacles—including police cars, Tim Shaw realized.

Tim Shaw shouted to Bob Bilsom, "Cut up over the curb, Bobby—here!" As the unmarked cruiser bounced over the curb diagonally and onto the sidewalk, blocking the south side of the street, Tim Shaw was already throwing open the door. The car's front bumper was about a yard away from the window of an expensive men's store—the window mannequins decked out in brightly colored collarless jackets and color coordinated walking shorts—just the sort of peacock-ish crap, Shaw told himself, he'd never get caught dead wearing. But he might get caught dead.

The armored car was barreling up the center of the

street cutting away passenger cars and motorcycles in its path. The grey van was skidding to a stop, sliding doors on both sides opening up.

Tim Shaw glanced behind him. Further along up the street, the convoy was on its way, the Shore Patrol escort cars and one of Eddie's SWAT vans with it. Uniformed cars would be joining it along the route.

Ed Shaw's voice crackled from the radio in Tim Shaw's left ear. "I'm gonna break out the grenade launchers against that armored car."

"Use 'em, Eddie," Shaw told his son. "Get somebody on a bullhorn warning the civilians."

"Right."

Men from the team were closing around Tim Shaw now. Shaw shouted to Bob Bilsom, "Bobby—get on PA and warn people to take cover and get off the street. Now!" Tim Shaw had his .45 in his right hand, his thumb poised over the safety, the little .38 Special out of his raincoat, and in his left hand. The rain was lashing across the street on a strong wind, blowing in cold angular sheets. The snapped-down brim of Shaw's black fedora was low over his face, but he still had to squint against the rain in order to see. "You two guys," Shaw ordered, "Get a grenade launcher goin' on that armored truck. We can get 'em in a crossfire. And stay down. Gonna be a lotta bullets flyin'." Shaw drew his raincoat closed around him, pocketing the revolver so he had a hand free for the buttons. The raincoat was made of bullet-resistant material. "You stay with Bobby here at the car and cover us," Shaw told one of the men, an ex-SEAL, turned cop, and one of the best guys in Eddie's unit. "Don't spare the suppressive fire." Then Shaw looked at the remaining six men with him.

"The rest of you guys, let's go."

His coat buttoned, the collar up against the rain and his hat screwed down tighter against the wind, Tim Shaw had the little .38 back in his left hand as he started off the curb and into the street.

He was the least well-armed of the group—the others equipped with shotguns, projectile-firing assault rifles and energy weapons.

Tim Shaw thrust the .38 Special revolver into his pocket and took a bullhorn from one of the men near him, squeezed the handle and talked into it as he walked. "This is the Honolulu Police Department TAC Squad. You in the grey late model van. You in the armored truck. Cease all vehicular motion at once. Step out of your vehicles with your hands raised over your heads and clearly in view, weaponless. This is a police order. Failure to cooperate might result in your death or injury. If you surrender now, you will not be harmed."

Then Shaw handed off the bullhorn, remarking as he did it, "Now we're through with that bullshit we can get to work."

The little .38 back into his hand, he kept walking.

The armored truck was steadily rolling down the street, still about a hundred yards off and going slowly now. The men in both open sides of the grey van weren't shooting yet and Shaw didn't want to have his men fire first, except at the armored truck, and that to stop it.

Shaw kept walking, closing the distance to the grey van.

He could hear public address systems on both sides of the street urging people to cover, warning them away. In a second or so, the first of the grenade

231

launchers would open up and, if the shooting hadn't already started, it would start then. Shaw and his six men were only a few feet from the central parkway which ran for miles along James Madison Way. There were synth-concrete benches that would make good cover against most types of small arms fire, including energy weapons. There were palm trees every few yards, their trunks good cover as well, because the trees were wide enough at the base.

And every man wore body armor.

The downside of that was that the bad guys would be wearing it too . . .

Marie wore nothing but a lace-trimmed cream-color slip. And Doring knew—he had watched her dress—that beneath the slip Marie wore nothing at all. Even if he had not watched her, such would have been readily apparent.

The way the garment draped over her body, the crack between the cheeks of her rear end was visible, as was, in profile, the nipple of her left breast.

She stood beside the apartment's solitary window, the curtains pushed back. Rain smudged across the glass in long grey streaks, the volcanic ash which fell when the rain did not, combining with the water to make mud.

Her fingernails were pressed lightly against one of the panes, and every once in a while Doring could hear a faint tapping noise which was not the sound of the rain.

Doring watched her for a second longer, then went back to watching the all-news station on the video screen. There was almost nonstop coverage of Kialuaea's continuous erupting. But when the attack on the convoy took place, there would surely be an interruption. And that should be at any moment.

Working through his island contacts, he had worked out the attack plan to the smallest detail, then let the Nazi sympathizers "engaged" for the operation run it themselves. If the operation proved successful, Doring could use the same system again, saving his own considerably diminished force for political assassinations and major acts of more subtle sabotage. If the operation failed, it would still terrorize the populace here in Hawaii and doubtless claim some police and military lives.

Doring was violating his mission parameters, but under the circumstances he had no choice. He, along with Marie and the men, had been infiltrated here as a totally independent unit, hence untraceable if the Americans should prove successful in capturing personnel or records from among the other more conventional infiltration teams.

But along came an old man, a policeman in a funny hat who did not play by the rules of the game. He thought like a general, fought like a commando, killed like a terrorist. Totally without warning, this policeman and the Honolulu TAC Team had raided the safehouse where Doring and his people had been staying. In one raid, the policeman was responsible for the loss of half of Doring's unit.

If the policeman, Inspector Tim Shaw, proved successful this time, before anything further could be done, Shaw would have to be eliminated.

His radioset near him (he was waiting for word from

a street observer who would alert him once the attack on the missile convoy was in progress) and his eyes on the video screen, Doring could do nothing now but wait.

Marie, he thought, just shaking his head. Women were so wonderfully, admirably simple. She could wile away her time by watching rain drops streaking dirty windows, nothing of consequence on her mind. She would stand there in her underwear just awaiting his pleasure should he wish to take her to bed again (which he intended to do soon). There were no real worries for her, except perhaps if her hair was properly brushed or she was physically pleasing in the sheets.

Perpetual children women were. In a way, such a life must have had its charms, of course, but to be a woman, Doring thought, would be worse than being dead.

The radioset beside him crackled with static and Doring picked up his earphone; he felt a smile beginning to cross his lips . . .

Several things happened at once. The grenade launcher from Ed Shaw's side of the street opened fire, the armored truck slow enough and well in range of it. The men in the grey van started shooting, energy weapons mostly, but at least two conventional projectile-firing submachineguns. The grenade launcher from the south side of the street, where Bob Bilsom had wedged the car, opened up.

Tim Shaw and the six TAC Team men with him moved for cover, already returning fire as they ran.

The .45 in Shaw's right fist fired twice, then twice

again as he dropped down on his knees into the mud behind the cover of one of the synth-concrete benches positioned in the parkway along the median strip of James Madison Way. And Shaw snapped, "First time I wore this suit since it was cleaned—shit." He snapped off another three rounds, then a fourth and tucked down to make a tactical magazine change.

"You guys all right?"

It was his son's voice coming to him through the earpiece for his radio.

The armored truck was picking up speed again, big clouds of grey smoke and some falling debris from the grenade impacts on either side of it. But the truck was seemingly unaffected and was coming right at them. "In about sixty seconds we won't be, Eddie. Take the grenade launcher yourself and put a pair on 'em, try knockin' out the front tires. And hurry it up."

Tim Shaw told himself to ignore the armored truck, then proceeded to do it. "Okay, you three with me, you guys, go for the other side. We close in on the van from both sides. Give us fifteen seconds then go for it." And Tim Shaw was up, running, the guns in his hands spitting lead toward the open doorway of the van on the side nearest him. He reasoned that as long as he was moving, chances were slimmer that the armored truck would pile into him and the longer he left things with the van, the worse they'd get.

A grenade fired, then another and another.

Shaw glanced to his left, grinning ear to ear. The armored truck was stopped, the front tires blown off on both sides and the armored synth-glass windshield smudged black.

The guys in the armored truck would have to wait.

Shaw's little .38 was empty and he dropped down behind another one of the benches, the distance to the grey van now less than twenty yards. Heavy automatic weapons fired and energy weapons' blasts were impacting the palm trees, the bench, the muddy grass.

One of the TAC Team guys with him was wounded in the leg, but still operational.

"We're closing in right down the middle in a car, Dad," Eddie's voice came through the earpiece again.

Tim Shaw had both pistols loaded again. He ordered the wounded man, "You stay here, Bill, and lay down a shitload of suppressive fire, but nice and high up 'cause we're gonna be under it. We're goin' in. Now!" Shaw was up and running.

The police car, windows down, guns firing out of all four positions, was coming dead on at the van, from the front, at a bad angle for the men inside the van to return fire. Tim Shaw saw a flash of movement on the far side, the rest of his men closing. Shaw held his fire, Bill's suppressive fire from behind him keeping the men in the van back.

"Gas grenades. Get 'em ready!"

They were five yards from the van now.

A man with an energy rifle threw himself into the doorway, firing it from hip level. Tim Shaw dodged left and fired both pistols from shoulder level, knocking the man down as the last of the energy bursts tore into the street near him. Shaw was moving again.

Shaw heard the whooshing sound of the gas grenades launching into the truck, clouds of tear gas billowing outward on the wind. The gas would be of little practical use, but would at least further confuse things inside the van.

And Shaw needed that as he reached it. There was a TAC Team man on either side of him. "Spray the van!" Shaw ordered, holding back for a second or two while the TAC Team men responded. One had a shotgun, the other a rifle, both men peppering the sides of the van with fire. Then Shaw went the last few feet and jumped, up and into the van, shouting into his radio, "Cover me but don't kill me! Hold fire!"

Inside the van, a nearly fully loaded gun in each hand, Tim Shaw opened fire, his eyes starting to stream tears, but enough vision left to him to get the job done. A man with an energy rifle took two from the .45 in the thorax and in the forehead. Another man with one of the submachineguns took two 158-grain lead hollow-point semi-wadcutters from the little .38 in Shaw's left hand, the submachinegun discharging as the man— one hand clasped to his chest—stumbled back. Bullets tore through the van's roof.

Shaw fired the .45 and the .38 simultaneously, killing the second submachinegunner.

The van was starting to move.

Shaw lurched, fell to one knee.

The other men in the van were dead or wounded.

There was a flash of gunfire from the driver's compartment.

Shaw could barely see any more, but he stabbed the .45 toward the origin of the gunfire and zigzagged the muzzle up and down and side to side as he emptied it. The passenger side front window blew outward and the body of the shooter went halfway through it.

The van was wheeling hard left.

Shaw stabbed the empty .45 into his pants, grabbed for the roof of the van, stumbled forward.

The driver was fumbling for a pistol.

Tim Shaw put a .38 into the man's right temple, dove rearward, then threw himself out of the van.

As Shaw hit the pavement—hard, his left shoulder aching, his back reminding him he wasn't that young anymore—the van jumped the median strip and crashed through one of the synth-concrete benches, then started climbing the trunk of the palm tree near it.

But it rolled onto its side, flames coming from the engine compartment.

Tim Shaw got up to his feet.

His son's voice was in both ears, Eddie running toward him from the police car and shouting, but his radio still on, "Dad? You okay?"

Shaw started loading his guns. "Bill's wounded—took one in the thigh—back over there," and Shaw gestured toward the bench from behind which Bill had provided cover. "Get him some help. Whatchya gonna do?" And Tim Shaw gestured toward the armored truck.

"Just a sec." Tim Shaw turned away, looking after the van. Some of the TAC Team people were pulling bodies out of it, living and dead. The fire was spreading, but slowly. Fire extinguishers started coming out. "Got Bill taken care of?"

Tim Shaw shoved the little .38 into his belt, the .45 cocked and locked, back in his right fist. "So?"

"We try rocking her over on the side with trucks after some volley fire from the grenade launchers to soften 'em up and some gas before that to confuse 'em. Of course, that's after we ask them if they want to give up."

"Your turn. I got to feel stupid the last time."

Tim Shaw's son nodded. There was a bullhorn suspended from a sling across Ed Shaw's chest. Ed brought it up to his mouth. "Attention to those personnel in the armored truck. Your vehicle is disabled. You are surrounded. Come out with your hands up. You will not be harmed if you cooperate. You have one minute."

"Pretty generous of ya," Tim Shaw remarked to his son.

"Hey, I'm all heart."

Tim Shaw looked at his wristwatch . . .

His right fist ached. Marie screamed. Perhaps he should have hit her instead of the wall, Doring thought. "Shut up, Marie! Go into the bathroom and shut up!"

"Yes!" And she ran from him.

His eyes went back to the television screen. Remote video from drones overflying the scene showed the armored truck to be out of commission, unable to move, the men in it trapped with their explosives. Perhaps they would have the courage and intelligence to detonate, turning the vehicle into a gigantic fragmentation grenade.

Doring himself would have done that.

And the other vehicle, the van, was destroyed.

There was ground camera coverage now, a long shot coming in on a group of men standing off to the side of the armored truck, almost equidistant between it and the van. All of the men were in black battle dress utilities, except for one. He wore a black fedora hat, a black raincoat, and in his right hand there was a handgun. The man was lighting a cigarette.

239

"Damn you!" Doring hissed through clenched teeth.

The first order of business would be to kill this man, Tim Shaw, this policeman.

They had tried killing his daughter, to send him a message. But Dr. Rourke had disrupted that. This time, however, there would be no message and no Dr. Rourke. And, Daimler vowed, no hirelings. He would take care of this American policeman himself, make certain that he could never interfere with their plans again.

Doring walked across the room, standing in front of the screen. He could still see Shaw, the half-amused look on the mongrelized face. "Laugh while you can," Doring told the screen. "While you can."

Thirty-Seven

There was no reponse from the men inside the armored truck and the time limit—one minute—was long since up.

Ed Shaw was running it, Tim Shaw keeping his mouth shut on his son's play. "Here's what we do," Ed Shaw began, a dozen of the TAC Team men assembled around him, Tim Shaw keeping off to the side. "We have to get the guys to come out of the truck because we can't get inside to get 'em, right? So they probably have masks, but it's worth a shot to try some gas. It won't make things better for them, that's for sure."

Tim Shaw's eyes were still tearing from the gas he had endured, but he still didn't trust to rubbing them because tear gas caused blood vessels in the eyes to distend and if the eyes were rubbed the blood vessels could rupture. Instead he turned his face into the wind again.

Ed Shaw was still outlining his plan. "If we launch gas in through those firing ports—and I know it won't be easy, so don't bother mentioning it—they'll figure that's our play for the moment. But it won't be. Once the gas is inside, we fire grenade launchers, trying to get the grenades under the truck. While the guys inside the truck are figuring out what's happening, they'll be away from the firing ports. And we need that. I've got three SWAT vans lined up on auto program so there won't be any drivers to get killed. They're electric, right, so we don't have to worry about fire. So, the vans ram the armored truck and, if we're lucky, flip it over. Then we pour everything we've got into the underside of the truck. While we're doing that a bunch of us come up on the truck from the roof side where the guys inside can't see us. Onto the truck, then the nasty part."

Tim Shaw was enjoying this. His son, Ed, had a natural head for tactics and a gift for the bizarre. Putting those talents together made for a terrific field commander, which Ed was.

"Nasty part?"

Ed looked at the man who fed him the line. Ed smiled. "I've got industrial-sized chemical fire extinguishers coming up. Each man who goes to the trucks will have two of them. I figure a dozen of those can fill the interior of the armored car with foam making it impossible for the men inside to hold their positions because the foam will cover the respirator filters on their gas masks and the smell of the foam along with what's left of the tear gas will force them out after they pull off the masks.

"Soon as they open the doors, we've got 'em," Ed Shaw concluded.

It was a good plan. A little more complicated than Tim Shaw liked, but a good plan and just crazy enough. No one inside the armored truck would be able to anticipate it. And that was even better.

Getting six gas grenades inside had consumed better than fifteen minutes and a good dozen more grenades were on the street, clouds of the tear gas still spewing up from them, the wind driving the rain, blowing the clouds down the street.

The three remotely operated SWAT vans were in place, but not ranked, so as to conceal from anyone watching from inside the armored truck what the plan was.

The grenadiers were starting to open fire against the undercarriage of the truck, and Tim Shaw held his ears against the sounds of the explosions as they started almost in series.

Beside Shaw, who was behind the cover of another of the vans, a shotgun rested, borrowed from inside the van. Logic, as opposed to legality, dictated that once the armored truck was overturned, instead of loading it up with chemical foam from fire extinguishers, they should load it up with lead from their guns. But police were supposed to arrest bad guys, not execute them, unless the latter was unavoidable.

They'd try the foam. If it didn't work, they'd still have the guns.

Hardly anything in the way of identification was taken off the dead and injured from the grey van. There was a driver's license on the man Tim Shaw had shot just before himself jumping from the van. One man had an Eden passport. Contract Nazi-sympathizers, gangsters with political axes to grind, they were just about as talented.

These weren't the same men who had hit the Country Day School or tried for Emma at her house, but Tim Shaw would have bet his pension check that they had the same leader. And if he could make himself as obvious as possible just maybe he'd become such a pain in the ass that they could make a try for him. If he could keep knocking off the soldiers, the general would come out of his hole and then Tim Shaw could get him. That was why Shaw hadn't waved away the news cameras. He wanted his face on the screen.

It was saying to the leader of these guys, "Come and get me asshole."

The grenade sequence was finished, more tires blown out, the body of the armored truck blackened, the vehicle otherwise appearing undamaged.

Shaw could see his son getting the TAC Team men ready for the assault as soon as the armored truck rolled over. Tim Shaw saw his son. He thought about his daughter. Ed might be in more danger than Emma, but at least it was a known, not an unknown.

Ed was going with the assult team. Tim Shaw was going too.

Ed gave the hand signal for the three trucks to be started out, the drivers aboard them getting them rolling then jumping clear. Ed Shaw started his team at a tangent down the street. Tim Shaw, the riot shotgun in his hands, running beside them. Tim Shaw's left shoulder ached. He was too old for this sort of life but he loved it—not the killing. If he ever started liking that he'd join a monastery. But he liked the action. Too many people these days—maybe it could have been said at any time in history—were too ready to sit back and let the world run by them, let everyone else take the risks, fight the fights, do what had to be done.

The three SWAT vans were in perfect synchronization now, picking up speed but obviously in low, coming dead on at the armored truck.

The TAC Team personnel forming the assault unit, Tim Shaw in the middle of them now, were nearly into position.

The three black Honolulu PD TAC Team SWAT vans hit and there was a shriek of metal against metal like nothing Tim Shaw had ever heard before, the armored truck starting to rock. In one dark little corner of his mind, Tim Shaw realized he'd have about six feet deep worth of reports to fill out because he had allowed the semitrashing of the three SWAT vans, but there'd be time enough for that later.

The armored truck seemed to balance itself for a second on the rims of its blown-out tires, then it started to fall.

Eddie shouted, "Let's go." And Tim Shaw quickened his pace.

The armored truck hit the pavement and flopped, the street vibrating under Tim Shaw's flat feet. The rain seemed to be driving down harder now and despite the lights that instantly flicked on from the other police vehicles, the darkness of the sky threw everything into such silhouette that movement seemed in slow motion, like the vid-tapes of the old pretalking pictures—jerky, distinct, clipped.

They were at the roof of the armored truck now, its

245

camel color blackened and smudged, the pavement cracked beneath the roof corners from its impact, a smell of dust and tarmac in the air despite the rain and the wind. Eddie was the first one up. Tim Shaw clambered onto the cab. A gun protruded out of the slit in the driver's side window. "Gun! Watch it!" Tim Shaw shouted.

Tim Shaw racked the pump with his left hand, torquing the shotgun, then ramming its muzzle toward the firing slit. A shot was fired, then another. Tim Shaw punched the muzzle of his gun through the slit and pulled the trigger, the shotgun's recoil almost breaking his wrist.

There was a scream, almost nonhuman, from within the cab. Tim Shaw pulled the shotgun back, pumped, rammed its muzzle into the slit again and pulled the trigger.

Eddie and the other men of the assault unit were already up onto the side of the van, unlimbering the fire extinguishers they carried.

Tim Shaw pulled back on the shotgun, freeing it from the firing slit, jumped away, clambered onto the side of the truck and was up beside Eddie and the TAC Team assault unit. He was breathing hard. The first of the extinguisher hoses was down into the side firing slits, pumping foam into the truck's interior from their tanks.

"Be ready if they bolt!" Tim Shaw advised his son and the others.

Ed Shaw nodded, alerting two of the assault team, "Be ready to fire down into that doorway just in case they try making a run for it!"

246

The rain seemed to be getting heavier, drenching Tim Shaw everywhere above and below his raincoat.

There was no let up in the rain predicted by even the most optimistic forecaster. The particles, that were constantly being pushed into the atmosphere by the nearby volcanic eruption, were, of course, the ideal material around which water vapor could condense. The islands, surrounded by water as they were, had a constant supply of vaporization. The cycle of rain could go on unendingly.

As a cop who started out on a beat, worked his way into being a detective and had always chosen the streets over a desk, Tim Shaw was used to lousy weather. It somehow magically occurred in perfect synchronicity with any operation which would require spending time outdoors. A raincoat was such a matter of course for him that half the time he wore one when the weather was bright and sunny. He was so inured to rain that he never spent a dime more than he had to on shoes because they were always the first things to go.

As he crouched there on the armored car near his son, the rain coming in torrents, he couldn't help but think of his shoes. Every time he moved his feet water flushed out of them. But unlike in his youth, there would be no one waiting at home against whom to get warmed.

Tim Shaw had a bet with himself that the men inside the overturned armored car wouldn't surrender, were fanatics who would rather die than be taken alive.

In less than a minute, he was proven right.

The doors below them moved, one falling open and downward, men from inside, half-covered with foam, emerging. The respirator vents on their gas masks had foam clinging to them. The men had to be choking inside their gas masks. They stumbled or crawled out, firing upward toward the assault team, some of them getting to their feet, running for it into the lights, guns blazing in order to take out as many of their enemies as they could before they were brought down.

Tim Shaw fired his shotgun, putting down a man who had just nailed one of Eddie's men with an energy rifle blast in the leg. There was answering fire from the police personnel ringing the overturned armored truck, its volume tremendous. Tim Shaw's ears rang with it. The men who had fled were cut down in mere seconds, dead or wounded.

Shaw's son directed that the infusion of the chemical foam be halted, then started down to the street level, Tim Shaw behind him.

They did the usual thing for door entry, only this time rigged a couple of slings together so that when they opened the now uppermost side door of the armored truck, the door could be held back instead of slamming down.

Then they went in, Tim Shaw and his son right behind the three men who were the first inside, all of them not only vigilant for lurking enemy personnel but careful of their footing in the overturned vehicle, the slippery foam clinging to everything.

There were crates of explosives visible in the flashlights of the TAC Team men, the crates wired in series and ready to be exploded. There was a detonator rigged, but the detonator was covered with foam, as were the battery terminal leads.

"You made a lucky guess with the fire extinguishers, Eddie," Shaw announced. "Good tactics. Glad I hired you. If they'd blown this shit, we woulda been sittin' on the biggest fragmentation grenade in history." And Tim Shaw walked out, back onto the street knowing he was no longer needed. And, he was tired.

His shoes were covered with white foam, his raincoat and his trouser legs were mud-stained and he was wet and cold. Then he started whistling as he walked away from the overturned armored truck and toward the police lines.

A woman reporter from a video news crew which had evidently slipped through the lines accosted him as soon as he neared them. Instantly, she started firing questions. "Who were these men, Inspector Shaw?"

Tim Shaw stopped whistling, cutting the melody in midphrase. "We have reason to believe they were terrorist saboteurs. There was some evidence of explosives inside the vehicle, but we have no definite data at this point on if or how those explosives were to be used. There'll be statements released as soon as possible outlining the progress of the investigation. So I'm afraid you'll have to wait and see."

"What will happen to these men?"

"It's too early to say. The wounded will, of course, be given the best possible medical attention. Beyond that, the situation is still very fluid. A number of charges will probably result."

"Were there any police casualties?"

"Very few, and no fatalities which I'm aware of, thank God."

Almost as an afterthought, the reporter asked him,

"What were you whistling, Inspector Shaw?"

Tim Shaw grinned. "Gilbert & Sullivan, from *The Pirates of Penzance*—you know, 'a policeman's lot is not a happy one.'"

Thirty-Eight

This meant openly invading the community, of course, but there was no other option left but to blast their way inside. Using every sensing device available to them aboard the Nazi V-stol, no other chink in the walls of the mountain was discernible. It was clear that the occupants of the mountain redoubt were either capable of utilizing a technology those living beyond its walls could not suspect or else they simply never went outside.

Where the main entrance to the onetime War Retreat had been, there were now thousands of tons of rock. The age of the rock slide was impossible to ascertain. Rourke supposed there might be still another alternative, that the occupants were trapped inside. But, that hardly seemed possible. And the gas could not have been natural.

And, with the presence of the lethal halucinogenic gas, he and Paul and their unlikely temporary allies would not have been able to risk moving about inside the mountain without chemical warfare gear, which would have made their presence rather obvious anyway.

"What if these people are perfectly peaceful, John? This is wrong."

John Rourke turned away from the laying of the explosives, put his hand to Paul Rubenstein's shoulder and started walking off with him, leaving the party of men planting the charges and moving toward the V-stol. "That fact hasn't escaped me. If we don't cooperate long enough to get the remains Zimmer wants, we have no real bargaining chip at all for the return of Sarah. After all, what if Michael's identity is discovered? There won't be any shooting unless it's in self-defense, and that wouldn't be morally justified either, I know. This may very well be wrong."

"You know I'm with you, regardless."

John Rourke nodded, wishing his own trepidations were as easily set aside. He was uncertain as to his rectitude, a feeling which troubled him greatly. He said nothing more of it, however, because Hauptsturmführer Gunther Spitz was coming straight toward them from the V-stol.

"So, Herr Doctor! How goes it?"

"It goes well."

"The explosives?"

"Nearly in place."

"Good," Gunther Spitz said, walking on then.

Paul, his voice little over a whisper, said, "He's being too friendly."

"Agreed."

"What if—"

"It isn't all that it appears?" John Rourke interjected, preempting his friend. "That thought has crossed my mind. What if, for example, they merely gave us a convincing-sounding lie, hmm? But, there's no way to know short of blasting our way in through the side of the mountain, is there?"

"So," Paul observed, "either way—"

"The expression I think you're searching for," John Rourke noted, "is we're either damned if we do or damned if we don't, but in any event, damned."

Paul Rubenstein beside him, John Rourke started back toward the base of the mountain, where the laying of the explosives, indeed, was nearly complete.

Thirty-Nine

The noise came from below her.

Emma Shaw crouched in the mouth of the cave and stared downward into the night, toward the river in the gorge below.

And she realized the noise was the whinnying of a horse.

There was a small fire glowing below, very small, as though built by someone exceedingly careful not to be observed.

Emma Shaw debated what she should do. To stay here in the cave was definitely the most prudent course of action, at least when viewed simplistically. Stay in the cave and whoever was down in the base of the gorge would move on.

Yet, two factors mitigated against her deciding to do just that. First, what if the fire were from the Land Pirates and they decided to stay put for a while? She couldn't remain hidden in this cave for more than a few days without running out of food. And the cold would eventually get her, because the solar batteries in her sleeping bag would be discharged and could not be recharged in the darkness of the cave. And building a fire would generate smoke which would draw attention to her position.

Also, the idea of a horse appealed to her considerably. With a horse, she could make it down river no faster but considerably more safely.

If she waited until morning, her options might well be fewer. She might, indeed, find that she was trapped, or that the possibility of stealing the horse had eluded her. Yet trying to navigate the side of the gorge at night might precipitate danger of another sort, either a fatal fall or a broken limb, which would—just as surely as it had so often for the old pioneering mountain men of the early part of the nineteenth century—insure her eventual death.

Emma Shaw lit a cigarette and tried to weigh her possibilities . . .

The V-stol was airborne and John Rourke had made a decision.

There was no sense in attempting to hide his conclusions from the Nazis who made up the rest of his and Paul's party, because the Nazis themselves would play an intrinsic part in what would happen if John Rourke's idea proved correct.

Rourke ordered that the V-stol land some twenty-five miles away from the mountain, then called a meeting, both the pilot and copilot present for it as well.

Outside, there was nothing but darkness, the moon—it should have been three-quarters full—

256

totally obscured by heavy cloud cover. Their aircraft, the window curtains drawn down and all running lights off, would only be visible for its heat signature.

Hauptsturmführer Spitz lit one of his cigarettes from the case which had the built-in lighter, leaning back as he said, "So? Why are we not activating the explosives, Herr Doctor General?"

Rourke ignored Spitz's use of the contrived-sounding title. "The explosives are in place and all we have to do is detonate. If our mysterious inhabitants of the mountain do have sensing equipment, they'll know it, be prepared for us to blast our way inside, or at least attempt to do so. There are two possibilities, of course: either that the explosives will do the job and get us in or merely cause some damage and we'll be unable to enter. I've been giving the present situation a great deal of thought," Rourke said, not about to mention that he and Paul had also considered that the very intent of their mission might be a ruse. "In order for that synth-concrete-style cap to have been put in place over the exhaust system for the lethal halucinogenic gas we discovered, someone had to get on top of the mountain to construct it, right?"

Gunther Spitz leaned forward in his seat, flicking ashes from his cigarette into the palm of his hand rather than looking away to use the ashtray. "I am intrigued, Herr Doctor."

Rourke smiled thinly. "I thought that you might be. The American short story writer and poet, Edgar Allan Poe, was of course best known for his tales of horror. But he also pioneered the detective story, predating Conan-Doyle's Sherlock Holmes with his own character, Dupin."

"'The Purloined Letter,'" Paul almost whispered. "The object which is in contention is in plain sight."

"In a manner of speaking," Rourke said, nodding to his friend.

"Letters? What do such things—"

Rourke looked at Spitz. "What if your people have been so intent on finding an entryway to the mountain redoubt that they have ignored the obvious, hmm? What if, instead of an entryway into the mountain itself, there are access tunnels coming into the mountain from underneath? The material like synth-concrete which was used to construct the cap over the gas outlet piping could just as easily be utilized to build tunnel walls. What if your aerial observations were so committed to looking for the subtle that the obvious was ignored?"

"Passageways," Spitz said.

John Rourke glanced at Wolfgang Mann. Mann seemed attentive, but there was a look in his eyes that seemed inexplicable. And suddenly, John Rourke realized that not only had the Nazis ignored the obvious in their search for the subtle, but so had he. And a chill, more properly called an involuntary paroxysm, ran along John Thomas Rourke's spine and made the hairs on the back of his neck feel to him as if, indeed, they were standing on end.

Rourke exhaled.

Paul said, "Then we should go airborne and utilize the colder evening temperatures to assist us in looking for heat signatures from tunnel openings which might be hundreds of yards, maybe even miles away from the base of the mountain."

Rourke looked at the pilot, then the copilot.

"Gentlemen, you've worked a long day. Can we do a few hours of high altitude observation before calling it a night?"

The pilot answered for both men. "Yes, Herr Doctor!"

John Rourke stood up, adjusting the positioning of his Scoremasters in his belt. "Good. We'll all help however we can, of course. I can spell either one of you on the V-stol's controls—for level flight only, however, since I've never checked out on one of these. While the inhabitants of the mountain, if they are aware of our presence, await our doing something with the explosives we've set, we'll look for another way inside."

Spitz smiled. "You are, indeed, Herr Doctor, magnificent!"

John Rourke said nothing.

Forty

Her father had always told her she was reckless, and she could almost hear Tim Shaw's voice in her ear telling her, "Watch out you don't break your damn fool neck, kid—excuse my language." And the thought of her father just then brought a smile to Emma Shaw's lips as she angled her way into a little defile, wedged herself there for a moment and rested. The little campfire was closer now, but it didn't seem much larger. Whoever had set it wasn't building it up for the night, perhaps was letting it go out.

The fire was her beacon and, just in case the fire was about to extinguish itself, Emma Shaw started moving downward again, trying to quicken her pace as much as she dared.

She heard the sound of a horse again, the clicking of hooves on rock and soft whinnying in the night. As Emma Shaw worked her way downward, picking her way with great care because the rocks were sharp and unevenly spaced, she felt warmer. And, it was more than her own exertion. Her father had always kidded that girls never sweated, only glistened. She'd kept the joke going with him over the years. Now, she was "glistening" quite heavily. She kept moving.

In addition to the sight of the fire, there were now two other sensual keys, both its smell—good, actually—and its crackle, almost friendly in the night. Soon, there was still another smell, one which was unmistakable. It was the smell of freshly made coffee.

Soon, Emma was able to discern shapes just at the boundary of the firelight, one of them very large, the horse. The other seemed to be a man. This latter moved about, as if tending to chores in some regular pattern. The smell of the coffee was stronger.

A small stone dislodged under her left foot, then started a cascade of stones down into the gorge and Emma Shaw froze, realizing that she might have alerted whoever it was beside the fire. And she was relatively certain that it was only one person. But the person's movement pattern seemed uninterrupted.

She waited, crouching there uncomfortably amid the rocks, her eyes focused intently on the fire. The man shape seemed to settle in, back toward her, she realized, because the figure's outline was silhouetted by the flame. She could make out no detail, only blackness.

By the face of her wristwatch, she ticked off the minutes, seven going by before she felt that it might be safe to move again. Then, move she did, but more slowly and cautiously now, feeling each step out lest she cause more sounds in the night. She reasoned that perhaps the rolling of the river—there were small rapids all along its length in either direction as far as she had been able to see before dark—had obscured the noise, thus leaving whoever it was beside the fire unalerted to her presence.

Emma Shaw hoped.

At last, she was nearly to the bottom of the gorge, her improvised backpack made from the parachute pack weighing heavily on her, her right hand sweating inside the insulated glove. In her right hand, which was balled into a fist, was the .45 automatic.

She started to ease her way down to the comparatively level surface of the river bank.

There was a series of four clicks and a man's voice from behind her saying, "Stop where you are."

Emma Shaw came close to pissing in her panties.

Forty-One

Emma Shaw's mind raced. He used English, not one of the bastardized dialects of the Land Pirates. The way the words were said, there was a definite sign of education, again totally atypical of the Land Pirates. And, a Land Pirate would have shot first, because in the darkness and with her helmet on, she would most likely be mistaken for a man.

Emma Shaw decided to risk it, spinning around to her right, her thumb sweeping down the .45's safety. She was nearly fully turned around when something hard struck her on the shoulder near the right side of her neck and her arm went suddenly numb and she started to go down.

Her gun fell from her fingers, but she launched her weight against the legs of the man who had just struck her and they both fell onto the snow-splotched rocks. She head butted the man, and as her helmet made contact, she heard him exclaim in a kind of low growl, "Damnit!"

Then something was grabbing hold of her helmet,

265

snapping her head back and dragging her up to her knees simultaneously, her helmet pulling free of her head, her hair falling out from beneath it, a fist—it seemed huge—coming toward her face.

And it stopped.

"A girl!"

Emma Shaw seized the opportunity, crossing toward his jaw with her bunched up left fist, his head tilting away in order to dodge the blow, her fist missing the underside of his jaw, catching him at the flat of the bone just forward of the ear.

He was better at this, she realized in one fleeting instant as his left arced up toward her and darkness swept over her after an incredible flash of light.

John Rourke sat at the V-stol's copilot controls, his eyes scanning the instrument readings for any sign of a heat signature. This was their fourth sweep, and even John Rourke was beginning to despair of finding the theoretical tunnel openings. The craft was fifteen miles out from the mountain's center.

One of the Nazi enlisted personnel brought him a cup of coffee and Rourke nodded his thanks, then sniffed at the coffee before sipping at it. It smelled like nothing but coffee.

"Take it out another two miles only." Rourke told the pilot.

From behind him, he heard Spitz's voice. "I am beginning to think, Herr Doctor, that your idea, however clever, is mistaken."

"Perhaps," Rourke said, sipping again at his coffee. "Perhaps not. Time will tell, as the saying goes."

"But time is of the essence, is it not?"

Rourke didn't look at Spitz, still watching the instrument array. But he answered him. "Your Führer's remains have been inside the mountain, according to Dr. Zimmer, since immediately following the conclusion of World War II. That was in the middle of the fourth decade of the Twentieth Century. I shouldn't think a few hours will make much difference after almost seven centuries, would you?"

Spitz seemed to sigh. "I suppose not, Herr Doctor."

"Why don't you get some rest; we'll all need it, whether we blast our way in or we find a tunnel—"

John Rourke didn't finish what he had been about to say. As the pilot tacked tangentially outward to the two mile mark, John Rourke's eyes detected a heat signature on the thermal scan . . .

Emma Shaw opened her eyes but did not move. Her head was resting on something and she was stuffed inside a thermal sleeping bag identical to her own, but it didn't quite smell right. There was nothing bad about the smell, but it was different, a hint of tobacco about it.

As she turned her head to the right—her jaw hurt a little—she saw the figure of the man whom she'd fought. She still couldn't see his face. "Sorry I decked you, Commander Shaw," he said.

Her hands moved over her clothes inside the bag and she found that her Lancer pistol was still holstered to her body. He couldn't have missed it.

Her name he would have gotten off her helmet.

Emma Shaw debated about reaching for the second

267

pistol. After a second or so, she asked, "Who are you?"

"Long story, really. The name's Alan Crockett."

Emma Shaw laughed. "Yeah, right."

"Ever dawn on you, Commander, that there are some things for which military training is not always the answer? Well, that's why I really am Alan Crockett and I'm not in Hawaii, but I'm here instead."

"Alan Crockett died three years ago."

"No. Alan Crockett was made to appear to die—and it will be exactly four years ago in another month."

"That's crazy," Emma Shaw said, sitting up too fast and her head aching a little because of it. She moved her jaw. No teeth felt loose or damaged, but the jawbone was a little tender. "What the hell would Alan Crockett be doing out here?"

"The phrase is 'military intelligence,' which, as we all learn eventually, is an absurdity because the two words are mutually exclusive."

His voice did sound like Alan Crockett's voice, now that she thought of it. She had attended a series of lectures he'd given for the Navy survival school, on wilderness survival after going down. But Alan Crockett died in an avalanche while on a field training exercise in New Germany. His body was never recovered. "How come you're not dead?" Emma Shaw asked. "And where's my gun?"

"Here's your gun," he told her, turning around and handing it to her. As he offered the .45 to her, butt forward, the light from the fire caught his face and she could see it clearly. He had a mustache, wavy hair poking out beneath a broad brimmed hat. And the bridge of his nose had a bump where it looked like it might have been broken once, but never given over to cosmetic surgery. He looked like Professor Alan Crockett. "And I am here, Commander, I daresay, to advance the same cause in the service of which you are here. We're doing our patriotic duty for Uncle Sam. In my case, that meant pretending to die so I could move about unmolested in North America. In your case, I suspect it was a little less planned. Bombing run?"

"To get away from some missiles I had to trash my aircraft."

"Flying a Blackbird?"

She wasn't going to tell him that.

He laughed after her long pause. "I'm really not an enemy, Commander, but you can be as secretive as you like—if that makes you feel more comfortable."

"What did you hit me with?"

He laughed again. "My fist, and I am very sorry; the blow you delivered wasn't exactly a love pat, though."

"No." She flexed her fingers around the butt of her just returned gun.

"I emptied the chamber by the way for safety."

She nodded her head. "What'd you slug me with, when you hit me across the shoulder?"

He was still crouched by the fire, the smell of coffee from the pot near him sensually overpowering. "This." His right hand moved and just as if it had appeared there by magic his fingers were curled around the butt of a long barrelled handgun.

Emma Shaw had seen enough old cowboy videos to know what it was that he held in his hand. It was a six-shooter. She'd seen them at Lancer's showroom. And something started to click at the back of her mind, something from one of Alan Crockett's lectures. She repeated it aloud. "When you are in a survival situation, you want your weapons to be as easily user-serviceable as possible. Therefore, those which are overly complex should be avoided."

"Not quite a direct quote. I would have said 'one' rather than 'you'. And which handguns did I recommend?"

"All the old ones."

"Hardly. But all of the ones which I did recommend were, indeed, replicas of original cartridge arms."

"The Government Model .45—"

"Yes, and evidently you heeded my advice," he said.

"Someone else's advice," Emma Shaw told him—it was John Rourke's advice, actually. And her father always used one.

"Then your someone else is wise."

"He's not my someone else." But Emma Shaw wished that he was. "So I thought revolvers were complicated," she said, hurriedly changing the subject.

"They are, inherently, more complex mechanisms. Some, however, are quite easily serviced. Colt Single Action Army, Lancer reproduction, of course, but made to my own specifications."

"So, you know a lot about Alan Crockett. That doesn't make you Alan Crockett."

"No, it doesn't," he sighed. "Why don't you just call me Alan, and we can worry about the Crockett part later? All right, Commander?"

"Emma."

"E. Shaw. Emma, then. Were you planning on killing me and stealing my horse?"

"I thought I might."

"How about having some coffee? It's decaffeinated."

"Coffee out here. Real coffee." It smelled marvelous,

but she wasn't about to mention that.

"Once every sixty days, I make it my business to be at one of several specific sets of predesignated coordinates. Supplies are waiting for me. If I need something special, I'm out of luck. It's always the same. So, no herbal tea, I'm afraid."

"Very funny," she told him. She racked the action of the .45, just to see what he'd do. His shoulder tensed slightly beneath the huge winter coat that he wore, but other than that there was no reaction. His gun was already put away inside a black leather flap holster on his right thigh.

"Hungry? I can fix some bacon, some—"

"Aren't you afraid of the Land Pirates, I mean assuming you are who you say you are?"

"As a matter of fact, Emma, I hold a healthy respect for their seeming fascination with death and destruction for its own sake. But there aren't any Land Pirates for at least fifty miles, unless you brought some with you."

"You heard the rocks I dislodged, didn't you? And why aren't there any Land Pirates here?"

"Because there is something worse, and I knew someone was coming down the side of the gorge long before you dislodged those stones."

"What's worse than the Land Pirates?" Emma Shaw pressed. "Nazis? Eden Defense Forces?"

"If I were to tell you, Emma, one of two things would result. You'd either believe me and keep me up all night explaining, or you'd think me a liar. We'll talk about it tomorrow." He offered her a cup of coffee. "Here, it's a clean cup."

She took it.

Forty-Two

It was another vent and they wore CBR (Chemical/Biological/Radiological) protective gear as they approached it. But there was no gas emerging from it, other than carbonmonoxide, a by-product of the burning of carbon-based fuel or synth-fuel. Yet their sensors read out other warnings to them: high frequency microwave transmissions. At the same instant, Wolfgang Mann was speaking about how he missed New Germany.

The frequency of the transmissions was so high, their instruments nearly missed it. By the time that one of Spitz's men announced the interception, John Rourke realized that it was already too late, that they had fallen into two traps at the same time.

The only weapon Rourke had to hand was his HK-91 rifle. His right fist tightened on the pistol grip. He spoke into his radio, in German, ordering the pilot of the V-stol, "Rourke to aircraft. Rourke to aircraft. Respond. Over."

The pilot did not respond and there was only the

faint crackle of static.

John Rourke turned toward Hauptsturmführer Gunther Spitz half thinking that perhaps he should shoot the man and be done with it, but realizing that Gunther Spitz had been played just as he had, played for a fool. Rourke stayed his hand. "Let's get out of here," he said in English. "Quickly, but not running." They were within yards of the vent pipe which was the heat source that had been identified from the air, the aircraft a quarter mile back, having stood ready to come in for them should that be required.

John Rourke had a thought.

Now the aircraft was not responding. And they were too far away from it to be able to tell by sound whether or not it had taken off. But, Rourke knew that it had.

"What is happening, Herr Doctor?"

Rourke looked at Spitz, rasped into his radio, "Give me a straight answer to this, Hauptsturmführer. Do you have any form of sealed orders which were to be opened upon penetration of the mountain? Tell me now, because you may not have the chance later."

Gunther Spitz said nothing for a moment, but his radio was open, Rourke could hear him breathing.

The HK-91 in Rourke's hands felt ridiculously light, as a weapon sometimes did when its use seemed somehow, inexplicably imminent.

Rourke heard Paul racking the bolt of his sub-machinegun.

At last, Hauptsturmführer Spitz said, "I have such orders but I do not know their content."

"Tell me about Generaloberst Mann. Is there anything you know about him that I do not?"

"I do not know what you mean, Herr Doctor."

Rourke rasped, "Is Herr Doctor Zimmer experimenting with cloning?"

"What?"

They were moving together in a brisk commando walk, Spitz's men flanking them on either side, assault weapons at the ready.

"When your people raided the cryogenic center in New Germany, did you have all the details? A complete layout, all the data concerning sentry positions, movement. You had an inside man?"

"But he was killed; that was the instruction, Herr Doctor."

"You only think you killed the contact; you only killed one of his underlings," Rourke said. "The cryogenic chamber had been raided before, even before Dr. Zimmer awakened from his own cryogenic sleep, but by his orders nonetheless."

Paul cut into the conversation, saying, "Will somebody tell me what the hell is going on?"

Hauptsturmführer Gunther Spitz's voice held not its usual condescending tone when Spitz replied. "I do not know, Herr Rubenstein."

"We've been set up," John Rourke remarked. "Spitz, keep your men on a tight leash, follow what I do."

"I do not—"

"We will be attacked. If it's a gunfight, we all make a run in the direction where the aircraft was. The rocks west of the aircraft could make a suitable defensive position. If we're outnumbered and outflanked—" As if John Rourke could somehow predict what was about to happen—to have had that ability would have been a curse, he'd always thought, despite its being handy at

275

times—the ground below their feet began to move leftward.

"What is this!" Spitz shouted, Rourke's ears ringing with the sound of the man's voice.

But, before John Rourke could answer, there was a voice, the English very American and perfect. "You are surrounded! You will stand still. Do not raise your weapons or you will be cut down. You are surrounded!"

Then Wolfgang Mann began to speak almost as if his voice were disembodied. "There is an entryway opening at coordinates—" And he recited degrees, minutes and seconds of longitude and latitude. John Rourke could not risk movement. He said into his radio, "Are we getting a microwave transmission reading?"

"Hurry!" Spitz shouted.

The enlisted man burdened with the communications equipment stammered in response, "It is—it is in the high—"

And John Rourke had one of those moments of instant clarity, when all stood naked and revealed.

And he spoke through his radio set to Paul, Spitz and the others. "Do as they say. We're surrendering."

"We—" Spitz began, but did not finish.

Forty-Three

The enlisted personnel were led away separately, only John Rourke, Paul Rubenstein, Spitz, and Doctor Mentz kept together, surrounded by two dozen men armed with assault rifles of a type John Rourke had never seen before.

Rourke's only visible weapon, the HK-91, was taken from him, as were the issue rifles of the other men and Paul's German MP-40 submachinegun and M-16. But no attempt was made at a search, almost as if any weapons which might have been secreted on their persons would not have been worth bothering with.

Each of the enemy personnel wore some sort of environmental suit and respiratory equipment. And they were the enemy; of that, John Rourke was certain. On the shoulder of each man's uniform there was a brassard sewn or otherwise attached. The symbol adorning the brassard was a white cross surrounded by a golden sunburst, the cross superimposed at the junction of its cross members with a black swastika.

Nothing of the guards' faces could be seen under

their breathing apparatus.

Rourke, Rubenstein, Spitz, and Dr. Mentz moved at their center, the enemy personnel filed on either side of them and ranked across both front and rear. The enemy personnel, weapons at a stylized high port, marched with parade ground snap and in perfect step over the snowfield and toward the massive mawlike opening in the ground before them. The enlisted personnel, likewise surrounded, had gone in first, two of the enemy—presumably military or political officers—conferring for some time before John Rourke and the others were started into motion.

Hauptsturmführer Gunther Spitz began to ask Rourke a question, but Rourke snapped, "Radio silence; I'm sure they're reading our transmissions." And inside John Rourke there was a deep and gnawing fear. Should Paul Rubenstein be discovered as a Jew, perhaps through some careless or intentional remark of one of the Nazis, push might instantly come to shove.

John Rourke had urged surrender for two reasons. They were vastly outnumbered by a well-armed force, which would have made escape dicey at best, and escape to where was part of that; and he needed to get inside this facility in order to find out why he had really been sent. Sarah's life, that of Wolfgang Mann, the lives of Michael and Annie and Natalia as well, might all hang in the balance.

But at last it was clear to John Rourke what had been done—not why, though. Prior to Deitrich Zimmer's own awakening from cryogenic sleep, along with Martin, or perhaps even prior to Zimmer's taking the Sleep, Zimmer's personnel had carried out very specific orders. These orders involved the theft of cellular material from Wolfgang Mann's body, and Sarah's as well.

A simple skin cell was all that was needed. In John Rourke's day, more than six centuries ago, frogs and other animals were replicated in this manner, called cloning, but—to Rourke's knowledge at least—never any higher animals. Each cell contained the DNA code for replication of the entire organism, a duplicate, like a Xerox copy.

Unlike in some science fiction, however, there was one inherent problem with cloning, other than moral concerns. That was that even though the physical characteristics would be identical between the original and the replicant, as of then—and, he assumed, still today—there was no means by which the contents of the original subject's brain could be transferred or duplicated within the replicant.

It was all so abundantly clear that John Rourke cursed his own stupidity for not having seen it earlier.

Seeing indeed.

Deitrich Zimmer saw with two eyes.

Deitrich Zimmer had had himself cloned, the replicant grown to adulthood, then its left eye—the ultimately perfect tissue match—removed, given to him to replace the one he had sacrificed in order to fake his own death a century earlier.

And Wolfgang Mann's bizarrely subdued behavior.

What had, in the final analysis, made John Rourke realize what Zimmer had done was that Wolfgang Mann, no matter how poorly he felt, no matter how slowly he was emerging from the effects of the Sleep, was at once a gentleman and in love with Rourke's wife, Sarah. From either motivation, Wolfgang Mann would have done what he did not do, ask how she was.

This Wolfgang Mann either already knew or didn't care.

And—a chill again ran along the length of Rourke's spine, terminating in the hairs at the nape of his neck—the Sarah whom John Rourke had seen in her recovery was probably not Sarah at all.

They were in the maw, now.

And it was no simple synth-concrete tunnel through which they moved. Rather it was more like a landing bay of enormous and, at least to John Rourke, unprecedented proportions. The interior surface was all rust-colored metal, with buttressed supports vaulting upward into the darkness of the domelike ceiling, extending from side to side as well. The span at surface level where they walked was more than two hundred yards across, their guards staying to the north side of the structure.

There was a muted roar, and John Rourke's eyes followed toward it across the vast expanse. There were aircraft of all sorts there, as though somehow they were a collection rather than a fleet. One of these was taxiing forward now. And in one instant of recognition what had remained a mystery to John Rourke and his entire Family for well over a century was resolved.

On the occasion when Michael originally discovered the survival retreat where Madison's people had lived, Michael had set out not to find a colony of survivors, but instead to find an object he had seen in the sky. He found it, too. The mysterious object was an ordinary aircraft, extraordinary in that it definitely dated from the period Before the Night of the War, or was at least a faithful duplicate.

The aircraft which moved forward now was such a craft, a U.S. F-14 Tomcat. But there were aircraft of all modern vintages, even propeller-driven models dating from the period of World War II. And there were the most modern aircraft as well, either purloined or cloned from state-of-the-art warplanes in the air forces of the world.

But how was it that such aircraft had never been detected by the Nazis who so carefully observed this mountain and its environs? Or, had they?

Rourke's eyes were on the apparent leader of the group which surrounded them. A man, presumably enlisted, walked in the fellow's wake, Rourke's rifle and Paul Rubenstein's submachinegun slung at the man's left side.

Although most of Rourke's usual arms were beneath the protective suit that he wore and would be slow and difficult to reach, John Rourke planned ahead. The A.G. Russell Sting IA Black Chrome, minus its usual sheath, was taped under the flap of the CBR suit's utility pouch, instantly accessible. It was only a knife, but one of the best in the world, and it would be enough.

There was no evidence to suggest that the atmosphere here in the landing bay area was at all unbreathable, that the environment suits worn by the military personnel surrounding Rourke, Rubenstein and the others were anything more than a precaution.

But John Rourke did not feel like taking chances with anything not requiring risk. He would maintain the integrity of his suit, just in case, but before their situation became more difficult, he would take steps to alter the odds.

Paul Rubenstein walked beside him, and as Rourke glanced toward his friend, their eyes met. There was wariness in Paul's eyes, and a look of amazement, too. John Rourke imagined that Paul's eyes mirrored his own. Whoever these people were, they were technologically sophisticated in at least a quirky sort of way, and somehow he felt they were very powerful.

Forty-Four

Since she could not sleep, Emma Shaw lit a cigarette.

The self-proclaimed Alan Crockett, his big single-action revolver in his right hand, slept opposite her, on the other side of the dying fire.

Electronic surveillance sensors were set up about the camp's perimeter. She had her guns. Emma Shaw should have felt secure.

Instead, she did not. If this man really was Alan Crockett—and the more she studied his face, the more pronounced the resemblance seemed—he was in some ways a modern-day John Rourke. Crockett, unlike John, was not a physician, nor had he been in the Central Intelligence Agency. Indeed, there was no Central Intelligence Agency in this century, only the various internal divisions of ONI, or the Office of Naval Intelligence. But he was a survival expert in his own right, and a weapons expert as well. Crockett, however, was an archaeologist.

Unlike the assumed stereotype of his profession, Crockett didn't look bookish, nor did he usually spend his time (although he had to occasionally, surely) pouring through old musty books and vid-tapes. He was, perenially, in the field.

It was Alan Crockett who had uncovered the ruins of the Louvre Museum at the bottom of the frozen shallow lake where Paris, France, had been Before the Night of the War. He had discovered the Mona Lisa and numbers of other presumed lost original pieces of pre-War art in a hermetically sealed vault.

It was Alan Crockett who, by means of ground-breaking underwater archaeology techniques, recovered the Crown Jewels of England (and nearly lost his life doing so).

Name some ancient artifact and Alan Crockett, if he hadn't already found it, was hot on its trail. Until the accident. Through historical records (he had found those during his unauthorized foray into Eden-protected territory to what had been Chicago), Alan Crockett discovered that on the Night of the War there had been a naval disaster of what normally would have been considered epic proportions. Apparently as the result of a missile strike against a United States nuclear submarine operating clandestinely in the North Atlantic, a wave of incredible size swamped and overturned the passenger liner SS *Triumphant*.

Aboard the *Triumphant*, as the story which appeared after Alan Crockett's death recounted it, was an exhibit on loan from the British Museum to the Field Museum of Natural History in Chicago, entitled "Treasures of Empire," artifacts from Egypt, India and all over the British Empire from the period of its height during the Victorian Era. Its worth in money would have been enormous, but its historical value even greater. While searching for the *Triumphant*, Alan Crockett supposedly perished.

Emma Shaw's attention focused on a large, orange ember, glowing hotly in the darkness. She could draw an imaginary line between the glowing red tip of her cigarette and the still-burning wood. But her concentration lay elsewhere, still, on the story this man—who said he was Alan Crockett—had told her. And he hadn't told her much.

After she accepted his offered cup of coffee, Crockett said, "You see, because of my field work over the years—and I suppose in some small part due to an undeserved reputation for a certain recklessness—the intelligence people thought that I would be ideal for their job. I didn't quite agree—what they needed was a SEAL Team group. But I took the job anyway."

"I don't understand," she'd said. "Intell like they'd want can be gotten from the air, either by overflights or satellite."

"Evidently, Commander Shaw, that is what the intelligence people thought, too. Until they realized that there were gaping holes in their North American coverage. And they had no idea why."

"Gaping holes?"

He'd lit a cigarette after offering one to her (her father the cop had taught her not to accept cigarettes from strangers because they might contain drugs). She declined. "Not holes in the literal sense, of course, but anomalies, shall we say. Vapor trails from jet aircraft, but no sign of the aircraft. Things like that. What was happening?"

"Why are you telling me this?"

He'd smiled at her. It was a good smile; she had to

give him that, whoever he was. "Aside from occasional satellite uplinks through a scrambler—or, unless you count some rather unpleasant interaction with Land Pirates over the last two years—I haven't carried on a conversation with another human being in more than a year. My horse there—his name is Wilbur, a sort of left-handed salute to some vid-tape nostalgia I always found oddly amusing—is the last of my original companions, as it were. There were three of us, myself, an intelligence officer named Hal Weatherby and a SEAL named Dan Collins. Weatherby was a bright man, but followed directions poorly. He wandered off in a blizzard and we found him two days later, frozen to death. That was only three months after we'd inserted. In fairness to Weatherby, it was one of those freak storms that just come up around here.

"Then Dan Collins died as a result of a rather protracted gunfight with a gang of Land Pirates. They only killed one of us and we killed seven of them, which I guess made us the winners. On the other hand we accounted for twenty percent of their number and they accounted for fifty percent of our number. I buried Dan, just like he and I had buried Hal Weatherby— only a little more gracefully positioned, actually. Hal was still frozen and we had neither the time nor the means to thaw him out.

"After Dan died, it was me alone, except for Wilbur and the three horses remaining in the remuda. The last of those horses broke a leg and I had to kill him. That left me alone with Wilbur. I talk to him quite a bit, but as yet he hasn't answered me, which I suppose is a good thing. We're on our way out. In another fourteen days exactly, there will be an aircraft meeting me near the site of old Albany—that was the capital of New York State Before the Night of the War. But if the plane isn't big enough for Wilbur, they'll just have to go back and get another aircraft. I don't abandon friends."

"You don't know that John Rourke is alive then, do you?"

And then he started to laugh, so hard that Emma Shaw thought he would choke. "John Rourke's alive?! What do you take me for, madam? A fool?"

"He was in cryogenic freeze. All the stories about his being dead were a cover-up." Like the stories about Alan Crockett being dead? She wondered. She added, "I know him, personally."

"Well, good for you. I thought I saw Jayne Mansfield one night during a blizzard about six months ago."

"Jayne who?"

"She was a rather underappreciated blonde actress of the mid-Twentieth Century, actually—at least I think so—a rather fine comedienne. She was most noted for her unique profile."

"Ohh, I see."

He shook his head indulgently, saying, "I seriously doubt that you do."

"I do know John Rourke. We're very good friends. He's a wonderful man."

"He'd have to be. He was around in the mid-Twentieth Century as well."

Emma Shaw said no more on the subject, and neither did Crockett. But she asked, "So?"

"So?"

"Did you find out what was going on? I mean, about

those 'gaping holes' and everything?"

He snapped the butt of his cigarette into the fire. "I ration myself, because the only supply I get of these is from my pickups. Neither Weatherby nor Collins smoked." He exhaled loudly, and it sounded like half a yawn. "Yes and no, actually. I have, on a multiplicity of separate occasions, found myself beneath such a vapor trail. When looking straight up, I saw nothing leaving it; or, at least, nothing which my instruments could detect. That was unnerving, to say the least. And I pieced together some data over the last two years, mostly from the time I spent among the Land Pirates."

"Yeah, right." Emma Shaw exclaimed, laughing.

He shrugged his shoulders, "Choose to believe me or not; that's academic. At any event, a little way east of here there is, purportedly, a mountain. The vapor trails—according to the Land Pirates with whom I've spoken—sometimes seem to originate from near that mountain, or dissipate near it. Anyone who goes near that mountain never returns. If it is the same mountain, Before the Night of the War, it was once a Presidential War Retreat, then abandoned. So, it should have been habitable inside."

"Is that all you found out in two years?"

"All?!" He leaned forward, shaking his gloved right index finger toward her nose. "My dear Commander, aside from getting—and then satellite uplinking— video on Eden's newest fighter aircraft, Eden's latest surface warfare tactics, troop strengths in North America above the thirty-fifth parallel, discovering a safe route across the radioactive zone which severs the continent at what used to be the Mississippi River and getting detailed strength and movement reports on the larger Land Pirate bands, I think that is enough. Don't you?"

"Well, I mean—so, are you going to go to this mountain and check it out?"

"No," he told her. "We are. Wilbur is the only remaining horse. Short of bumping into Land Pirates and stealing a horse from them, he's it, as far as transportation. I imagine you have a survival raft and were planning on using it to get you downriver, right?" He didn't wait for a reply. "Well, don't. About fifty miles further down, there's a band of Land Pirates called the Deadlanders. They have their base of operations right on the riverbank. They kill everyone who isn't a Deadlander. In your case, you might not be that lucky. With that helmet off, you're quite attractive. So, if they took you alive, they'd probably keep you alive. A healthy woman like yourself might survive two, possibly three months before the overwork, the undernourishment and the continual forced sex caused you to die of exhaustion."

"So, I shouldn't use the raft."

"Exactly. You shouldn't use the raft. We're going to see the mountain. Together. We'll learn all that we can and then you and I—and Wilbur, of course—will head for Albany and the airplane. And I'll be very happy. You'll be very happy. Even Wilbur will be very happy. Now, I am going to get some sleep. I suggest that you do the same. We have a few long days ahead of us."

Emma Shaw pretended to go to sleep, watched him draw his cowboy gun, watched him go out and check the perimeter alarms, check his horse, then slip into his sleeping bag.

Whoever he was, this man who called himself Alan Crockett had an interesting story to tell.

But how much of it was true?

She snapped her cigarette butt into the fire, lay back and tried to sleep. Her eyes just didn't want to stay closed.

Forty-Five

About five hundred yards into the vast structure, and perhaps one hundred feet down, maybe a bit more, the troops guarding John Rourke, Paul Rubenstein, Hauptsturmführer Gunther Spitz and Doctor Mentz stopped before large double doors. The doors were made of the same material as the walls, the support beams, the ceiling and the floor, the same sort of rust-colored metal.

Rather than an entrance into another chamber or anything like that—when the doors opened with something akin to a pneumatic hiss—beyond them John Rourke saw another tunnel.

This tunnel was appreciably smaller in height and width. Its purpose was clear. It was a tube through which something akin to a subway system travelled. To Rourke's right, nearer to the outside, there seemed to be a switching yard of some sort, but the lighting was dim between where he stood on a sort of platform—the same rust-colored metal—and the yard, making the recognition of detail difficult.

There was a car coming from the right, out of the switching yard. And, it was most curiously shaped. John Rourke remembered such cars from his boyhood. It looked like a trolley car, save for the fact that it ran on a single rail—probably magnetic—and there was no trolley apparatus extending upward from the roof.

The color of the car was a muted, almost faded shade of red. And, true to its image, at the front of the car there was an antique-looking lamp; it cast a dim yellow light before the trolley car, only faintly illuminating the solitary rail.

"Welcome to Oz," Paul said in a low voice. Rourke said nothing, only nodded. No brick roads yet, of yellow or any color, but indeed there was an almost surreal quality to the place.

And the guards. Why had they not searched their prisoners rather than just taking the visible weapons? Were personal weapons unknown here? Or, was fear of the outside atmosphere so pronounced that an environment suit was inviolate?

And, aside from the message given, notifying Rourke, Paul, Rubenstein and the others that they were surrounded and outnumbered, no other words had passed between captors and captives.

The car was slowing down now, and Rourke assumed that soon they would all be boarding it. That would likely be the moment to recover their weapons and disarm or kill the enemy personnel. When Rourke saw the shoulder patches worn by these men, any softness in his heart eroded fully. Nazis like Gunther Spitz and Dr. Mentz were evil; but, even more evil, if that were possible, were those who masked race hatred beneath the guise of a religion a principle tenet of which declared that God is love.

Killing unnecessarily was the mark of a brute; but, if it came to killing these men, John Rourke would do it remorselessly. They would kill him, perhaps joyously.

The trolley car stopped.

Doctor Mentz asked, "Where will this take us, Herr Doctor?"

Paul answered, "To the wizard's office, possibly."

John Rourke had already transferred the A.G. Russell Sting IA Black Chrome knife from beneath the flap of the accessory bag to his right hand.

The doors on the side of the trolley car at the front and rear opened. There were steps going up into the car.

Posted on a little round seat was a motorman.

But the motorman was not real. Neither was the motorman some sort of sophisticated wonder of modern science. The motorman was, in fact, an audioanimatronic robot, not really a robot at all, but an articulated mannequin with mechanically operated facial expressions and hand and body movements and a prerecorded series of messages to imitate a human voice.

As the lead elements of the military unit surrounding Rourke, Rubenstein and the others started aboard the trolley car, the motorman's voice twanged out in something roughly like Midwestern standard, "Careful to watch your step there! Find a seat and stay clear of the doors, please!"

Paul was shaking his head, either in disbelief or disgust, perhaps both. John Rourke found the thing faintly amusing, but rapidly passing round the bend of what might ordinarily be thought bizarre.

As Rourke stepped up into the trolley car—the leader of the unit and the man carrying Rourke's and Paul's weapons were already seated—Rourke's eyes took in how the audioanimatronic motorman was attached to the car's controls. The right hand rested on the controller and the left hand on the door bar, the feet set to be working pedals. Unless there were wireless connections, however, the motorman seemed to function as a real motorman would, merely to operate, not as an integral part of the controls.

John Rourke remarked through his radio to any and all listening, "When I was a boy, and we'd be bussing it for some school function, I remember that some people always picked the bus as the place for getting violent." Paul was now up into the trolley. Spitz and Mentz were not.

But someone would be needed to deal with the enemy personnel still on the platform.

"Violent," Rourke said again. "Now!"

Forty-Six

Paul Rubenstein mule-kicked his left foot back and upward into the testicles of the armed man behind him and the man, at last, spoke. "You—" Paul's right elbow snapped back and whatever the fellow had been about to say was terminated in the same instant. Paul's elbow contacted teeth and bone and there was a squeal of pain.

John Rourke was a blur of motion. The little black A.G. Russell knife was in John's right hand. It pistoned forward, burrowing into the neck of one man, then withdrew to thrust into the chest of another. John elbow smashed one man, knee smashed another. Paul realized he was needed more elsewhere. The radio receiver beside his ear was feeding him grunts and groans from the two Nazis who were still on the trolley platform. Paul twisted round on the little rubber-treaded step and, supporting himself on the chrome-plated grab rails to either side, swung his feet outward, catching one of the guards in the chest, slinging the man back into two more of the guards.

Even if Mentz and Spitz were Nazis, there seemed to be nothing slow-witted about Hauptsturmführer Gunther Spitz. Spitz had already brought one of the guards down and was decking another with the butt of one of the peculiar-looking assault rifles the guards carried.

Paul Rubenstein jumped down from the trolley car, onto the backs of two of the guards, these men battling with Dr. Mentz, Mentz handling himself against them gamely enough, but ineffectively. Under his breath, Paul hissed, "Why am I helping this son of a bitch?" But there wasn't time to ponder the question any further. Paul bulldogged both of the enemy personnel to the platform surface. He slammed one man's forehead into the metal of the platform, shoving the second man away. As this man made to bring his rifle up, Dr. Mentz struck the fellow a sincere-looking but apparently wholly ineffectual blow to the jaw. The guard wheeled away from Paul Rubenstein, toward Dr. Mentz instead.

But Paul was already moving, hurtling his body weight from the rear against the guard's left knee.

The guard stumbled, toppled forward, and Gunther Spitz buttstroked the man across the side of the head.

Four men were down inside the trolley, only the officer who led the party still in motion. John Rourke took steps to correct that problem, dodging the muzzle of the officer's rifle, slapping it aside. Rourke thrust forward with his knife through the protective suit and just below the respirator unit, into the throat.

Rourke pulled back on the knife, Rourke's right foot snapping upward, its instep catching the officer in the testicles. As the man's body doubled forward, Rourke stabbed the knife downward just below the nape of the neck, finishing him quickly.

John Rourke stepped back, moved over the just-dead man and unlimbered his own HK-91 from another of the bodies, this one draped half over the back of a chair. It was suffocatingly warm inside the environment suit after the exertion, but Rourke had no way of knowing whether he could risk removing the protective mask, even for a few seconds, just to cool his skin. Not knowing, he dismissed the idea.

Rourke was already down the steps, racking the bolt of the HK just in case the chamber had been cleared. The already chambered round flew outward, onto the track bed.

But there was no need to fire. Between Paul and Spitz and Mintz all was quiet on the platform.

Rourke held a finger to his lips, signalling silence. Their radio transmissions might be monitored by the enemy.

Rourke jumped down from the trolley and onto the platform then from the platform to the track bed. He retrieved the rifle cartridge—he'd always believed in the old aphorism about wasting not and wanting not—then clambered back up to the platform.

John Rourke pointed toward the trolley, resisting the impulse to shout, "All aboard!" But it would have been inappropriate, at any event.

As they started up, Rourke removed the magazine from the HK. He reinserted the loose round he'd retrieved. There were two magazines bound together with a clip, giving him twenty rounds, then another twenty, very fast.

As he reset the HK's safety and started about the business of separating the audioanimatronic motorman from the trolley's controls, Rourke judged that he could well be needing all the firepower he could lay his hands on here. And that might well not be enough.

And the man who looked like, sounded like and claimed to be Generaloberst Wolfgang Mann climbed aboard.

Forty-Seven

Thorn Rolvaag needed sleep, but he needed answers still more. And analysis of the data at hand via computer modelling was the only hope.

The computer room aboard the USS *Cherokee*, the United States Navy's only floating laboratory, was immense, big enough to house the old mainframe computers of the mid-Twentieth Century. He'd seen a vid-tape of a still wonderfully funny film from that period, which had starred Katherine Hepburn and Spencer Tracy. In the film, there was such a computer (or more likely, a mocked-up representation). Other films of the period, as well as still photographs, had shown these huge machines which dominated entire walls, running on enormous reels of magnetic tape.

This room within the bowels of the submarine USS *Cherokee* was enormous not because of the computers but because of the number of very small laptop-sized machines like that on the desk before him. The room could service up to one hundred researchers each working at a separate task, each drawing (simultaneously if need be) from the same memory banks, working independently or on line.

But Thorn Rolvaag was the only person in the room, his machine the only one turned on, his needs the only ones the memory banks served.

A man given over to panic would have looked at the enormity of the trench beneath the Pacific and declared in desperation that here, at last, was the beginning of the end of the world. If the trench kept spreading that was exactly what might result, of course. But, Thorn Rolvaag was not given over to flights of doomsaying. He saw a problem and took steps to correct it. Such would be the case with this trench.

If it continued—it was expanding at an ever-growing rate—it would grow exponentially in length and, in a relatively short period of time, reach the end of the Pacific Plate and impact against the North American Plate, around the new coast of North America where, Before the Night of the War, the San Andreas fault had been. The resistance given by the North American Plate would either stop the fissure completely or, as Rolvaag assumed to be more likely, cause it to split and spread.

That was the scenario for terrestrial destruction, that the entire Ring of Fire would go. In that event, any number of deadly possibilities loomed, some scenarios clearly indicating that there would be the cessation of all life on the planet.

But, if the fissure could be blocked and closed before reaching the North American Plate, in a slow, controlled manner, then the fissure might be stopped.

Disaster might be averted.

The key to closing the fissure would be the successful

employment of nuclear explosives. And that required no computer scenario. To convince the powers-that-be that nuclear devices could be utilized in a manner which matched their original intent—the peaceful use of atomic energy to create harbors, level terrain, help mankind—would be beyond Herculean. And it was frightening to realize that the United States, unless it used virtually every single nuclear missile at its command (including those seized from the Soviets more than a century ago, which would have to be upgraded for practical utility), would not have enough nuclear material to do the job.

Small nuclear charges would have to be placed all along the hundreds of miles which the fissure already covered, and every day that went by would add to that number of required charges. If the United States used its entire inventory of nuclear weapons, Eden and her Nazi allies would attack, and the United States and the other members of the Trans-Global Alliance would be powerless to stalemate Eden and the Nazis, subsequently powerless to repel the inevitable invasion. Because Eden's stockpile of nuclear material would be intact.

Mankind was faced, Thorn Rolvaag realized, with its greatest challenge.

Weeks would go by before the attempt to halt the growth of the fissure could be made, even if full cooperation were assured immediately.

And, there would be a point of no return. If too great a quantity of nuclear explosives were utilized when the fissure reached the North American Plate, the same disastrous result would be precipitated as if the fissure reached the Plate.

Thorn Rolvaag thought of his wife and children when he closed his eyes. Even with his eyes closed he could still see the computer monitor's screen. The scenario the computer was running was what he had mentally labelled Megadeath. It was the scenario which called for the chain eruption of the volcanoes surrounding the Ring of Fire and the total destruction of the planet Earth.

Forty-Eight

The main body of sensing equipment was gone, with the enlisted man who had worn it, taken away along with the other enlisted personnel.

But there was a small, hand-held sensing unit that Doctor Mentz had. John Rourke was forced by circumstances to rely on that. While Rourke piloted the trolley car along its single rail through a rust-colored metal tube toward he knew not what, Mentz took readings. "The atmosphere, aside from having rather high traces of ferrous substances, seems perfectly normal. There is no presence of gas."

Rourke nodded, made his decision. Spaced every ten yards apart, there were glowing yellow lights, illuminating the tunnel, the lights inset directly overhead. These lights, coupled with the yellow headlight of the trolley itself, combined to make huge, ghostly looking shadows all around them, even inside the car (which was also illuminated in yellow lights). Rourke pulled off his mask.

Rourke's face felt suddenly cold, and the rush to his

303

senses made his head swim. He controlled his breathing carefully as he instructed, "Unsuit as much as you need to for whatever additional weapons and gear you think you'll need then resuit, wearing those materials on the outside. The chance for contamination will have to be run." And that was the real danger. The more Rourke considered what had been encountered atop the summit, especially in light of the shoulder brassards worn by the soldiers here, the greater was his certitude that the lethal hallucinogenic gas was utilized as a means of execution, not as a weapon. The suits the men had worn, although there had been no time for detailed examination of one of the dead, seemed to be entirely superfluous, at least from any practical considerations.

A society isolated from all the rest of humankind for well over six centuries would have developed its own immunology and perhaps its own diseases, to which other humans would not be immune. That was obvious—the more restricted the gene pool, the better the chances. Several genetically related diseases, for example, had been outbred at Mid-Wake. Among blacks, for example, sickle cell anemia had ceased to exist.

Paul was beside Rourke already stripping down enough of the protective suit which he wore to access the Browning High Powers, his knife and other gear.

While Rourke still controlled the trolley he called back to Spitz. "Spitz, those sealed orders. Will you open them now and read them to us?"

Spitz said, "And if I am ordered to keep the contents from you, Herr Doctor?"

"You'll have to make that decision yourself. I need to know what's inside. I will know. We didn't come here

304

for some crazy genetic scheme based on cloning Adolf Hitler. That may be a fringe benefit as your Dr. Zimmer sees it, but not the real reason. That should be obvious by now. We came here because of this place, not Adolf Hitler's remains. If those remains are here, they're only a secondary objective to Zimmer. When this fellow claiming to be Wolfgang Mann announced those coordinates to the pilot of the V-stol, our mission here was done. Zimmer sent us as decoys, to find the way into this place so Zimmer's personnel can follow us and penetrate the facility themselves. You have to understand that by now."

"You are, it would appear, correct, Herr Doctor. But surely Herr Doctor Zimmer's plan need not be readily discernible to us. We only serve—"

Paul, out of his mask by now, said, "Give it a rest, huh? What's the matter with you? Your Herr Doctor Zimmer sent us all out to get killed, and you don't care? I admire loyalty, but there's loyalty and then there's stupidity."

"I will open the orders." Gunther Spitz declared, not sounding as though he had warmed to the idea at all. But perhaps despite being a Nazi, the man had some semblance of common sense. John Rourke glanced back over his right shoulder in the same instant that Spitz took from beneath his tunic a device about the size of a pocket calculator. It opened almost like a book. As it did so, there was the faintest hum.

Rourke was already turning his eyes back toward the tunnel but from the corner of his eye he saw Paul starting to move. And then Dr. Mentz shouted, "Hauptsturmführer!"

Rourke instinctively dodged and dropped shouting

to Paul, "Look out!"

There was the pulse of a high-yield energy weapon. Rourke released the controls of the car, wheeled. The deadman's switch was already starting to slow the car. Paul crouched midway between Rourke and the rear of the car near to the steps.

"John!" Paul threw one of the two Browning High Powers he carried and John Rourke caught it—it was the second gun—not the battered old one Paul had carried since just after the Night of the War. Rourke racked its slide knowing that Paul would never have thrown the gun had it been chamber loaded.

Hauptsturmführer Gunther Spitz was flat on the floor of the car. Dr. Mentz lay over him, the center of Mentz's back burning from the close-range shot. And Mentz was obviously dead, the smell of burning flesh only slightly more nauseating than the exposed spinal column. There was a small energy pistol in the right hand of the man claiming to be Wolfgang Mann. Paul was shouting, "Hold it, Mann!"

The imposter stabbed the pistol toward Paul. John Rourke fired over Paul's shoulder hitting the man who claimed to be Wolfgang Mann twice in the chest, then twice more in the thorax, Rourke's ears ringing with the flat cracks of the 9mm Parabellums in the confined space.

"You killed Wolfgang Mann?" Paul was shouting.

"No, I didn't," Rourke rasped, getting to his feet. "Paul. Stop the car. Brake control on the left just like an automobile."

"Right—but then who the hell is—"

Spitz was getting to his feet, recoiling from the smell of burning flesh, Dr. Mentz's body still smoldered as

306

Spitz crawled from beneath it.

"What is this!" Spitz shouted.

"This is a clone of Wolfgang Mann," Rourke said as he moved past Spitz, stepped over the corpse of Dr. Mentz and looked down at the man he had just shot to death. "A clone, with some sort of implant in his head that allowed him to be programmed for certain responses. When you opened your orders—some sort of computer?"

"Yes?"

"When you opened the case or powered up—I imagine it powers up when opened. But that was a signal for the clone of Generalobest Mann here to kill you and anyone else from the party that he could. Remember when he recited coordinates just as we were taken prisoner? That wasn't a flash of inspiration for the heroic aircrew that would go for help. That was to alert Dr. Zimmer's invasion force, which is standing by somewhere near here.

"And," Rourke added, "we'll be caught in the middle and you know too much, Spitz, so if we make it out of here alive, Zimmer'll want you dead anyway. Zimmer's ability to clone human beings is a power he'll jealously guard and it's only a power as long as it's a secret."

"This is madness."

John Rourke ignored Spitz's comment, his concentration focused on the clone of Wolfgang Mann. Skin elasticity was a little too good for a person of Mann's biological age, even considering the salubrious effects of the Sleep. Already Rourke was dragging the dead body toward the trolley door.

"Why are we stopping?" Paul called back.

John Rourke was acting on a hunch. And he said as

much. "If I were Zimmer and I were diabolical enough—not to mention sufficiently talented—to clone a human being, then utilize computerlike microcircuitry in order to program certain responses, I'd equip my weapon with a fail-safe device which could itself be turned into a weapon when needed."

"I do not understand you!" Spitz almost shouted. "This is madness!"

"Perhaps. Help me roll him out. Much as I'd like to examine him, I don't think there'll be time. Paul!"

"Yes, John?"

"Be ready to step on it when I tell you to. We may need to distance ourselves as much as possible from this body. And keep down low. If I'm right, no telling how powerful an explosive might be inside some body cavity or another."

"Yeah—right—"

Paul worked the door control.

Spitz, shaken, ashen-looking, grabbed the other end of the body, Rourke's hands already under the armpits. They carried the dead man down and into the railbed. "Here. Place him over the rail. If he is a bomb, may as well get some good out of him. Come on. Hurry!" And together Rourke and the Nazi officer ran to the trolley and up the steps. "Go for it Paul."

The trolley started into motion, John Rourke swinging down in the stepwell, his eyes cast back toward the body they were leaving behind, but his face and body shielded. Almost two minutes had passed since bringing down the clone of Wolfgang Mann. The delay might be another sort of fail-safe device. Either that, Rourke realized, or he had read too much science fiction in years gone by and would have the proverbial egg all over his face.

The explosion came, Rourke swinging back fully inside, body parts flying everywhere amid a burst of bright yellow light, the tunnel walls—metal—reverberating with it, the rail beneath the trolley vibrating, the noise all but deafening.

As the noise subsided, Spitz gasped, "God in Heaven!"

"More likely the work of a devil from hell," John Rourke shouted back. The clone was, technically, an innocent man. Deitrich Zimmer had something else to pay for now.

And John Rourke felt himself choking back tears which he did not wish to show, because he realized now that the woman he had seen, had thought was his wife Sarah, was—in all likelihood—not his wife at all but another of these, a clone of his wife's flesh made to entrap him and eventually kill him.

His own voice sounding odd to him, John Rourke managed to say, "We'd better get back into our masks and full protective clothing. If the enemy didn't know we were loose, they'll know it now. Our radios were off, but chances are the tunnels here are somehow monitored. They'd know of the explosion. They might use gas."

"What arc wc to do, Herr Doctor?"

Rourke looked at the Hauptsturmführer. "Let me see those sealed orders for starters. Then, we try to intercept the rest of your men. They were walked off, maybe to a trolley line paralleling this. I don't know. Then we get the hell out of here for the time being. Otherwise, we'll find ourselves trapped in the middle of a war when both sides want us dead."

Paul started to laugh, the laughter tinged with obvious bitterness.

John Rourke, fully inside the trolley now, the door closing behind him, just looked at his friend, not understanding for a moment.

Paul said, "Some things change, but some things always stay the same, don't they?"

Forty-Nine

At the first trolley station they neared, there were armed men standing on the platform. But the men were not soldiers.

Rourke ordered, "Every ounce of speed this thing's got, Paul, Spitz, stay by the rear end of the car!"

The armed men wore dark blue slacks, light blue shirts, dark blue ties and blue hats with silver cap insignia and gleaming black visors. The gunbelts these men wore were the type John Rourke had last seen on Chicago Police Officers. Garrison straps with Jordan-style holsters. Each man had a revolver in his hand. And a badge on his chest.

Behind the men were police barricades, painted blue. Behind those were huddled a few spectators. But beyond them lay a city.

There was a voice shouting over a blue and white plastic bullhorn. "This is the police. You are ordered to throw down your weapons! Stop the trolley at once!"

All of this—including the words said over the bullhorn, which came and went in a Doppler effect—

was a blur as the trolley sped past. Gunfire came toward the car. Rourke shouted, "Fire over their heads!" And Rourke dropped the trolley window.

"But!"

"Just do it, Spitz!"

Rourke triggered off a string of shots from the HK-91, firing into the roof of the trolley station, the roof more decorative than functional. Spitz fired an energy pistol.

A string of small fires started as the energy bolts impacted the station, and Rourke suspected that what looked like wood was, most likely, some form of plastic.

Then the trolley was past the station and there was no more gunfire.

Two windows had been shot through. There was a bullet hole in the seat beside Rourke.

"What was all that? It looked—"

"Normal?" Rourke asked. Paul's radio transmission still echoing in his ear. "Pull off your headgear, but keep it handy."

They would need to talk.

"Should I slow us down?"

"Yes. Good idea." John Rourke had changed magazines in the HK, was reloading the partially spent one from the clipped-together brace he had removed. Safing the rifle, he set it aside, leaned between his thigh and the seat. With the little Executive Edge pen-shaped folding knife from his pocket, Rourke dug the bullet from the seat. When he had the bullet, even before he put the knife away, he found himself just staring at it.

"What is it?" Spitz asked, joining them at the front of the trolley car.

"This, Spitz, is rather like having a dinner party and finding out that one of your guests happens to be a Neanderthal. This is a 158-grain Round Nosed Lead .38 Special."

"I do not know a great deal about firearms," Spitz admitted freely.

"Briefly the .38 Special round which got everyone discontent with the .38 Special by the late mid-Twentieth Century is this round. Underpowered, prone to ricochet, terrible manstopper, it was the standard police service round in the United States for decades."

"John?"

Without looking at his friend, Rourke's eyes still on the recovered bullet, he said, "What is it?"

"My eyes were pretty much on the track here, but did I see what I thought I saw?"

John Rourke smiled, "Middle America sometime in the last quarter of the Twentieth Century? Looked like that to me."

"What?" Spitz asked.

John Rourke's mind raced. There was no way in which the three of them could fight off an entire civilization. When the attack by Zimmer's forces began, there might be the chance to escape in the confusion. "Here's what we're going to do. When Zimmer sent us in here, he said something about Paul and me being able to blend in with the society here. I dismissed the remark—sort of a typical thing for a racist to think, that people with similar backgrounds will all behave similarly. But I realize now that Zimmer had inside word on this place. Which is good for us, because that means there must be a way out that one or

two or three men could take. We just have to find it."
And Rourke outlined his plan.

The SS personnel Zimmer had sent to accompany
John Rourke and Paul Rubenstein had not worn
uniforms, but instead cold-weather casual clothes. The
trolley was parked near what appeared to be an access
into the trolley tunnel. John Rourke stripped away his
protective clothing, stuffing it into the teardrop-shaped
rucksack which had been on his back. The rifle would
be another matter. But it wasn't an immediate
problem.

Beneath the protective gear, Rourke wore snow-
clothes over boots. Aside from the fact that he was
sweating in them, because it was too hot with them,
they were sartorially inappropriate as well. He stripped
these away. Beneath the snow gear Rourke wore a
long-sleeved black knit shirt and black slacks bloused
over combat boots.

John Rourke had planned ahead.

Paul Rubenstein had done the same. Paul was
already stripped down to a grey long-sleeved knit shirt
and black slacks.

Rourke took his battered old brown leather bomber
jacket from the teardrop-shaped rucksack, pulling it on
over the double Alessi shoulder holster that he wore.
Paul was setting his second Browning High Power into
a black ballistic nylon double Tri-Speed shoulder rig.
Rourke had one of these at the Retreat. This one was a
duplicate of the Twentieth Century original acquired
from—who else?—Lancer.

Rourke had the snow gear and environment suit

314

packed into the rucksack.

For the moment, his gunbelt went around his waist, but that would have to be stashed away too if this thing he planned were to work.

"I do not like this," Spitz proclaimed.

"Don't worry; you should love these people," Paul observed.

Spitz made a mocking laugh. "Yes, but you will not, heh?"

"None of us will, if you open your mouth with a German accent," Rourke noted. "Let us do the talking if we make it that far." Spitz was stuffing a pistol beneath the ski sweater that he wore. The pistol was another Lancer, presumably a duplicate of the Walther P-88 9mm Parabellum. "Get that when the Lancer warehouse in New Germany was broken into?" Rourke had heard it mentioned by Emma Shaw's father.

Spitz smiled enigmatically, saying nothing.

Paul pulled on a leather jacket. "Ready."

"You and Spitz take care of the trolley."

"This is a disgrace," Spitz remarked.

"Nazi or no, Dr. Mentz struck me as a good soldier. I think if he were able to comment, he'd agree." Paul said.

Spitz just shook his head, but started for the trolley.

Rourke caught up his gear, slinging the rucksack over his left shoulder, the rifle in his right hand. And, he started into the accessway.

Fewer than three yards into it, he required light. From his bomber jacket, Rourke took a small size mini-Maglite loaded with German batteries (they had a projected life of two thousand hours of use, and an anticipated shelf life in excess of seventy-five years,

315

hence would last longer than John Rourke thought that he would, especially given the current circumstances). With the little flashlight shielded by his left hand, Rourke moved cautiously along.

While he investigated this little tunnel Paul and Spitz would be completing the rigging of the trolley. Dr. Mentz's body would be left in it. The audioanimatronic motorman might be remotely disabled. Instead Mentz's body would be lashed to the controls, his weight keeping the deadman's switch—a quite literal description in this case—from activating and stopping the train. Enough explosives were set that the trolley and anything near it would be all but vaporized. The charges were preset for three minutes.

From beyond the mouth of the accessway, Rourke could hear the trolley starting out.

Ahead, in this barely shoulder-width tunnel, Rourke saw nothing within the beam from his flashlight except more tunnel. He moved on, reminding himself that it had to lead somewhere.

Fifty

John Rourke had guessed right, on both accounts. The accessway, indeed, led out of the trolley tunnel. And as he had suspected, the trolley tunnel (after they had covered the distance between the hidden entryway and the mountain itself) had been leading them not in a straight line, but progressively downward. The trolley system, it appeared, went from ground level to some point far below, too far for Rourke to clearly discern as he looked over the edge into the manmade abyss. And perhaps, he was better off not knowing at the moment.

Above, however, the central core—it was buttressed expertly at every level—seemed to narrow. It was more than optical illusion. Perhaps it narrowed to a tunnel leading upward? But to what? What John Rourke supposed was a death chamber from which the lethal hallucinogenic gas was expunged into the atmosphere?

Racism and murder. It was a stupid simile, Rourke realized, but they went together as naturally as ham and eggs—except they were poison.

There was a chasm to cross, only eighteen or twenty

feet wide here but wide enough that it could not be jumped by anyone but an Olympian with a good deal of luck. On the opposite side was a metal-runged ladder leading upward and downward periodically terminating when it reached one of the core levels. And some fifty or so feet above and a nearly equal distance below, there was a covered synth-concrete-looking span, perhaps a pedestrian walkway from one of the trolley stations.

But the nearest of these walkways was at least a hundred yards away laterally. How was this tunnel, at the mouth of which he crouched, accessed?

Two things happened simultaneously and John Rourke did a third. He heard Paul and Spitz coming up behind him arguing. He saw a man armed with some sort of submachinegun-sized weapon flying toward him harnessed within some sort of personal minicopter and John Rourke dove back into the tunnel in order to silence Paul Rubenstein and Gunther Spitz and avoid being seen.

As Rourke threw himself back, from just below the lip of the tunnel mouth, a platform began moving outward.

"Quiet! Stay down!" Rourke rasped to his friend and their unlikely ally.

This was how the accessways into the trolley system were reached, by these personal helicopter devices.

As Rourke crouched beside his suddenly silenced companions and the armed man in the flying rig hovered over the just-extended platform, Rourke glanced at the Rolex on his left wrist. The three minutes would just about be up.

The armed man touched down with a little jump, the blades from the unit into which he was harnessed thrumming suddenly more slowly. The explosion shook the very fabric of the accessway. The enemy soldier or whatever he was wheeled toward them with his weapon.

John Rourke drew the A.G. Russell Sting IA Black Chrome and dove toward the man. If he fired, the man and his flying rig would tumble off the platform extending from the tunnel mouth and the flying rig would be lost.

John Rourke kept his body low, avoiding the rotor blades. Rourke's left shoulder impacted with the gun and the man at waist level, the weapon discharged, sounding for all the world like a suppressor fitted HK submachinegun, flat, barely audible. Rourke's little knife gouged deep into the man's upper abdomen and angled upward into the sternum to Rourke's right and the man's left.

There was a groan from inside the gas mask the man wore and the body fell limp beneath Rourke.

Rourke pushed himself away from the body. It lay half extended over the platform, the rotor blades from the bizarre personal flying rig clear of any contact with the platform, the rig apparently wholly undamaged.

"What have we gotten ourselves into?" Paul hissed.

John Rourke wasn't quite certain, but it seemed like the combination of an unfathomably ugly future and an eerily familiar past . . .

When both John Rourke and Gunther Spitz found

themselves insisting on using the flying rig, Rourke realized the sound of reason when he heard it and let Paul have his way. Paul was harnessed into the flying rig, standing halfway out along the length of the platform. Around his waist was the climbing rope which had been lashed to Rourke's rucksack.

Should the flying rig prove inoperable to someone not trained on it, Paul would cut the power and ball himself inward in order to avoid the blades. The rope— unless he fell so rapidly that the rotor blades would still be moving with sufficient force to sever it—would save him from a fall to his death.

"You sure you want to do this?"

Paul looked at him and smiled. "No; I'm sure I don't want to do it but I'm closest in build to the guy we took this off, so it seems logical."

John Rourke ducked below the rotor blades and clasped his friend's right hand in both of his. "Good luck."

"I'll try to make it to the lower crossover if something goes wrong. Otherwise—"

"Otherwise," Rourke said, nodding, "get across to the other side and tie off the rope." Above them by about twenty feet and on the other side of the chasm formed between the central structure and the outer shell where they stood now was what appeared to be an opening into one of the levels of the central core.

As Rourke stepped back and Paul Rubenstein powered up, Gunther Spitz said the most curious thing. "Good luck, Jew."

And Paul Rubenstein answered saying, "Right."

The rotor blades slicing through the air at what

looked like full power, Paul half-stepped, half-lifted off the platform.

And there was a sickening feeling in the pit of John Rourke's stomach when, for an instant, his friend nearly vanished from sight. But then Paul—jerkily not smoothly like the dead man from whose body the flying rig was taken—rose, started across the chasm.

Fifty-One

Emma Shaw awoke feeling a human hand over her mouth. Her pistol was in her right hand—the .45—and she nearly had the hammer back when she heard Alan Crocket's overtly sexy-sounding whiskey voice rasping to her. "Keep still; I have to silence my mount. We have company up above; don't move."

And the pressure over her mouth eased. She rolled onto her abdomen, smelling smoke. What had remained of the campfire was evidently just struck, snow that was still not fully melted to water heaped over it.

And, above her, she heard sounds too, now.

Machine sounds.

Aircraft, perhaps, but if so at considerable altitude. Motorized vehicles definitely, and close.

To her knees, her tiny right fist was balled tighter on the butt of her pistol.

She was still fuzzy from sleep and the exhaustion which had come before—that was why she hadn't awakened when the noise began. And three questions dominated her consciousness. What kind of man called his horse Wilbur? Why did she now think of this man as actually being Alan Crockett, who was supposed to have been lost at sea after all? And what army was making the noise at the height of the gorge above them?

She wriggled out of her sleeping bag. Perhaps her senses cleared a bit because another question reared its very ugly head. Had whoever it was up there seen them? Emma Shaw shivered, lying to herself that it was just the sudden exposure to the night air making her so cold . . .

Gloved hand over hand, John Thomas Rourke worked his way upward along the tied-off rope.

Beneath him, if he slipped, he calculated there was at least a thousand feet before his anticipated trajectory would bring him in contact with one of the crossovers. And kill him.

John Rourke kept moving.

Paul, the submachinegun in a ready position but his eyes on the rope, crouched on a narrow ledge beside a low camel-colored synth-concrete wall.

Rourke looked below and behind him, Gunther Spitz waiting to cross after him, guarding their backs. For the moment it was in Spitz's best interests to cooperate, be a loyal (however ephemeral) ally. The moment would come when Spitz could not be counted on, and Rourke counted on that.

Paul reached out toward Rourke now and Rourke clambered toward his friend's hand, grasping it at last, fingers barely touching, then hands locking over wrists. Rourke pushed himself off as Paul braced himself. In the next instant John Rourke was crouched beside him. "A lesser man would say he was getting too old for this shit," Paul observed.

"Or possibly just a brighter man," Rourke answered smiling.

As Rourke signalled toward the accessway, Gunther Spitz swung onto the rope. Rourke loosened the sling on his HK, bringing the rifle to a close crossbody hold. Rourke's thumb poised beside the selector, ready to move it from safe to fire.

Spitz seemed admirably fit, moving quickly, agilely. Paul said, "I'll give him that—he's in good shape."

Rourke smiled again. "Not to mention in his mid-twenties."

"Excuses, excuses. My mother used to say that excuses weren't worth the powder to blow them up."

"Everybody's mother used to say that," Rourke noted.

"Did your mother make chicken soup with little matzoth balls?"

Rourke choked back a laugh. "The soup, yes, but you've got me on the matzoth balls."

Spitz was at the midpoint over the chasm now. Paul was watching him, so Rourke slowly, cautiously peered over the low wall. As he had approached, the angle had been wrong to see anything. Now, however, he had a reasonably unobstructed view. The wall was some four feet high. There was a sidewalk, wide enough to be a driveway just beyond it. It bordered the wall and, on the far side, a park. The park was green, inviting, tree-dotted. There was a bench, a drinking fountain. Beyond the park lay another sidewalk, this one of more conventional width.

And beyond that lay a street. On the street moved

horse-drawn wagons and carriages, the clatter of the animals' hooves sounded almost melodic. Some pedestrian traffic crossed from one side of the street to the other. Rourke followed with his eyes.

On the far side of the street began a system of streets, it seemed, extending—it appeared—inward, toward the hub.

Lining the street directly opposite John Rourke's position was a woman's clothing shop, on one side of it a store bearing a sign which read "Mountain Market." To Rourke's right of the market lay an animal hospital. Beside that was what appeared to be a public library. Beside the library was a stairwell, treads leading up and down.

There was a street sign, Rourke trying to make it out without pulling his binoculars. At last he thought he had it. It read "Sector A, Level Five."

Rourke's eyes drifted back toward the windows of the women's apparel store. He had never been much of an observer of women's fashion, but the clothing he was able to see seemed somehow reminiscent of the sort of thing the Beaver's mother or Donna Reed would have worn, dresses with what seemed to be buttons down the front to the waist and full skirts which looked packed with petticoats beneath. And the mannequins all wore little hats.

"Take a look," Rourke suggested to his friend.

But Paul was busy helping Gunther Spitz off the rope, Spitz murmured grudging thanks. Attached to Spitz's belt was a second cord. It was knotted across the chasm to the tail of the hitch they had used for tying off the rope on which they crossed. Rourke took this cord and gave it a brisk sharp tug. The knot, just as Rourke had hoped, pulled free and the rope started to the wall. Paul and Spitz caught at it, pulling it up from the near end as quickly as they could.

"And now?" Spitz asked.

"I think we'll go visit middle America." John Rourke said.

Fifty-Two

Considering the hour, it seemed not at all remarkable that the stores were closed and there were few people on the street. If the people of this mountain community kept to any sort of truly circadian rhythm, it was three or four in the morning here.

And, as they left the park, the matter of time was resolved.

A clock on the window of the veterinarian's read a little past two-fifty, unless it was off resolving the question handily.

"I do not like leaving our weapons behind," Gunther Spitz said through clenched teeth.

Rourke, walking between Spitz and Paul Rubenstein, said, "I'm not partial to the idea, either. But we'd attract instant attention if we didn't." Rourke was gambling, a pastime in which he preferred not to indulge. His bet was on the size of the population here and how close it might be to what it appeared. If the mountain held in excess of a few thousand people, strange faces might not instantly be noticed. And—so far, so good it seemed—if male attire encompassed the "casual look" their clothing might even pass.

There were no women in evidence on the street, and only a few men, these in workingmen's clothes, waist-length jackets and slacks, some few of the men even carrying lunch pails. Some of the men were bare-headed, some others wearing fedora-style hats or caps.

In the few carriages that had passed along the street while Rourke, Rubenstein and Spitz had hidden their weapons in a dense row of hedges, Rourke had seen the occasional "well-dressed man" type, dark suit and hat, but that was it. The wagons mainly seemed to be carrying sacks or crates of produce, perhaps en route to stocking a market.

Every face was white.

Rourke had anticipated that.

They stopped in front of the women's apparel store. Indeed, the fashions worn by the mannequins and visible through the windows in the shop within confirmed Rourke's earlier observation. Paul put it best, saying, "I wonder if David and Ricky's mom shopped here?"

"Possibly."

"What is this—"

"This," Rourke responded, "is indicative, perhaps, of a society which sees itself returning to 'traditional' values; then again, it may be nothing more than the vagaries of fashion." Rourke looked off to his left. "Let's check that mailbox at the corner, then see what's down the block." Without waiting for acquiesence, Rourke starting moving.

A man wearing grey workpants and a windbreaker looked at them oddly, but nodded a greeting. Rourke nodded back. He stopped at the mailbox. It was painted green, as mailboxes had been when he was a boy. On it was stenciled, "United States Mail" and beneath that was a white card with pick-up hours printed on it.

Rourke looked down the street to his right. More stores, and beyond that houses.

Rourke started walking. Paul said, "This reminds me of Albuquerque just after the Night of The War."

"In more ways than one," Rourke agreed.

Spitz said nothing.

"Shopping are we?" Paul asked.

John Rourke only smiled.

The street was well lit, but by street lights and shop windows alone. Was there some sort of artificial daylight during "daytime" hours?

As they passed a bookstore, Rourke spotted three uniformed men on bicycles coming their way, but down the center of the street. "Cops—get into the doorway!" And Rourke, Rubenstein and Spitz flanking him, moved quickly into the doorway of the bookstore. Rourke's right hand was under his bomber jacket, to one of the two ScoreMasters he carried in his waistband. With the exception of the Model 629, the Crain LSX knife and the HK-91 rifle, John Rourke had all of his weapons.

The policemen pedaled by without even looking their way, either otherwise engrossed or grossly inefficient. Paul started away, but John Rourke pulled him back, saying, "Look in the window." There were a variety of novels, some of them appearing to be romances, some mysteries, all by unrecognizable authors. But there was also a collection of nonfiction.

One of these books was *The Annotated Mein Kampf*, complete with a new introduction by United States Senator Charles Breen. The dust jacket featured a quote which read, "For those truly interested in Hitler the man as well as the brilliant philosopher and charismatic leader, this is the best yet." The quote was attributed to Dalton Cole, President of the United States.

Gunther Spitz laughed aloud. "These are my people!"

Paul Rubenstein's jaw tensed, the cords in his neck slightly distending.

John Rourke glanced over some of the other titles (*The Race War Without*, *The Coming Cleansing of Earth*, *Christianity and The White Race*) as he told Spitz, "If you feel like getting killed, go right ahead and run after those policemen. I have a feeling you might not be any more welcome than we would, 'Heil Hitler' and goosestepping notwithstanding. And for God's sake don't tell me that all Nazis are brothers. That would be absurd even coming from you, Gunther."

Rourke started back onto the sidewalk.

And across the street in the middle of the block, he found what he'd been looking for. "Come on."

Paul said, "Shopping."

Fifty-Three

As John Rourke knotted his tie in the mirror—it was a solid blue in color and felt like silk—he listened to the radio. The music, although the precise tunes were unrecognizable to him, was the sort of thing he remembered from his boyhood, light 1950s pop music. Rourke liked much of the real music of that period. Songs sung by Sinatra, Torme, Clooney, Crosby and others were part of his now inaccessible music collection at the Retreat. This, on the other hand, sounded like bad elevator music.

On the half hour, at three-thirty (Rourke's Rolex read somewhat differently, but he made a mental note of the correlation), there was news.

"Good morning. This is Tom Fields with the early A.M. news on the Big Band Easy Sounds of WRPH AM. A spokesman for President Dalton Cole has confirmed that four of the Outsider saboteurs captured overnight by the Defense Forces are still at large in the city. Police are combing all levels and sectors and FBI Director Harold Hayes promises, and I quote, 'These killers will be found and brought to justice before they have the chance to do their dirty work.' Unquote.

"Police urge all citizens to be on the lookout for outsiders and report all suspicious persons to the proper authorities at once. Unconfirmed reports indicate the outsiders may be of mixed race and might be able to pass for white.

"In other news, Defense Forces spokesmen have released casualty figures for over the weekend. In a clash with negroes and Jews attempting to mount an attack force against the north entry site, thirty-two Defense Forces personnel were killed. Tempering that sad news is the fact that more than two hundred of the negroes and some seventy-six Jews, and a dozen more males of unidentifiable race were killed when the attack was repelled."

"What does he mean, this fellow?" Spitz said, pulling on the jacket from a grey single-breasted suit. "What negroes and Jews?"

Paul said nothing.

Rourke slipped his shoulder holsters on. "I think I may have finally added up some things which on the surface seemed rather confusing. The sum, unfortunately, is rather unpleasant."

"You speak in riddles, Herr Doctor."

Paul, knotting his tie, said, "No he doesn't. Think. The gas we detected on the summit. For executions, it would seem. These guys have a war-footing society here, but they don't have a war. So, they pretend they have a war. And even a pretend war has to have some real casualties. The 'good guys' can't always come through unscathed."

"Precisely," Rourke said, nodding. He slipped on the

double-breasted jacket of the blue pinstripe suit. "Notice that electronics shop next door? Lots of radios. Record players. Even some reel-to-reel tape recorders, not a single television—video to you, Gunther. Know why? Bet I do. You can stage still photos in a newspaper, maybe even some newsreel footage for use in a theatre. Not television coverage, or at least not so easily. So, no television. Just radio."

There was no weather report; that would have been ridiculous at any event. The music returned. Paul shut off the radio.

Rourke took the hat which he had selected—a dark grey fedora with broad brim and high crown, identical to the one his father had worn when Rourke was only a boy—and he placed the hat on his head, slightly cocked over his right eye. "What do you think?"

"That's you, John," Paul observed, grinning. Spitz, on the other hand, seemed in the blackest of moods; perhaps, Rourke thought, the Hauptsturmführer was beseiged with doubt about where his duty lay. As Rourke secured the two ScoreMasters in the waistband of his pleated front trousers, Paul said, "Just like Humphrey Bogart."

Rourke laughed. "Hardly, but you've already won my daughter's hand in marriage."

Paul started very seriously to laugh, leaning against the counter from which they had, all three of them, just liberated briefcases for stowing their regular clothes.

Spitz said, "I see no cause for mirth, from either of you. I am stranded here while my men may be enduring tortures for their fidelity to the Reich. And, if you are right, Herr Doctor, then an attack is about to begin against this place."

"Not much more than an initial foray to test the defenses here, I'd think," Rourke commented. "At any event, when we leave here we'll find someone to volunteer the necessary information that will enable us hopefully to find your personnel. Then we get them out at least, possibly ourselves as well. What exactly did your orders say, by the way?"

Spitz exhaled, long and hard, splaying his fingers over a glass countertop beneath which cufflinks, tie clips and watches with fake leather bands were displayed. "I was to locate two objectives within the city."

"And?" Paul asked.

Spitz looked at Paul, drew another breath, said, "And I was to place the two of you under arrest; failing that, kill you both."

"Then Zimmer doesn't care about his son," Paul remarked.

John Rourke lit a cigarette, stared at himself in the mirror. "I'd say Zimmer cares about his son a great deal, but not the man we have in the cryogenic sleep chamber." Had life been a cartoon, a lightbulb would have flashed over his head in that instant, Rourke realized. He had been played for a fool from the very first.

"John?"

Rourke shook his head. "You didn't know about the cloning, did you, Spitz?"

"I do not understand either of you."

"The man in the cryogenic chamber isn't Martin Zimmer," Rourke said.

Paul sucked in his breath.

Rourke wasn't about to divulge the fact that it was

336

actually Michael asleep in the cryogenic chamber left behind under guard of Natalia and Annie. But neither was it Martin Zimmer whom John Rourke had caused to die over the volcano, half a world away in Hawaii. "He cloned his son—my son—at the same time that he cloned Wolfgang Mann and Sarah—no, earlier. Of course," and Rourke inhaled on the cigarette, exhaled, making a low whistling sound as he did. "The image of Martin and the image of me, Zimmer's joke on the world."

"I fail to understand you, Herr Doctor."

"He's got the original Martin, and he's got copies, perhaps dozens of them," John Rourke almost whispered. "The basic problem with cloning a sentient being—aside from the fact that one cannot, at least at the moment I'd assume, copy the very thing which makes an individual an individual, his mind—is the morality of it. After all, once the clone exists, he or she is a separate living being, with all the inherent moral rights of a human being. He can't be used like a lab sample, or a spare parts source. But to a man like Deitrich Zimmer, the morality isn't a problem. And, with his undisputed mastery of advanced surgical techniques, the use of spare parts would be almost infinite."

"What—what are you saying?" Paul asked.

"I'm saying that Deitrich Zimmer can manipulate human life to his will." And John Rourke looked then at Gunther Spitz. He asked him flat out, "What were the two targets in your orders, Spitz?"

Spitz, whose complexion was normally very fair, looked slightly pale. He held one hand over his stomach as though it were churning. "The remains about which you were informed. They are here, the remains of the Führer."

"That's one target. What's the other?" Paul pressed

Spitz's eyes had about them a dispirited look something like the look Rourke imagined one would see in the eyes of a condemned man in the instant prior to his execution. "I do not understand why, but I was to take over a storage room which I was told would be guarded by the city's best-trained troops."

"No explanation as to the specific nature of the objective?" John Rourke asked.

"Only that if I had sufficient forces remaining which would enable me to secure one of the objectives, that was the one I must hold, lest it be destroyed."

Paul wrapped his fingertips against a glass counter top. They were in the rear of the haberdasher's, this portion of the store was cut off from the front and hence, out of view from anyone on the street by heavy curtains. It was here apparently that the higher priced items were purveyed. Rourke had disabled the alarm system with ease. Paul had mentioned that—"I know this isn't stealing—it's just resupplying in the field," echoing and at once parodying his reactions at the geological supply store in New Mexico following the Night of the War.

All three of them stood, as if waiting for some brilliant insight, Rourke thought. And then, he had that insight, its brilliance debatable but its importance paramount. "I know why we're here."

Both Paul and Gunther Spitz just looked at him.

Rourke spoke very slowly, not wishing to repeat anything, still working out the nuances of his realization as he said, "In the intelligence field, everything that's really important is on a need-to-know only basis. I'm sure that's the same for your people today, Gunther. Just as it was when I was part of Central Intelligence Before the Night of the War." It was as if the threads of John Rourke's life were being woven together into a pattern, and if he looked at it in just the right way he could discern it. But, if he blinked, its meaning might forever be lost to him. He stubbed out the cigarette—one of the noncarcinogenic German ones he occasionally smoked—and lit another in the blue yellow flame of his battered old Zippo windlighter. "You have to understand the Twentieth Century in order to comprehend, I suppose." Rourke pushed the fedora back off his forehead, began to pace the room, talking as he walked. "Science and technology never moved faster. I knew a man who was born in 1898. That was well before powered flight. As a boy, he helped his father hitch horses to a wagon because it was before the automobile. He lived what would be considered a relatively brief span of years by today's standards, when practically everyone's living well past a hundred. But he lived to see powered flight and even fly in an airplane. He lived to see men set foot on the moon, the reuseable spacecraft, all of that. Because technology never moved faster than it did in the Twentieth Century. The body of knowledge expanded almost exponentially, not just in the United States but in all the advanced nations of the world. And, sometimes, it went off at a tangent, this quest to know.

"Sometimes, like evolution, it went down a wrong turn which ended up in a blind alley. Sometimes too," Rourke said, his voice barely above a whisper, "it went where it shouldn't." He looked at Spitz. "Virtual

Reality—you understand it was in its infancy during the Twentieth Century, where someone could wear a clumsy helmet and a glove and perhaps stand on a treadmill and through primitive electronics, when compared to today, interact within a computer-generated environment. There was a man—I don't remember his name, but I heard about the work. It was for the Defense Department. They tried everything once, it seemed. The Navy was using psychics to assist in tracking enemy submarines. That sort of thing.

"This man who worked for the Defense Department," Rourke continued, "got the idea of recording human brain waves, on a huge scale, then digitizing them. He wanted to build a computer program that would allow reading of the human mind, and eventually programming the mind. Supposedly he had the brainwave research to a point where he could translate some element patterns. To test the possibility of practical application, he fed this data through a very sophisticated—for the time—very sophisticated computer array. He tried his theory on a volunteer, using the brainwave program in conjunction with virtual reality."

"What happened?" Paul interrupted.

John Rourke exhaled heavily, stubbed out the cigarette. "This was all rumor, but I found it intriguing, pursued it a bit. As best I was ever able to ascertain, the test volunteer went insane. Sensory overload. He used a sharp piece of equipment to slash his wrist. And there was a sort of elephants' graveyard for research data and equipment. It was somewhere in the eastern United States, in some bombproof facility. What if that was here? What if Deitrich Zimmer learned about those experiments through some reference or another

Coupling the potential of that body of research and experimentation with modern electronics and computer capabilities and Zimmer's own work with cloning, he could create human beings almost at will."

"The power of God," Gunther Spitz murmured.

"In the hands of the devil," Paul whispered.

John Rourke picked up the briefcase which contained his clothes and boots and musette bag. "We'll find your men, Spitz, if we can, then find that facility. And then you'll have to decide. If the research really is there, do you want a hand in turning earth into hell? Or will you help Paul and me to destroy it?"

John Rourke started walking toward the back door.

Fifty-Four

More personnel and equipment were arriving almost by the minute, landing at areas at the four major points of the compass. Deitrich Zimmer's plans were not on schedule, they were ahead of schedule. It would be dawn soon, and merely because it was the classic moment (his personnel were equipped with state-of-the-art night vision accessories), then the attack would begin.

Everything was, at last, coming together.

The conspirators within the Nazi Party would soon be eliminated, the attack on Pearl Harbor, Hawaii, would soon be begun and very soon—computer simulations projected a victory within seventy-two hours—he would possess what was the ultimate power, the power to create and manipulate life.

Within his airborne command post were only the most trusted of his personnel—and the traitor, Graham, who had brought him the knowledge of this power's existence.

Graham sat over the portside wing, staring out into the yellow-orange line along the eastern horizon. Deitrich Zimmer engaged the fellow in conversation, standing up from the couch on which he had lain to rest. He walked toward Graham, saying to him, "And so, you are ready for history to unfold before your eyes?"

"Yes, Doctor. It will be wonderful. The destiny of the white race finally fulfilled."

"Yes, indeed," Zimmer said in agreement. There was white and there was white. Graham, like the others within the mountain redoubt from which Graham had escaped, was the product of mongrelized inbreeding and, as such, was not as pure as he supposed.

The city within the mountain was a fluke, really, an accident.

Zimmer sat down on the opposite side of the table from Graham, studying the man's features. The dark eyes, the too black hair, the very pale complexion. There was a definite Slavic influence, and the name itself was from the British Isles. No racially pure fellow this.

"Coffee, Graham?"

"No, Doctor, thank you."

Zimmer nodded, signalling to an aide that he alone wanted coffee.

The coffee arrived. Zimmer added cream to it, the color, the taste, almost everything about the coffee changing as he did so. That was the way with race. Once purity was violated, it could not be regained.

Zimmer, however, liked cream in his coffee. He sipped at it.

The city within the mountain had come about in the oddest way. "Tell me again, Graham, how your civilization came to be."

Graham took odd delight in this and Zimmer's eyes were tired from staring at computer terminals. He stared at his coffee while Graham began to speak. "Well, like I said, Doctor Zimmer, our ancestors were white people, Christians all, and decent. We were tired of everything that was going on in America. Negroes were getting jobs and white men weren't. Jews were helping them. And women were being encouraged to be shameless sluts. It was time to do something." Graham was reciting the history of his people, something out of a schoolbook. "Folks who spoke up about what was wrong were branded. My people were being persecuted because they were God-fearing white men. We had to act or perish."

"An inspiring story—that's why I never tire of it. Go on, please," Zimmer told him, sipping again at the coffee.

"What you call the city within the mountain we call New Jerusalem. There weren't many of us at first in New Jerusalem. When the war started between the Commies and the Jew-controlled United States, well, it looked like it might be the end of white people everywhere. But some of our people had worked for the Jews in government, like secret agents, hating them all the while but pretending to do their bidding. And they knew about New Jerusalem; it was called the 'Alpha Site' because it was the first war retreat for the United States. Even though the war retreat was considered too vulnerable to a direct strike, and was moved later, the

Alpha Site was kept up as a storage facility for important government documents and things the conspirators who ran the United States government didn't want known—like the remains of Adolf Hitler being there.

"And our people," Graham went on, his voice a sad monotone, "were able to successfully infiltrate the staff that maintained Alpha Site. When it seemed that the War would be inevitable, our people took over Alpha Site. Before we had to lock down to avoid radiation, there were one hundred and seventy-nine good white Christian people inside."

Graham paused, as if he had just recited something holy. "And we nearly died, our people, but through perseverence and the work of our scientists, we survived. There are over thirty thousand of us now." And Graham lowered his voice. "But the leaders are afraid, now. They made up the war, and they kill our good young men to keep up making people think we can't go outside. They're afraid that we'll flourish on the face of the Earth and their power will end. It's a little clique of men, Doctor Zimmer. Some of my friends and me figured that somehow our leaders became corrupted, that they don't really believe we'll conquer the Earth.

"We kept hearing the rumors that there wasn't really a war, that there wasn't really an enemy. We didn't know what to think. And then one of the pilots from the scouter planes—they live in separate quarters because they might be contaminated from the outside, least we were told that—this pilot got word out to an old friend of his. He said there weren't any negro and

346

Jew armies outside.

"That's how our network started," Graham said, a look of pride glowing in his eyes. "With the help of some of the other pilots, we got to see some aerial photos. There were cities, that real big one you call Eden, Doctor. But New Jerusalem wasn't surrounded by enemy armies. And the glacier disappeared when you went further south. And the air was clean and fit to breathe, not poisoned.

"And that's when the plan was made. Five of us were supposed to go to the 'Front,' and we knew then that there wasn't a Front at all, and that some of us would be taken away and executed. We knew that because we had a man who got to talk to one of the Summit Guards. They're the Elite of the Elite, like I told you, Dr. Zimmer. Turned out, though, that the Summit Guards don't guard anything except our own boys brought up there through some sort of elevator. Then they killed our boys. This Summit Guard was sick of it.

"So," Graham said, "when our unit was going to move up to the Front—like I told you, nobody but the officers had a map or a compass and units were always exfiltrated at night—the five of us in the unit figured to make a break for it and see if maybe there were other good white people like us out there."

Deitrich Zimmer took a last swallow of his coffee. "Fortunate for you and your people that you survived."

"And that you're the greatest doctor in the world, Dr. Zimmer!"

Zimmer smiled indulgently.

When Graham was discovered wandering on the

347

glacier, Graham's feet were frozen and gangrenous. He'd been attacked by Land Pirates and left for dead rather than a bullet or an energy pulse being wasted to end his life. It was the Eden Defense Forces which found him, and through a stroke of pure luck (one of Zimmer's own liaison officers working with Eden Defense Forces) Graham's feverish babbling about a hidden city to the north was overheard and reported.

Zimmer personally flew to Eden, made up some story on how he could use the hapless fellow in his research and took Graham back with him.

Coincidence. Or, synchronicity. Deitrich Zimmer's lifelong involvement with the perfection of human genetic engineering had exposed him to vague references to the brain-wave research of Doctor Horace Patterson, conducted during the Twentieth Century. Other data had convinced him of the existence of "Alpha Site" as the repository of various items—including the remains of Adolf Hitler—which the United States government had wished to preserve but keep secret. Logic suggested that the results of Doctor Patterson's research would be there as well.

And, out of the blue, along came Thaddeus Graham, a discontented private soldier with racial theories more rigid than Zimmer's own, from a society that could easily be conquered and then set to work in his own behalf because it already shared his political ideals.

All that remained was to penetrate it, "liberate" it from its rather bizarre leadership and absorb it, rather the way the Third Reich had absorbed Austria in 1938.

He would be welcomed. He might even appoint Graham as some sort of administrator, either that or kill him and have him posted as a martyr, whichever seemed best at the time.

Deitrich Zimmer looked out the aircraft window he and Graham shared and Zimmer squinted his eyes against the advancing sunrise. In moments, his attack on the facility at the entrance that Dr. Rourke had so kindly and stupidly found for him would begin.

Fifty-Five

Alan Crockett led his horse Wilbur along the river bed, Emma Shaw walking beside Crockett.

The river bed here at the base of the gorge was still in grey darkness, like a room in daylight with all the curtains tightly drawn and light seeping in through cracks. But above them, to the east, it was nearly full daylight.

They followed the sounds of the army which had passed them in the predawn hours of the morning. Above them, as she looked up, there were squadrons of high altitude V-stol and helicopter aircraft. There was, of course, some miniscule chance that two human beings and a horse might be detected moving thousands of feet below, but that risk had to be run.

They would have been no safer, Alan Crockett had explained, had they stayed put. Emma Shaw agreed. If this were some sort of battle rather than a training exercise and any Trans-Global Alliance forces were committed, it might be possible to link up with them and escape this place.

Maybe.

Or, they might be walking into something neither of them could anticipate.

Each step they took brought her closer to the coastline, however. And, once she was there, it would be possible in one way or another to get off the continent. That kept Emma Shaw raising one foot after the other as she picked her way along the rocks. The horse with the funny name, of course, had to have the clearest portion of the riverbank lest it break a leg. Evidently, Crockett would feel better having to shoot her than his horse, Emma Shaw thought . . .

Annie Rourke Rubenstein awakened. Natalia was "sitting" guard beside the cryogenic chamber in which Michael slept. Annie had awakened several times during her brief respite from guard duty, hearing the sounds of military movement in the darkness around them.

As she looked outside, however, through one of the aircraft windows, she saw no change. The same tracked vehicles which had been posted around the aircraft ever since her father and her husband had left were there now. A few troops moved about on whatever business they had, but didn't look to be up to anything important.

It was almost as if the aircraft and the people aboard it were being ignored.

Annie looked away from the window, looked at Natalia—Natalia looked tired, drawn—and said as much.

"I've been thinking that, too, Annie," Natalia said,

lighting a cigarette as she stood up. Annie caught her friend's eyes as they glanced toward the transparent top of the chamber, looking at Michael, Annie's brother and Natalia's lover. "I think that Dr. Zimmer has somehow achieved his purpose for bringing us here in the first place, that our staying behind with the cryogenic chamber is somehow less important than John and Paul going off on Zimmer's mission to find Hitler's remains."

"Seems like an awful lot of trouble for what's left of a body after six and a half centuries. Can't be much," Annie suggested.

"Enough for Zimmer's genetic research, maybe. I don't know. But, I know I don't like this. There's something wrong."

Natalia echoed Annie's own thoughts, but there was nothing for it now but to wait and see—and pray for her father and her husband, and Natalia and Michael and herself, too.

Fifty-Six

John Rourke's eyes shifted from side to side as he walked down the street. Life started early here, it seemed, men dressed as factory workers gradually filling the streets. Rourke, Rubenstein and Gunther Spitz had split up, were searching the various levels of this cylindrically shaped city within a mountain. They would rendezvous—Rourke checked his wristwatch—in another ten minutes at the park at the original level and sector co-ordinates where they had entered the city.

As the early morning wore on, more persons dressed in business clothes, as Rourke himself was dressed—suit and necktie and hat—entered the streets as well. Rourke stopped in a coffee shop and had a cup, listening to the talk, glancing at the newspaper, spending some of the modest amount of money he had lifted out of the cash register at the men's store.

The cigarette leavings policed up, the alarm system reactivated, some time might elapse before the nocturnal visitation and the removal of three suits, three shirts, three ties and three belts and hats would be noticed. Similarly, he didn't clean out the cash register, merely taking pocket change.

The first time necessity in the line of duty had forced him to steal (a civilian car in Nicaragua), his conscience had been terribly troubled. Certainly, it was for what he perceived as the greater good, but that didn't ease the result for the man whose car it had been, nor would it now for the owner of the men's haberdashery.

Rourke's perusal of the newspaper proved about as interesting as reading any sort of propaganda with a dash of home town gossip thrown in. Circulation figures for the newspaper indicated that some twelve thousand copies were regularly sold.

Rourke had already mentally estimated the population here to be in excess of twenty thousand, and the circulation figures only seemed to support that number or better.

The coffee wasn't bad.

Some persons smoked. Rourke smoked as he walked, but a cigarette because he had seen no evidence of cigars.

By the time he reached the original level and rendezvous time was near, John Rourke had discerned many bits of intelligence. He stood on the street corner, waiting for the mechanical walk sign to go on, watching the horse traffic and the bicycling policemen—they travelled in packs—and listening to the street noises. Except for the absence of internal combustion vehicles and the presence of clopping hooves, this little town built in a spiral within a mountain seemed very familiar to someone born in the United States in the middle of the Twentieth Century.

Except for the news stories.

Those kept coming back to him. There was, supposedly, a bitter war raging outside the mountain, the entire economy, the entire society was on a war footing. There were posters in shop windows urging that people buy war bonds. Race, according to the papers, was the basis for the conflict. And race seemed a constant topic of idle conversation in the streets. Not a solitary black or brown or yellow or red face was in evidence.

A woman stepped up beside John Rourke at the curb. She wore a blue dress with a full skirt, the dress was made from a white polka-dot fabric. A little blue hat was perched atop her head, her hair short and tightly curled. Almost involuntarily as the light changed and she stepped off the curb, Rourke shook his head.

Fifties.

The woman stopped for a moment in front of the window of the women's clothing store, adjusted a seam in her hose and walked on. Rourke passed the shop, passed the Mountain Market and stopped at the animal hospital window. It was much too early for regular office hours, of course, but there was some sign of activity within.

He went past the animal hospital, his eyes on the park across the street. There was no sign of Paul or the Nazi officer, Gunther Spitz. Letting Spitz off on his own was dangerous, of course, but Rourke saw no other way in which to cover enough ground in a short period of time.

Rourke stopped at the Library, studying the donors' plaque beside the main door. The names were all good

Anglo-Saxon ones, and not a single woman's name appeared except as "Mrs." with her husband's first name instead of her own.

Here was a static, very stratified society, both in the figurative and literal sense of course. People knew their place here, did what their parents had done and made certain that their children would do it, too.

Juxtaposing the time on his Rolex with the time difference here, it was already almost seven-thirty A.M.

The streets were filling, more horse-drawn wagons and more carriages, some apparently private, some for hire. And bicycles, not just police but young people, the girls in bobby socks and petticoated full skirts and sweater sets, the boys in loafers, white socks and baggy trousers, hair slicked back.

A time warp.

The 1950s may have been the "good old days" to people who had never lived them, but John Rourke remembered them, albeit with the selective perspective of childhood. Air raid drills in school. Unemployment. Steel strikes. Two wars just over. Segregation was still in the law in many areas. Society was artificial. In that respect, the 1950s were perfectly recaptured here.

It was time for the rendezvous in the park.

John Rourke, lest he be arrested for jaywalking, returned to the corner, waited for the light, then crossed.

The 1950s, like the forties and thirties, had one significant advantage: men's suits. They were tailored of heavier fabric and worn looser, which made the concealment of firearms vastly easier. John Rourke wore six under his clothes, and the suit was merely taken off the rack. He smiled at the thought. The trouser legs had been in the rough, not cuffed. He'd found the sewing machine in the back of the shop and cuffed them himself, not only the suit that he wore but the ones which Paul and Spitz wore too. There was a sewing machine at the Retreat; Annie had used it to make all her own clothes. When Rourke installed it there, he taught himself how to use it so that he would understand its workings should he have to service it from the spare parts he had stocked.

This had not been planning ahead, but a lucky accident instead.

Rourke was across the street now.

He entered the park, no sign of Paul or Spitz yet.

From fragments of casual conversation and items in the newspaper, little details one who was trained in the piecing together of information might interconnect, he was relatively certain that they would find the rest of their party—Spitz's soldiers—in Level One, Sector A. That was above them. Level One, Sector A was the seat of government, and most particularly where this community's self-styled "FBI" was housed.

He'd known numerous real Federal lawmen Before the War, FBI personnel included. To a man, they would have cringed at being compared to what likely went on here—repression.

The hedges in which the long guns, the one-man helicopter like device and their other unmanageable gear were stashed seemed untouched. But Rourke did not approach them.

As he turned back toward the street, he spotted several bicycle-mounted police officers collecting near the corner.

And wagons, black and enclosed, drove up, their

horses reined in quickly, men clambering out of the backs through black double doors, the men in riot gear.

The staircase to the side of the library—Paul was there, starting out, but then falling back.

John Rourke's palms sweated.

He had judged wrong: Spitz was not only more vile but more stupid than John Rourke had supposed.

In the very moment when he thought the name, he looked toward a carriage which had just reined up near the curb. Sitting in it, beside a chubby-looking, rather officious-seeming man, he saw Gunther Spitz. Two uniformed policemen sat opposite them.

And Spitz stood up, extended his arm toward John Rourke, pointing Rourke out.

John Rourke turned on his heel and ran the few steps to the hedges and threw himself up and over, rolling across the grass in his new suit—but it was some synthetic which felt like wool and seemed sturdy enough. Rourke reached into the hedge, pulling against the rain poncho in which the HK-91 and the other gear was wrapped. He would need all the weapons he could muster.

He had misjudged Spitz but John Rourke had formulated a plan lest Spitz should perpetrate some treachery, such as he had.

Gunther Spitz's voice rang out across the park, shouting, "If he is there, the other filthy Jew cannot be far away!"

The corners of John Rourke's mouth raised in an involuntary smile. He could think of no finer man on earth than Paul Rubenstein, his best friend and his daughter's husband.

Quickly, as the uniformed police in full 1950s-style

riot gear—helmets and clubs and revolvers and shotguns but no visible body armor—ran in formation toward him, John Rourke checked his rifle, making certain it hadn't been spiked and left as a trap. It was as he'd left it, one of the hairs from his own head over the closed breech.

Rourke slung it, slung on his musette bags, Paul's as well, the combined weight considerable with the loaded magazines and loose ammo, but he could afford to leave nothing behind. He opened the sling on the HK rifle, ran the sling through the briefcase handle, then resecured it.

His gunbelt, with the Model 629 and the Crain LSX knife—he strapped it around his waist under his now open suitcoat. Screwing his fedora down tightly on his head, Rourke grabbed up the flying rig and Paul's submachinegun. The poncho was Nazi issue and Rourke didn't worry about leaving it behind.

As the policemen started to close, Rourke rose to his full height from behind the bushes, racked the bolt on the Schmiesser and fired, a long ragged burst cutting into the front rank of the riot police, putting down four of the men, the rest scattering, falling back.

Rourke ran, his burdens slamming against him, slowing him, ran for the low wall overlooking the chasm which surrounded the spiral of the city. He glanced back once as he heard shots. Paul was firing a pistol from each hand, cutting down the riot police from behind, drawing off their fire. Rourke turned as he ran, firing the submachinegun again, taking out another two men with a short burst. If Paul saw where he was going, Paul would have to realize what he planned—Rourke hoped.

Rourke reached the wall, putting down the flying rig, firing the German MP-40 submachinegun empty, taking out another three men. Pistol shots rang toward him now, Rourke letting the Schmiesser fall to his side on its sling, grabbing the ScoreMasters from his belt, thumbing back the hammers, returning fire.

Tear gas grenades were lobbed toward John Rourke, but there was no time to fish out the lightweight, ultracompact protective suit or the mask from his belongings. He fired again, killing two more of this twisted society's riot police.

In the same instant, there was an almost deafening roar from above.

Deitrich Zimmer's attack had begun . . .

Paul Rubenstein drew back into the stairwell, bullets whining against the synth-concrete surrounding him. John would try the flying rig as his means of escape, Paul realized. A fresh magazine up the butt of each pistol, Paul Rubenstein stabbed the guns around the corner and fired high, no desire to shoot at innocent, however perverted, civilians. He tucked back as more gunfire poured toward him. There was no way he could cover John without knowing the precise moment in which John would attempt to use the flying rig.

It was time to withdraw.

Ten rounds left in each pistol and more spare magazines secreted on his body, Paul licked his lips, screwed his "liberated" fedora down tight on his head and took off in a dead run up the stairwell, hoping some of the riot police would follow him.

As he hit the landing, he saw a flash of blue uniform.

Paul threw himself flat and rolled, a shotgun blast impacting the wall beside which his head had been a split second earlier. Paul fired, a double tap from each pistol, putting down two uniformed riot police, their bodies sprawling down the stairwell toward him. As Paul pushed up to one knee, two more men charged down toward him, revolvers in hand. Paul fired, catching one man with a double tap to the chest and thorax, the second with a shot to the abdomen and the left side of the chest, over the heart.

Paul thumbed up the safety on the pistol in his right hand, grabbed for the shotgun from the dead man nearest him, taking hold of it at the pump, snapping it to rack it. At the same time, he twisted his left thumb round behind the second High Power's tang, upped the frame-mounted safety, belting this pistol as well.

He had been taught survival in battle by the man who should have written the book on it. Never leave weapons behind you which can be used against you again. He grabbed up the police revolvers, shoving them into the side pockets of his suitcoat. He scavenged ammo for the shotguns and the revolvers as quickly as he could from the bodies of the men near him.

The second shotgun would be more than he could handle comfortably and there was no sling for it. Setting down the first shotgun, he cleared the second shotgun's chamber by working the slide release lever near the trigger guard—the gun was a copy of the Remington 870—and then inverted the gun, smashing it against the wall. Its synthetic stock splintered away. Paul flung the gun down the stairwell after him, then started up again, the first shotgun in his hands.

Beside the bodies of the second two riot police, Paul

paused, taking their revolvers and the loose ammo from the pouches on their belts. There were no police radios.

He kept going, the guns in his pockets dragging his suitcoat down at the shoulders.

He reached the next level. There were four police bicycles there, but no visible signs of more police.

Paul Rubenstein started up the next flight of stairs . . .

There were more explosions, now, every few seconds, at times the synth-concrete of the city spiral trembling under his feet. Sirens, like the ones from the 1950s which sounded once each week with clockwork precision for testing, sounded now, and the street behind the riot police, cordoned off, was the sight of a panic. Men and women poured from shop fronts and along the sidewalks.

Now was his chance, and he stepped from cover to the wall.

John Rourke was into the flying harness, eyeballing the controls while he pushed his gear as clear as he could. There was a central shaft which split into an off-angled *Y* shape. The frame was like a man's bicycle, the main strut rising straight upward to the main rotor past maneuvering controls set up like a solid triangular shaped handlebar. The secondary strut, to which the perchlike rest/seat was attached, extended aft, the tail rotor set into its end.

The rotor blades fanned upward and outward when powered up.

Riot police were closing on him now in a flying

wedge, their revolvers and shotguns blazing. With projectiles impacting off the wall near him, John Rourke stepped over and onto the ledge. The added weight of his burdens might be too much for the little craft. If it was, he would plummet to his death.

If he stayed where he was he would be shot to death.

John Rourke jumped, both hands on the control bar. There was a sickening rush before the rotor blades fanned out, the machine evidently not designed for so abrupt a start. As the blades opened, began to spin, there would be no hope. Keeping his legs rigid, elbows tucked in, he brought the machine to full power.

And no longer was he falling. But, he wasn't actually flying, either, more gliding and straight toward the wall on the opposite side of the chasm.

It was then that John Rourke made a decision.

Testing the controls gingerly but rapidly, he started the machine upward, nearly attaining the height of the level he had just left before the wedge of riot police reached it and started firing. Rourke stabbed the Schmiesser toward them and fired a long, ragged burst, no hope of accurate fire while he was strapped into the zig-zagging machine. But the riot police, unused to automatic weapons, it seemed, or any real combat either and without body armor, fell back.

The explosions John Rourke had heard, felt, came from above. Level One, Sector A had to be on ground level. As he and Paul and the others had been led to the trolley and the rest of Spitz's men had been led off in a different direction, they would have been taken straight ahead to Level One.

And that was where Zimmer's attack would originate, of course, because it was the only site for which

Zimmer had coordinates.

And it would be the only way out.

John Rourke kept the machine climbing, at last seeing Paul's face peering out over an identical wall to that on the level he had just left. But this was the ground level. And black smoke billowed out over the wall. Concrete dust fell everywhere in the chasm surrounding the spiral city now, and large pieces from the ceiling above were collapsing into the chasm. Rourke dodged the machine this way and that as best he could to avoid the rotor blades being struck.

Gunfire came at him from below, but he was powerless to respond to it. Above him, he could see Paul stabbing a shotgun downward, firing toward the personnel firing at him from below. The flying rig was straining at full power. But John Rourke was nearly there.

From his right there was a blur of motion. A man appeared, then another and another, in flying rigs identical to his own, but these men were unburdened with additional pounds of equipment and they knew their machines' capabilities, Rourke realized.

As the nearer of the three made a pass toward him, a submachinegun in the fellow's hands, John Rourke swung Paul's submachinegun forward, punching its muzzle toward the man. Rourke and the enemy trooper in the flying rig fired simultaneously. Rourke's burst of submachinegun fire struck across the tail rotor strut and into the tail rotor itself.

The man's flying rig started spinning, twisting and contorting, pieces of the tail rotor flying everywhere. Two things happened almost at once. The man's flying rig impacted the far wall of the chasm and exploded, a black and yellow fireball belching up hot and fast, Rourke veering his own machine away from it. And a piece of flying debris struck John Rourke's main rotor. The rotation speed immediately dropped, and the machine began to drop as well.

The remaining two enemy personnel in flying rigs arced toward John Rourke. As Rourke looked up, he saw Paul firing the shotgun. The man in the rig nearest to Rourke took a hit, man and machine slamming into the far wall, exploding.

John Rourke fired his submachinegun toward the last man.

Bullets whined off the metalwork of Rourke's flying rig. And still, it was falling. As the last man started a pass, Rourke fired what he judged to be the last few rounds left in Paul's submachinegun. Rourke and his opponent were so close that their rotor blades nearly touched. The burst from Paul's submachinegun struck across the handlebar control, sparks flying, bullets ricochetting upward and downward, peppering the man's chest and abdomen. Rourke banked left, still falling, the now-dead man's machine plummeting downward and downward into the seemingly bottomless chasm between the spiral and the outer wall.

Rourke's machine sputtered and stalled, started. Rourke's eyes shifted over the controls in a frantic search for some means by which he could avoid his enemy's fate, a killing fall into the chasm.

There was a fuel mixture control. Logic dictated that it would increase oxygenation, hence the burn rate. Rourke throttled back one quarter, then turned the mixture control to full rich, simultaneously cutting

367

power to half on his tail rotor, then throttling the main rotor all the way out as he angled his body toward the inner wall.

With a wrenching that tore at his spine, the flying rig lurched upward and began twisting so strongly that Rourke felt his lips curling back from his teeth. He was turning with the machine with the increased power from the main rotor and the diminished tail rotor revolutions, spiraling upward toward the ceiling above.

Explosions were rocking the interior of the mountain now, but Rourke was only vaguely aware of them, the sheer force of his movement pushing him toward blackout. In seconds, he would impact against the ceiling and crash.

The fingers of his right hand edged across the bar to the platform control. It had to be dismounted, aimed. There wasn't time for any of this, he was telling himself, but not to try was to give up, the abdication of life. His fingers closed over the remote and he wrenched it free, stabbing it outward, punching the control constantly, unable to see if he was having any effect, extending any of the minilaunch platforms used as take-off and landing pads for the flying rigs. They wouldn't be everywhere, might only be on the outer wall side.

He had not experimented with the platforms. Paul had not used one when Paul utilized the flying rig to cross the chasm.

John Rourke was nearly to the ceiling and nearly unconscious. He kept punching the platform control unit with his right hand and cut all power to the rotors with his left.

Still spiraling, he started to fall.

His right hand let go of the remote and his left fist punched against the quick release for the harness which was against his chest.

And he was free of the flying rig, tumbling, everything around him a blur now, black, edged with unconsciousness and nausea.

His arms flailed and hands groped.

The fingers of his left hand touched at synth-concrete. His body slammed against something hard and bounced away from it, no longer spiraling, just dropping. Rourke's hands clawed at the wall.

His right hand caught at something and the falling stopped for a fraction of a second.

He thought he heard Paul's voice.

He wasn't sure.

His right hand was holding something, like a ledge.

The blackness was closing around him. John Rourke swung his left arm outward and arced it upward, his left hand catching hold.

"Damn stupid of me," Rourke rasped.

He could barely breathe.

He looked up, nausea and fear gripping him tighter now, cold and wet on his flesh, because he had the chance to think.

As Rourke's eyes focused, he almost laughed. His fingers were locked over the lip of one of the four foot walls; all of his efforts with the remote platform activator were for naught. He looked down. There were platforms open everywhere on both sides of the chasm, but he wasn't near any of them.

Rourke looked up again. He was three levels down, and smoke billowed from the two highest levels. There was no sign of Paul.

Rourke looked at himself, his "liberated" suit in tatters.

His shoulders ached. He shook his head and spasms of pain shot through it. But the pain brought him back fully to reality.

And he started climbing upward. As he got his right arm over the wall, then started hauling his body after it, Paul was there. "You almost died!"

"I know."

"That was crazy! And then there you were, hanging onto this wall! Know what happened to your hat? You wouldn't want to know."

John Rourke was over the wall, half-collapsed into his friend's arms. More explosions. The smell of smoke. Muted screams, the frantic clopping of horses' hooves. Gunfire and energy bursts from above.

He looked at Paul. "So? What happened to my hat?"

"You're the luckiest man alive. A rotor blade sheered it away when you jerked free of the flying rig. An inch lower and it would have trimmed away the top of your head."

"Probably could use a haircut anyway." And Rourke rose to his full height, leaned against the wall and against Paul. "How much trouble we in?"

"The police are poorly armed. But the defense forces—or army or whatever—have a lot of firepower. Their tactics look like a Chinese firedrill in the making, but I think Zimmer's probe got more than it bargained for. Zimmer's people got into Level One from the tunnel—must be what happened to Spitz's force. They were brought straight in and we were taken downward by trolley. What passes for the FBI here is on Level One, but near as I can make out military headquarters is several levels down. Anyway, Zimmer's forces are being driven back. We're gonna be trapped."

Rourke pushed away from the wall. "Take some of this stuff, huh?" and he started dividing his burdens with Paul. "Toward the center of Level Five I saw a kind of spiraling street."

"I saw it too, but from Level One."

"Fine—ever steal a carriage?"

Fifty-Seven

The briefcase discarded, his clothes stuffed into his musette bags, his boots knotted together and slung over his shoulder and his leather jacket on instead of the tattered suitcoat, John Rourke ran along a service alley on Level Three, toward the street out front. Paul Rubenstein ran beside him.

Rourke's right hand was bleeding a little still, his skin scraped from the encounter with the wall, but when he had the time he'd use one of the antiseptic/rapid-healing sprays and bandaged it. Now he was running out of time.

As long as the battle raged, there was a chance of escape. Once it stopped, they would be trapped in the city.

The explosions still came, but more distant. Part of that was because they were near the inner core of Level Three, not at its outer edge. But the explosions were less frequent now, too.

The city itself was like a living organism, seemed seized with panic. Riot police battled civilians in the streets. There were overturned carriages and wagons and some small fires, perhaps from natural gas, perhaps electrical.

Zimmer's forces had not penetrated far, but they had disrupted this city's apparently fragile infrastructure so severely that all the 1950s-style self-control was gone, the panic of upwelling suppressed anxiety replacing it.

As they reached the street, coming out between a ma and pop style restaurant and a hairdressing salon, Rourke spotted a horse-drawn cab, the driver and two policemen fighting on the curb. One of the policemen tried to jump aboard the cab, but the driver pulled him down, fighting him back onto the sidewalk. Near to the cab were two bicycles.

"The cops are trying to steal that guy's cab!"

Rourke looked at Paul and nodded. "Let's prevent them from doing that, and take it ourselves. Come on!" And Rourke broke into a dead run down the middle of the street, Paul beside him. Rourke's HK rifle was in his right fist and he stabbed it toward the men fighting at the curb, shouting, "Everybody back up!"

Paul covered them as they stepped back, while John Rourke climbed into the driver's box.

Rourke let his rifle fall to his side on its sling, grabbing a pistol from his belt and pointing at the two policemen and the cab driver. "Stay back and you won't get hurt. Try to stop us and you'll die. Simple as that."

Paul scrambled up into the passenger compartment and Rourke handed off his rifle to his friend. "Use it if you need it, Paul. Keep them covered while I get us out of here."

Then Rourke started backing the team—a nice-looking matched pair of bays, looking more like saddle stock than harness animals—and got the cab fully into the street. There was a long-handled whip. Rourke pulled it out of its receptacle in the boot.

The spiraling roadway at the core was straight ahead. And John Rourke cracked the whip over the animals' heads and shouted, "Gyaagh!"

The team lunged forward and the cab was off into the street, Rourke's body thrown deeper into the box. But he kept his balance, half standing, feet spread wide apart, the reins in his left hand, the whip in his right. He'd driven a farm team once in Indiana and he'd ridden horseback ever since his childhood and considered himself a good horseman, but his knowledge of wagoneering was limited.

He didn't mention that to Paul.

Across an intersection now, nearly colliding with an overturned produce wagon. Policemen were dismounting their bicycles, opening fire. "Discourage them, Paul!"

Paul fired a burst from his submachinegun. Then he shouted to John Rourke, "What are we going to do if we get out of here?"

"Ditch the cab and the team and steal a vehicle from the Nazis, that or an aircraft. They should be in a row out there if we're lucky. We couldn't do anything else. We don't have clothes for the temperatures we'll encounter. Hang on!" And Rourke slowed the team, took it into a turn and they headed into the spiral at the core.

It was steep here, well paved, wide, but the turns quick and Rourke kept the team at the best speed he could. He had to save them for when they reached the tunnel leading out, because it was then that he would need all the speed they had.

They reached Level Two, passed it and went on.

The walls here were decorated with murals depicting the counterfeit warfare between the forces of this city and hordes of evilly drawn black men with savage looks in their eyes, amid them hawk-nosed grey-complected men with leering expressions, driving the black men onward.

The team was running evenly, not seeming to strain. As Rourke turned them into what he guessed was the final bend, ahead of the cab, half blocking egress from the spiral, he saw men in the environment suits of the military personnel who had captured them at the city entrance. The men were in a pack, not a formation, firing indiscriminately it seemed toward whatever lay beyond. "Stay down, Paul—and be ready!"

Rourke hauled the reins close against his chest, twisting his body against them, the team turning, arcing right, straight toward the soldiers. Rourke cracked the whip in the air over the horses' ears and they dashed ahead at top speed.

The fighting men of the city within the mountain fell away in a wave on both sides. There was some gunfire, the rattle of Paul's submachinegun part of it, but John Rourke could not divert his attention from the team long enough to look back. He cracked the whip again.

They were into Level One now, fires burning everywhere, smoke billowing outward from buildings on both sides of the street here. Bodies of men and some horses were strewn about, as though discarded. Rourke cracked the whip again. Men in Nazi uniform, evidently the ones who had been in battle with the men from the city Rourke had just passed, started running from the path of the team. There was more gunfire.

As Rourke hauled the team round a curve and through an intersection, he nearly lost control, tugging hard on the reins, swerving the team in order to avoid an overturned wagon which was on fire in the middle of the street, half blocking it. The front wheel on the offside hit the curb, rolled over it. The cab nearly overturned.

They kept going.

Ahead lay a barricade, intense fighting around it. And John Rourke saw their chance. On the other side of the barricade, perhaps five hundred yards distant along the tunnel opening beyond the barricade were two armored Nazi staff cars. The barricade was the problem, but John Rourke shouted to Paul, "We're shooting our way through! It's the only way!"

"I'm with you, John!"

John Rourke put the whip into his teeth, drawing one of his ScoreMasters with his right hand, thumbing back the .45's ring-style hammer. And he thwacked the reins over the horses' backs, urging them onward toward the barricade.

Small units were in knots everywhere, exchanging fire, energy pulses and projectile ammunition. Smoke, grey and acrid and foul, obscured everything to Rourke's right, two buildings on fire there. The team tore forward, Rourke crouched in the box, nearly but not quite seated.

And they were into it, Rourke relying heavily on the element of surprise. But he had no choice. As men raised weapons toward the cab, Rourke fired toward them, little hope of hitting anything. The horse on the

377

right faltered, nearly dragging the other horse down. But, it ran on, a wide bloody crease across its neck. An energy burst impacted the pavement in front of the team and the animal on the left reared, Rourke firing his pistol into the road surface behind the animal's hind legs, the horse bolting onward.

Bullets tore into the box.

The sounds of Paul's submachinegun, then Rourke's HK-91, boomed out behind Rourke. A man—one of the Nazis—ran toward the charging team, about to fire his energy rifle. Rourke emptied the ScoreMaster into the man's chest.

The man fell away, the right front wheel of the cab rolling over his body.

Rourke stabbed the pistol into his trouser band, its slide still locked open. And he grabbed at the whip, cracking it over the ears of the team. "Gyaagh!" They were nearly to the barricade now, a knot of soldiers from the city storming toward the cab, evidently to seize it and the team as their own means of flight. Rourke cracked the whip across the face of one of the men who was jumping for the box, driving him down.

The whip back in Rourke's teeth, the reins transferred to his right hand, he grabbed for the still-loaded second Detonics ScoreMaster. He punched its muzzle toward the face of a man grabbing for the reins of the offside horse. Rourke fired, then fired again, killing the man.

The horses ran wildly now, of their own volition, not from Rourke's urging he knew, running it seemed to get away from the gunfire and the energy weapon bursts and the smoke and fumes. More gunfire from the passenger compartment. A man charged toward the team from the front. Rourke could not fire, upping the ScoreMaster's Safety, stabbing it into his belt. As the animals started to turn their heads, Rourke cracked the whip, driving the horses over the man, trampling him. There was a hideous scream, the cab bouncing wildly as it careened over him.

A Nazi jumped toward the box on the right side, Rourke lashing at the man with his whip in the same instant that there was a burst from Paul's submachine-gun.

Rourke cracked the whip over the ears of the froth-soaked team, driving them onward, faster.

They were past the barricade, into the tunnel.

There were Nazis here, most of them retreating, some senior noncoms supervising them. But whatever swell of victory was being felt by the defenders here would vanish with the next attack, because this had only been a probe to feel out the city's defensive capabilities; from the paucity of equipment and personnel on the Nazi side, that was obvious. A knot of Nazi personnel raised their energy weapons almost in unison as Rourke drove the team near them. Rourke shouted, "Paul! On our left!" and put the whip back into his teeth, redrawing the second ScoreMaster. Rourke fired it out toward the men as he heard the heavier cracking of the HK-91 from behind him. Two of the Nazis were down, the others breaking and running.

Rourke belted the empty pistol, and as he looked forward grabbing at his whip, there was a blur of motion at the far right edge of his peripheral vision. A man in Nazi uniform, his bulk tremendous, sprawling over John Rourke and knocking Rourke back into the box's seat. The whip fell from Rourke's teeth as the wind was knocked out of him by sheer force. A ham-sized fist hammered toward Rourke's face, Rourke blocking it with his left forearm, his arm numbing for an instant from the impact. Rourke's right knee smashed upward, impacting flesh. There was a groan, the smell of hot breath, the Nazi's body slumping back.

Rourke threw his body toward the man, both of them on their knees, hammering at each other as they tried to stand. Rourke's right fist pistoned forward, once, twice, a third time, hammering at the man's abdomen. The Nazi noncom's right crossed Rourke's jaw, snapping Rourke's head back. Rourke stumbled, reached out, catching a handful of the man's uniform with his left. As Rourke threw his weight forward, he freed his fingers from the uniform, bunched his hand into a fist and short-armed the man with a left across the nose, smashing it. Rourke's right came up, catching the Nazi just under the tip of the chin. Rourke back-handed his left across the man's mouth, knocking him out of the box, between the team and the cab itself. The cab lurched as it rolled over the Nazi noncom's body.

Standing full upright in the box, Rourke cracked the reins over the animals' backs, shouting, "Come on! Come on! Faster!"

One of the armored staff cars Rourke had spotted was already in motion, escaping the tunnel to join a flow of vehicles well ahead of it. Rourke urged the animals onward, a spray of sweat from them like mist on the air. The armored staff car was picking up speed. Paul had read the intelligence data on these vehicles. Their gear ratio gave them horribly slow pickup, but they could top out over one hundred miles per hour on smooth, level surfaces. "Paul—jump for it! Be ready! Gyaagh horses! Gyaagh!" They were nearly even with the staff car, but in seconds its engine would outpace the team.

Rourke edged the cab closer. The staff car's turret hatch opened on top, a man with an energy rifle sticking up through it, about to fire. "Look out, John!" Paul shouted, firing a long burst from his Schmiesser. The Nazi's body snapped back, the energy rifle still in his hands, firing upward into the tunnel ceiling. In the distance, Rourke could see the interior boundaries of the airfield taxi zone, some from the number of this eclectic collection burning or already gutted to blackened ribs.

The team was running even with the armored car. Rourke glanced back and saw Paul jump. Paul caught hold of a grab handle, his feet dragging for an instant. Another man appeared at the turret hatch, a pistol in hand. As the man aimed his pistol toward Paul Rubenstein, John Rourke's left hand darted under his battered old brown bomber jacket, to the Detonics minigun under his right armpit. Rourke tore the little stainless steel .45 from the leather, thumbing back the hammer as he drew, then firing cross body toward the Nazi in the turret. Rourke's bullet struck the man in the face and he fell, rolling over the hood of the staff car and down to the tunnel floor. Paul pulled himself up, aboard at last.

Rourke safed the little Detonics and shoved it into his left front trouser pocket, then gave the reins one final crack, hauling right on them. Rourke balanced himself on the edge of the box and the seat, then threw down the reins and jumped. He missed his mark, landing hard, sprawling over the armored staff car's hood. His hands grasped at the barrel protruding from the gun turret above him. He clung there, the hood surface steeply angled, hard for his feet to find purchase there.

Paul was up by the hatch, firing downward.

Rourke hauled his body up, clambering over the gun barrel and onto the turret, beside his friend at last.

Rourke reached to the small of his back, grabbing for the old Metalifed Colt Lawman .357. It was the perfect gun under the circumstances, short-barreled against a close quarters scuffle, and powerful, loaded with 158-grain semijacketed soft points. Paul fired a last burst downward, nodded, shouted, "Ready!"

"Cover our backs!" And John Rourke grabbed to the turret ladder and vaulted through into the hatchway the revolver in his right fist, his left hand clinging to the rung of the ladder.

A half-dozen dead bodies littered the interior of the armored staff car, some of them officers.

A man, bleeding badly, sat at the automobile-like controls of the machine. He twisted round and began raising a pistol.

Rourke shouted in German, "Do not make me shoot!"

But the man punched his pistol forward, toward Rourke's chest.

Rourke fired first, double actioning the .357 only once, slamming the driver's body back against the control panel.

On the video monitor by which the man steered, Rourke saw the burning wreckage of one of the aircraft coming up fast—too fast. Rourke stabbed the stubby

.357 into his hip pocket as he threw himself forward, then wrestled the dead man away from the steering controls. The armored staff car was nearly into the flames.

Rourke cut the yoke hard left as he shouted to Paul, "Hold on tight, Paul! Hold on!" The armored staff car veered suddenly left, away from the burning aircraft, into the tunnel roadway.

Rourke dropped into the driver's seat and stomped the accelerator control pedal, the armored staff car picking up speed.

From behind him, he heard Paul Rubenstein asking, "And now? Zimmer's headquarters after we find an aircraft?"

There was the sound of the hatch closing as Rourke turned the staff car into the flow of traffic, minitanks, more staff cars, a few trucks. There was comforting anonymity here. On the indicator panel in front of Rourke, the hatch's sealing was confirmed and the environmental system automatically kicked in, a rush of pleasantly warm air surrounding Rourke.

Ahead lay the mouth of the tunnel, Nazi vehicles and foot soldiers funneling through it. It would be easy to continue to mingle with them, avoid detection—except for serial markings, all the staff cars looked alike. Already, Rourke was slowing down, letting the staff car drift to the rear of the force. He would break off at the first opportunity after they were outside.

John Rourke was thinking aloud. "We'll have to get in touch with the SEAL Team that's shepherding Natalia and Annie near Zimmer's headquarters, have them get the women and Michael out of there."

"But what about Sarah? And Wolfgang Mann? We'll

have to go in after them; Zimmer might kill them for spite."

Rourke nodded his agreement. "With that SEAL Team helping us, and assuming Zimmer's down to a significantly reduced garrison at his headquarters, it shouldn't be too bad. And after we get Sarah and Wolf out, then we destroy the place if we have to, or hold it as a staging area against Eden." Soon, Eden and its Nazi allies would attack. With any luck Eden City's bio-warfare facility was already destroyed, perhaps setting back the timetable for the attack on Hawaii—Hawaii and the United States forces assembled there, the true linchpin of the Trans-Global Alliance.

It was war again. John Rourke put one of his cigars between his teeth, but he didn't light it. "And then we come back here, Paul, to stop Zimmer before he makes himself invincible and we'll never be able to stop him at all."